Autumn Raga

Autumn Raga

JASKIRAN CHOPRA

NIYOGI
BOOKS

Published by
NIYOGI BOOKS
D-78, Okhla Industrial Area, PhaseI
New Delhi-110 020, INDIA
Tel: 91 11 26816301, 49327000
Fax: 91 11 26810483, 26813830
email: niyogibooks@gmail.com
website: www.niyogibooks.com

Design: Nisha Albuquerque
Editor: Gita Rajan
ISBN: 978-81-920912-8-0
Publication: 2011

Printed at: Niyogi Offset Pvt. Ltd., New Delhi, India.

For my parents
Surjit and Mahindar Singh Sarna,
and my brother Navtej,
from whom I learned to appreciate
the eternal music of life's seasons.

Acknowledgements

I am grateful to Ruskin Bond and Ganesh Saili for encouraging and appreciating my writing. I thank my son Karan for always believing in me. My beloved valley of Doon is where I found the serenity to give words to my feelings; there is no better place for inspiration. I am also grateful to all my friends who love Dehra Dun as much as I do.

"Dear old Dehra: I may stop loving you, but I won't stop loving the days that I loved you."

- Ruskin Bond

1

Faiz Ahmed Faiz had always been her favorite Urdu poet. His exquisitely crafted couplets had enlightened her in many situations in her life. Each Spring, she caught herself humming "*Gulon Mein Rang Bhare, Baad e Naubahaar Chale, Chale bhi aao ki gulshan ka kaarobaar chale*" and "*Na Gul khile, Na unse mile, Na mae pi hai, ajeeb rang mein ab ke bahaar guzri hai*". At parties and other gatherings, her friends would request her to sing "*Aaye kuchh Abr, Kuchh Sharaab aaye*" or "*Dono Jahaan teri mohabbat mein haar ke*" and she would happily oblige.

The concert the previous evening in the auditorium at the Indian Military Academy had made Sunaina nostalgic as the singer had rendered three ghazals by Faiz. She had gone to the concert with her mother who was extremely fond of ghazals sung in the classical style.

She could picture her nanaji listening to these ghazals (by Begum Akhtar or Mehdi Hassan) on his old gramophone and herself reading Faiz as a young girl. Thinking of Urdu poetry, she suddenly felt at ease. It had always made her feel peaceful. Sunaina often wondered how poets found the perfect words to express their exact states of mind, echoing everyone's emotions so beautifully.

Since their schooldays, her friend Tanuja had been saying that she lived in a dream world and walked in the clouds. When Tanu had gone to college to study Economics and she had chosen English Literature and Music, Tanu had remarked, "Well, what else could you have done?" wearing an expression that said that she had given up on her.

As she walked home at noon after taking classes at school she had many things on her mind. Among them was the thought that she had not met Tanu for more than a month while living in the same town. "What am I doing? How can I be so forgetful?" she said to herself.

After a little rest at home, she decided to go to the Public Library and then meet Tanu to catch up on the news. It was a Saturday and Tanu would be home by late afternoon.

It was October. The autumn scents were familiar to Sunaina. This was her favorite time of the year. With festive days at hand and thoughts of a long, beautiful winter lingering in her heart, she could face just about anything at this time of the year. She had taught the students Raga Malkauns today, and it had uplifted her soul. She drove to the Library, singing the Khayaal in Malkauns softly. "*Mohe kaahe bhool gaye sanware*."

When she arrived at Tanu's house, it was almost three and the sun, for October, was hot. She parked the car outside the familiar blue gate and rang the bell. The camphor tree, planted by Tanu's mother when the house was being built, stood tall like a guardian angel, spreading its sweet fragrance far and wide and providing a caressing canopy to the sprawling lawn.

Tanu was her usual self. Bright and energetic, full of smiles. "Well, its good you finally landed up. I was almost getting angry." She had been busy with guests and work and though she had missed Sunaina, could not find the time herself to meet Sunaina and catch up with news of each other.

"So Sunaina, your beloved October is here once again," laughed Tanu.

"I can feel it in my heart and sing it in my songs, Tanu," Sunaina replied, closing her eyes.

It was those eyes which made her father choose this name when she was born. They were not large but had a certain charisma about them. Deep brown, mysterious, trusting and beautiful! "Sunaina! The one with the beautiful eyes! That's who she is," her father had said. She had heard this story innumerable times from her mother and her grandmother but was never tired of hearing it.

Though her mother sometimes called her "Naina," her dad had always called her Sunaina. He was no more but his gracious voice, calling her name softly, stayed in the deepest recesses of her heart.

Life had moved too swiftly, or so it seemed to Sunaina. How had all that time flown! The schooldays when all that concerned her and Tanu was homework and exams. Cycling every morning to school in their maroon and grey uniforms in winter and maroon and white dresses in summer, they would dream of a world where there were no classes, exams or teachers. They wondered why grown-ups had all the luck in the world and consoled each other with the idea that they, too, would grow up one day.

Remembering her schooldays was one of Sunaina's favorite pastimes. "Tanu, do you remember that peevish-looking girl who joined us in Class Nine and was always asking for notes from everyone?" she asked Tanuja once.

"Well, I can vaguely remember her but cannot quite place her name or her face," Tanu replied casually.

Even twenty years after she had left school, Sunaina dreamed of those days and could feel that innocent joy even in her sleep. She could hear her mother asking her, "Don't you have to go to school today, Naina?" and her father indulgently telling her mom to not be so insistent.

Those days Tanu and her brother Shridhar lived nearby and would come to her house every morning. The three would cycle down to school. Shridhar was in the boys' school close by and would carry on from their school, alone. Tanu still lived in that house.

School was great in many ways. The Irish nuns with their rare combination of compassion and discipline, old teachers who were institutions in themselves and an atmosphere of calm and safety made school feel like a haven to Sunaina. She often yearned to go back in time to be able to enjoy it all once more.

Today, as she looked at those roads, at the school building and at herself, she could not believe that all that had happened here itself. It seemed much too far away! Too much had happened to her and the little town she had grown up in. She felt old already and could feel the exhaustion of the town which had been forced to expand overnight from a sleepy little town in the Himalayan foothills to a bustling capital city.

"Poor little Dehra, where have you gone?" Sunaina would say aloud. She wanted to go to its rescue and make it come alive. She longed for a glimpse of the town where her childhood and youth lay hidden. For the town which now lay mirrored in the depths of her soul, and in her beautiful, warm, brown eyes.

2

It was Tuesday and she had three classes. She reached school at 10:00 and sat in the Music Room, tuning the instruments, doing some riyaz and sipping coffee.

She loved this room in the mornings. Students who had spare time came and helped her with doing up the cosy room with its high wooden ceiling and the olde world look. When she led her students in hymns at the morning assembly, Sunaina reached school at 7:30 in summers and 8:30 in winters.

Sitting on the diwan in the Music Room, she was lost in thought remembering how she had first met Ranvir in college. It had been during one of the University Music Festivals on a cloudy winter day in Delhi.

She was in second year and he in third. While he was a student of Economics, she was studying English Literature and Indian Classical Music.

Ranvir sang at almost all college cultural events and occasions. He had never learned formally but had a fine voice and a natural sense of rhythm. The winter music festival was hosted by her college that year and Ranvir was one of the contestants. So was she.

That was their first meeting. Many more followed. They met in each other's colleges, before classes, after classes, at the college cafeterias, at the university dhabas and at the bus stops, not to talk of the University Special buses. With each meeting, they realized how similar their interests were. Also how different they were in some ways.

"Ma'am, the girls have all come," Smriti's voice brought Sunaina back to the present. She quickly brought out her books and began the theory lesson. Smriti and Rewa were good singers, exceptionally talented, while the others required a lot of guidance.

Rewa reminded Sunaina of her own youth, when she was emotional about life and music, wide-eyed with wonder at the depth of ragas and always ready to work hard at lessons. Listening to Rewa sing Raga Yaman, Sunaina envied the girl her dreamy-eyed look. Sunaina wished life had not dealt such harsh blows to her own dreams so early in life. "How fortunate to have one's illusions about life intact!" she often thought while interacting with her young students.

She was back after experiencing life, having lost all her dreams and trying to renew her interest in life. Back in Doon, her beloved hometown. But even Doon had changed. The surrounding forests had thinned, the increasing traffic and pollution had marred the pristine beauty of the valley and the lovely, tree-lined roads were now bereft of trees. The vast open spaces were disappearing. Like her, Doon too had lost its dreamy-eyed look. It had hardened, like her soul.

Tanu had called the previous evening. She was organizing a small get-together in her lawn to welcome autumn, the season of festivals and the promise of winter, to "revive the garden culture of Doon". Those were the words she had used, albeit jokingly. Sunaina felt a pang of sadness. "Why was everyone talking of reviving the simplest things about life? Why had they been forgotten and lost in the first place?" She felt angry with Tanu, herself and all the other people who had made it necessary for the simple pleasures of living to need reviving.

"I'll come at five and help you with the preparations," she promised Tanu. Shridhar was in town from Mumbai for a week and she looked forward to meeting him. He was with an IT firm and well-settled. His wife and daughter had not come with him as he was here for a meeting.

"Good to see you, Sunaina!" It was Shridhar as he was placing chairs and tables on the lawn. He hadn't changed much in five years. Sunaina was happy to meet him. He rarely came to Dehra Dun and when he did, he kept talking about how good life was in Mumbai. The debate would then escalate and, Sunaina would give up. And the way things were going, there wasn't much truth left in her claims, or her praises regarding Doon, anyway.

"Can you imagine, Shri, flats have actually come up! All around this place! Flats! In Doon!" This was Tanu cursing all those who were ruining the quiet valley, thinking flats were the ugly symbols of development.

"That's what I have been noticing and now, all of you here have no more reason to be so proud of your city," Shri was quick to put in his verdict.

Well, Sunaina could not but agree with Tanu and Shri that Doon was fast losing its characteristic charm. "It's a shame!" she replied, feeling terrible that she could no longer counter Shri's remarks.

"And to think that when we were in school, October was actually cold!" Tanu went on. Before Sunaina could say anything, the guests began arriving and soon there were about a dozen people. Coffee was served first with the trademark "Pista" biscuits which were so missed when not served with tea or coffee in Dehra Dun.

Sumeet, Tanu's husband, was in Mussoorie for business and would be back the next day. Their son, Shashank, was in a boarding school in Mussoorie and Sumeet would be bringing him home for the autumn break.

The party over, Tanu and Sunaina sat together for a relaxed cup of tea and a heart to heart conversation.

They talked about Sunaina's husband, Prashant Singh, who lived in Delhi.

It was not as if Sunaina never loved Prashant. She had grown really fond of him over the years and his presence was often comforting. Their little daughter was a bond between them and things had moved well for some years after marriage. But, gradually, the differences in their temperaments had begun to emerge strongly.

It had become quite a nightmare for her to carry on in the strained relationship. The humiliation she was facing had broken her joyous spirit. He had taken it upon himself to underrate her thoughts, her actions, her views. Demeaning her seemed to give him a strange pleasure. Many a time, she would try and sweep the problems under the carpet, but soon enough, they would reemerge, stronger than before, and uglier. She just could not have taken it any more.

Eight year old Roop was with her now. Prashant was working in Delhi and it was not easy for him to think of shifting to Dehra Dun. He was a big city boy and even the thought of being near his daughter was not enough temptation for him to think of leaving his life and work and moving to Doon. He had a battery of servants and a huge company house in Delhi and was so busy that he hardly had time to miss anybody much. And he was not sure whether his moving out of Delhi would be a solution to the problems they had with each other. In fact, he knew well that it would not resolve anything yet.

They had first met at a new year party held in Sunaina's maternal aunt's home. Prashant had been her cousin Adi's friend. Sunaina was then teaching English at a school in Delhi and stayed with her aunt. Her parents were in Doon. Her father taught English Literature at a local college and her mother was a Librarian at a scientific institute. It was from her mother that Sunaina had inherited her love of music.

As soon as her studies were done, Sunaina had longed to return to Dehra but her father had asked her to continue in the job in the Delhi school as it was a prestigious institution and the experience would be good for her career. Reluctantly, she stayed on in Delhi but missed no opportunity of going back to her hometown whenever possible.

Her music classes continued in the evenings with Mrs. Sugita Guha of the Banaras Gharana, who lived in Green Park and was extremely choosy about her disciples.

Meanwhile, she waited for Ranvir to make up his mind about marriage. She waited for four years but Ranvir could not gather the confidence to take an important decision against his parents' wishes. They had decided on a girl for him, their friends' daughter, and constantly pressurized him to marry her. Ranvir had joined the Indian Excise Service by then. Sunaina waited for Ranvir to tell his parents what he actually wanted and gradually understood that he would never stand up for her.

"I know that I can never be happy with Megha. But I am in such a dilemma, Naina," he would say, expecting her to resolve the dilemma. How could she?

And finally, he married Megha. Whether he was happy or not, his family was delighted.

Somewhere Sunaina felt that she had lost respect for Ranvir when he had begun expressing helplessness regarding the possibility of their marriage. "Had he really loved you, he would have gathered the courage to tell his parents so," Tanu had tried explaining to her when she visited Doon just before Ranvir's wedding. "Even he didn't know what he wanted."

Sunaina was shattered. First she was numb and then she could feel nothing but the pain of being left alone by Ranvir. She felt that she was nothing but a bundle of pain and misery. Negative thoughts and emotions kept pulling her down into a sea of bleakness, regret and loss He had left her, bereft of love, standing at a crossroad from where she did not know where to go. Young as she was, the pain was too intense to bear. She was sure he missed her as much as she missed him. He had always said that she was his only reason to live, his very life breath. How had he suddenly transformed into this other person, one with whom she could not relate at any level? The grief seemed everlasting. It seemed the end of the world to her.

Her riyaz gave her peace to an extent but the moment she stopped singing, her mind would get entangled in a web of memories ... of the winter mornings spent at the university, of the summer evenings spent with Ranvir at music concerts in Delhi, of the morning shows at a cinema near the university. Some of the films she had seen there were extremely close to her heart and she could not bear the thought of seeing them again. It pained her greatly. Visits to the Coffee House and the British Council Library with Ranvir were routine and she even dreamt of them for years after. She had stopped going there. All the time, Ranvir had been telling her how much he cared for her, how much she meant to him, how he would die without her. Now she knew.

3

The Principal, Sister Martina called Sunaina to her office that morning. "Mrs. Singh, we are planning to hold a concert next month."

"Sounds great, Sister. What theme do you have in mind?"

"We have thought of staging the various ways Dussehra is celebrated all over the country." The drama teacher can chip in and you can both sit together this afternoon and work out a rough plan."

"We'll do that," said Sunaina, thinking all the while of her own school where she had participated in singing Christmas carols and the golden oldies of the 50's and 60's. Once, she had even played a chef in a play called "The Poet Tasters of Isfahan" and had been extremely unhappy with her role. "I just cannot do it," she had told Sister Florence, her drama teacher. "Child, don't be naughty now. Please try to understand what I am telling you and get down to practicing," Sister Florence had replied gently. She had listened to her and finally, on Parents' Day, her role had been appreciated.

Another time, she took part in a declamation contest. The topic was "Time and Tide Wait For No Man." She could recall clearly her rehearsals for the contest where her meticulous English Teacher, Mrs. Reeta Manchanda, helped her get the right nuances and stresses. The speech began with a quotation, "Time, you Old Gypsy Man, will you not stay? Put up your caravan just for one day." The more she tried, the worse it sounded. "Please do not say it in a sing-song way, Sunaina! For Heaven's Sake!" shouted Mrs. Manchanda, desperately. It took Sunaina three days to say it the way her teacher wanted.

At that time, she did not know that she would call to mind the quotation, time and again, at various moments in her life ... Time, you Old Gypsy Man, will you not stay? Put up your caravan, just for one day!"

Roop was studying Hindi that evening. Her pretty face was tucked into the books. Her face was oval-shaped, her complexion fair and she had waist-length hair. She looked more like her father and had his shiny black eyes. Roop missed her dad but with Sunaina's mother around, she felt pampered. "Naanu, please tell me the meaning of *swabhimaan*," she asked her grandmother who was helping her with her homework that day. The way she said "swabhimaan" made it sound as if it were the name of a warplane.

Sunaina had always hoped Roop would be interested in music but until now, she had not shown any particular interest. She liked to listen to her mother practicing but Sunaina wasn't sure that this could be construed as love for music. It could as well be love for her mother.

Prashant came to meet them now and then but did not stay long. He always had a packed schedule. They went to Delhi during the school vacations. Whenever they did, Sunaina informed her guru, Madhavrao, that she would be taking a few classes with him. Mrs. Guha had passed away two years ago, Madhavrao was one of her old students who now ran his own music school.

"Mom, will we be going to Delhi in the autumn break?" asked Roop.

"I'll drop you there, baby, and be back, as I have to prepare for a concert here," she replied, while having her evening cup of coffee.

"Will you come again? To bring me back when my vacation ends?"

"I think Dad will have to bring you back," Sunaina said.

So many people asked her why she did not live with her husband. Sometimes she tried explaining but most of the times, she did not feel the necessity especially if the question came from people she did not know well. Prashant's visits to Doon silenced people and the questions grew less frequent and insistent.

Tanu often persuaded her to try harder to get Prashant to start his work in Dehra. But Sunaina knew that Prashant's priorities in life were different from hers and he would feel suffocated here. Doon was not exactly a small place any longer but compared to Mumbai and Delhi, it was small. People still knew and cared for their neighbors.

Ever since she had shifted here and joined school, Sunaina felt that the relationship between her and Prashant had improved and they had started understanding each other's worldview better. In Tanu's words, she and Prashant were a living example of the adage, "Absence makes the heart grow fonder!"

The concert practice picked up speed. Group Dances and solo songs based on classical music were rehearsed by the girls. One of the compositions was based Raga Bhairav, the enchanting early morning raga.

Sunaina found Bhairav soul-stirring every time she heard or sang it. An old film song by Lata Mangeshkar in Bhairav, "*Jaago Mohan Pyaare*" from the film *Jaagte Raho*, had mesmerized her even as a child.

"*Bhor Bhayi, Chhaaya Ujiyaara*" sang Smriti, Rewa, Mishka, Tuhina and Saakshi, the best singers in senior school. Not a single false note could be heard in their rendering. It was sheer magic! What could match the magic of ragas, she often wondered. Each raga created a special world where the singer as well as the audience was transported for the time it was being rendered.

This was what gave her joy. Listening to her girls singing the true notes of life, celebrating the beauty of eternal sound. She wouldn't trade this happiness for anything! Closing her eyes, she sat back and absorbed each nuance, each "meend" and "murki" of the "bandish".

"Okay, go for the fruit break now and get back in twenty minutes," she told the students. Dulari, the school's ancient maid, brought Sunaina a cup of coffee.

Tanu always thought coffee was the answer when she saw Sunaina looking tired or listless. "I think you need coffee," she would say when she saw her looking sad. And then they would look at each other and laugh like giggly schoolgirls.

Good old Tanu! What would Sunaina have done without her? Exam jitters? Tanu had the cure. Monday morning blues? She had the formula. Tiff with Mom? Rush to Tanu. Boyfriend trouble? Well, who else but Tanu would find a way out? Through thick and thin, through joys and sorrows, through smiles and tears … Tanu and Naina had been through it all … had grown up from cherubic girls with long black plaits tied in red ribbons to attractive young women who broke many a heart and on to confident women who went out into the world knowing that they could always bank on each other, whatever the problem might be. Wasn't that enough to be happy in life? She believed that it was.

4

Sunaina planned that she would leave Roop in Delhi on Friday evening and be back in Doon on Sunday night. The very thought of being away from school and from Doon scared her. She had never liked traveling, just like her dad. She just loved being at home for as long as she could, sitting with her parents, studying or listening to music. Given a chance, she would never travel. She was more given to dreaming about traveling. But actual traveling, she found tedious. The only place she looked forward to visiting was Mussoorie, just an hour's drive from Doon.

"How can you be so very boring?" her mother, a keen traveler, would ask. When Sunaina was a young girl, her mother would go on short trips with friends while she and her younger brother, Ishaan, stayed back home with their dad. How they used to enjoy those times! She felt guilty thinking about it now. With her mother gone to nearby Rishikesh or Haridwar with her friends for a day or two, Sunaina would take charge of the house and order Ishaan around. Ishaan, who was six years her junior, had no choice. He did as commanded.

Yet they were a team. Together they would cook and clean, then wait for Dad to get back from college. They would serve him and wait for his words of praise. He would call them "My Little Master Chefs" and reward them with chocolates, pens or even a late night show of the latest movie running in town.

Her mother would admonish Sunaina. "Look forward to the future. Leave the past behind. One has to live in the present in order to succeed," she would say in the warm, husky voice which her daughter had inherited from her.

Sunaina knew she was right but found it extremely difficult to follow this well-meant advice. She could not get herself to break away from her world.

Bhairavi Bakshi, Sunaina's mother, had retired from the institute five years ago and had now devoted herself completely to music which she had practiced throughout her life, from the age of four. Sunaina's grandfather, Pandit Sachidanand, had been a well-known vocalist who had made his three daughters learn music from an early age. He had even named them Sursudha, Bhairavi and Geetmala to keep their links with music unbreakable.

Her mother wanted to be a professional singer but had been too busy with household responsibilities to accomplish her goal. She had been the eldest daughter-in-law in a joint family for several long years in Lucknow before Professor Bakshi finally came to Dehra Dun. Sunaina was five then.

But Bhairavi had never stopped singing. Even now, a music teacher, a man of seventy with a flowing, hennaed beard and a white cap, came twice a week to brush up Mom's singing. Murad Ali was his name. "Call me Ustad Saàb," he insisted when they met him first. Roop and Sunaina called him that but Mrs. Bakshi would sometimes address him as "Guruji".

Sunaina rarely got a chance to learn from him due to pressures of work. But Ustad Saàb sometimes asked her to sing and he would then give her his own version of the bandish. Sunaina found him a bit arrogant but, on the whole, he was a good soul. Simple and content.

As a student in Class Eleven in Doon, she learned sitar and vocal music from Master Swarup. In the school, they had a teacher, Miss Anjana Verma, but she taught in a text-book manner with no original flair for music. She was too methodical for Sunaina's liking. Sunaina preferred Master Swarup who could get into the very heart of a melody and taught her how to do the same. It was from him that she had learnt "*Madhuban Mein Radhika Naache Re*", the famous Mohammed Rafi song from the film *Kohinoor*, the song Ranvir had sung at the college fest and won the second prize. Sunaina had sung a ghazal (*Aankh se aankh milaata hai koi, dil ko kheenchey liye jaata hai koi*) written by Shakeel Badayuni and originally sung by Lata Mangeshkar. She won the third prize while the first prize went to Pawan Kumar from Delhi School of Economics, a versatile classical singer. That year, he had sung "*Laaga Chunari Mein Daag*" sung originally by Manna Dey.

These songs always took her back to college, the lush green lawns, tutorials outside in the sun during winter, scrambled eggs on toast in the college cafeteria and the imposing corridors of her college with their exquisite woodwork. At times, when she missed her college too much, she used to go to the Forest Research Institute building in Doon, a majestic piece of architecture, which looked similar.

Sunaina loved studying English Literature but it was music she wanted to teach youngsters. Sometimes, when the English teacher was on leave, she used to take a few classes discussing poetry. Prose she liked to read by herself. Analyzing a book was not her cup of tea and she would prefer describing the finer points of ragas to critiquing a prose work.

Tanu, Sumeet and Shashank came over for dinner that night. Shridhar came too. It was Wednesday. Roop had already begun packing her bags for Delhi. They would leave on Friday evening by train.

She had prepared a South Indian dinner of lemon rice, idlis, coconut chutney, sambhar, plain rice and rasam. The children as well as Tanu were fond of these dishes.

Shashank was ten and got on well with Roop. "Roop, take Shashank to the TV room if you wish to watch something," Sunaina told her daughter. But the kids sat with Uncle Shridhar who always had a bagful of exciting tales, most of them quite spooky. In fact, Tanu and Naina, during their schooldays, had to stuff cotton wool into their ears when they wanted to avoid his ghost stories. Naina had never savored spooky stuff and used to plead with him not to tell such stories.

But Roop loved them and at her request, Shri was repeating the old story of Mussoorie's English Saab who could be seen on horseback many a night near the old graveyard where he would ask passers-by for a light for his cigar. "Oh! Is that so?" squealed Roop. "Shashank, have you met him? Does he live near your school?"

"I have heard of him but have not met him yet. Thank God!" said the little boy.

"Roopsi, Shashank, please come and have your dinner first," called Sunaina's mother. "See, I have fried small papads for you."

The grown-ups talked about Mussoorie, taking their cue from the spooky tale. Sunaina was just as fond of Mussoorie as her dad had been. Mussoorie, close to Doon, was an ideal weekend getaway and, with his family, Professor Harshvardhan Bakshi spent many weekends there, returning to Doon on Sunday evening.

"Can we go up to Mussoorie sometime after the concert?" she asked Tanu who had worked at the Mussoorie branch of her bank for a couple of years and often said that going to the hills for a holiday was much more fun than working there all the time.

"Sure, we can go on a Saturday or Sunday," Tanu replied.

"Mom, please wait until I'm back from Delhi. Then we can go and meet that Englishman with the cigar," piped Roop.

"Okay Roop, we'll do that," she said looking indulgently at her adventurous little girl.

5

Delhi was quite warm even though it was end October. Sunaina and Roop had reached there the night before and were picked up by Prashant's chauffeur. Prashant was at a dinner. Roop was disappointed not to see her dad at the station. She spoke to him on the phone and he apologized profusely. "I'm really sorry, my darling! I'll be home soon after you reach there," he assured her.

Sunaina was already feeling strange, as always when away from Doon. What was it about that town which captivated her, she often thought and could only put it down to her attachment to her childhood memories, the wondrous adolescent years and a spiritual closeness to the hills all around the valley, the forests and the rain, the sounds and scents of the little town which had suddenly expanded. This always reminded her of Roop when she tried wearing Sunaina's saris to look grown up, using a dab or two of foundation and lipstick. And that is why she loved Dehra and Roop, with great intensity and feeling.

"You've come to Delhi after a very long time!" Prashant said at breakfast. As it was Saturday, the office would close by three. He would get time to spend with them.

"Four months or so," Sunaina said, "But you have not been to Doon even once."

"I'll be coming to drop Roop on the seventh," he said. Roop was going over to spend sometime with her Uncle Sushant, Prashant's younger brother, and his wife, Ananya. They had a daughter who was a year younger than Roop and a son who was three. On his way back from the office, Prashant would bring Roop home. "But I want to go over to your office one day too," Roop insisted. "Theek hai, you can come along and we'll go out for a Chinese lunch that day," her dad agreed.

After breakfast, when Roop was in the bath, Prashant sat with a cup of tea on the verandah cane swing next to her chair. He neither smoked nor drank, qualities she liked best about him. Just like her dad, she would think.

At times, Sunaina wondered how she could have such puritanical ideas. She wished she could be more flexible but some ideas were so deeply ingrained in her that she could not change them. For her, smoking and drinking could never be acceptable.

"So, have you thought about us?" came the question she always dreaded hearing or answering.

"Thought what?" she asked, deliberately obtuse.

"You know very well what I mean. Any plans to come back?" he asked, gently but firmly.

"I really do not think I can see myself living and working here, losing track of myself and everything else. I am really sorry Prashant but I cannot bring myself to leave Mom and home for Delhi," she said, measuring every word before uttering it, a bit scared of his reaction at the same time.

"I know what you mean," he said, taking her by surprise. "For the last few months, I have been trying to see things from your point of view and have decided that gradually I can plan leaving this city and considering some other option."

Sunaina was taken aback! Completely so! Was this Prashant, the man who had once given her an ultimatum that if she went away from Delhi, he would give her a divorce? The man who would fret and frown over all she said and did, intolerant of almost everything. She would be terrified of expressing herself before him as she knew he would be scornful, without a reason. He always maintained an air of superiority and smugness, thinking that all she thought held no meaning. And now he was actually trying to see things from her point of view! Well, wonders never cease, she thought, smiling inside. She felt almost guilty at listening to him talk like this. She would have felt better if he had lost his temper, as usual.

"I really don't know the answer. I have thought for months on end and still do not know what to do. I hate having to take tough decisions like this," she said, almost apologetically.

"Okay, we can talk about it when I come to Doon. Don't worry. You are here just for a day. Relax, go shopping. We can all go out. I'll take you both out when I return from office," he said, rising to get ready.

She felt greatly relieved. Things were fine, then. For the last two years that she had been away in Doon, Prashant had kept raising questions to which she had no answers. And she felt dreadfully cornered. But something inside stopped her from trying to come back to Delhi. Too much had happened to her in this city and this home. There had been nights when she had stayed put in the verandah, sobbing for hours. Prashant would be harsh with her and when she cried her heart out, sitting in the verandah, he would not bother to come and call her in. The wall between them was getting stronger and higher every day. There were no major issues as such but his way of dominating everything in the house and treating it like solely his possession gradually created deep resentment in her heart. Perhaps, had it not been for Roop, she might have opted out of the marriage.

There was no need to panic. There was no other crisis around the corner, she assured herself, as Prashant got ready to take them out.

When Sunaina arrived in Doon on Sunday night, she felt a bit lost without Roop but was glad to be back. She slept as soon as she reached home. There was school on Monday and then concert practice in the afternoon.

It was almost the end of October and the mornings and evenings in the valley were getting chilly though throughout the day, the sun was strong and quite hot. Mrs. Bakshi had begun taking out the woolens and airing them. People in this city spent some time doing this in November, and then putting them away for summer, after thoroughly sunning them for days in April.

"There are two letters for you," her mother told Sunaina in the evening. "One is from Ishaan while the other is from Delhi."

She was hearing from Ishaan after a long while. He was posted at a station in the North East as a Major. His wife, Neera, and his little son, Abhisaar, were living in flats for separated families in Meerut where Neera's parents also lived. Ishaan and Neera had also met at Delhi University, just as Sunaina and Ranvir had.

The thought of Ranvir still saddened her. She often wondered whether they would have had a better married life than she had with Prashant. She would never know that but tried imagining what things might have been like. Their intense love for music was a great bond between them. And music has the power to bring people really close together, spiritually and mentally. As singers, they had never tried to compete with each other. They loved each other's voices. The jealousy would come from other reasons.

"Sometimes, I get jealous of your favorite ghazals, you are so passionate about them," Ranvir had often said while they were sitting in University Coffee House, discussing various subjects but mostly music. How naïve they both were!

Believing that life would go on like this, between tutorials, lectures, library, music concerts, picnics and drinking endless cups of coffee.

Ranvir was about five foot ten, extremely good looking, with a wheatish skin, wavy hair and large, expressive eyes with long, curling lashes. "Well, I am jealous of your eyelashes. They are so beautiful and entirely wasted on you!" Sunaina would often tease him. Sunaina's friends at college often referred to Ranvir as the "Greek God". And she used to love that. Though he was called Ronnie by most of his friends, Sunaina always addressed him by his name – Ranvir. She loved saying his name – Ranvir. It was so clear and sounded sweet. She did not like shortening it in any way. She loved the man and loved his name. For her, this name would always be special, she thought. And the meaning, the brave one of the battlefield, was good too. Though sadly, he turned out to be so weak in his battle for her!

Sunaina was tall too, almost five foot seven, and had long, wavy dark brown hair which she tied up loosely in a pony tail or in a bun. On special occasions, she would leave it loose and received several compliments at how nice it looked like that.

Her eyes were her most attractive feature, lighting up her round face. She had a cleft chin – her friends remarked that she must be a great flirt. Well, she didn't know but was quite fond of her chin. "It's much better than your boring old long chins," she told her school or college friends when they teased her.

"What has Ishaan written?" her mother asked, cutting into her reminiscences. "He says he is doing fine and will be coming to Doon and Meerut in January," said Sunaina getting up and giving the letter to her mother.

The other letter was merely a subscription reminder from a Delhi music journal.

6

The concert went off far beyond her high expectations and the parents of the girls were all praise for her and for Mrs. Lalita Prasad, the dance and drama teacher. Sunaina had presented a solo item singing parts of "Madhushala" by Harivansh Rai Bachchan and some excerpts from Gopal Das Neeraj's poetry which she had set to music. This item of hers was a special presentation amid the "Dussehra-based" songs and dances presented by the students.

One of the Rubaiyees of Bachchan she sang sounded apt when used to describe the deteriorating condition of Doon. "*Ek samay santusht bahut thha paa main thodi si haala, bhola sa thha mera saaqi, chhota sa mera pyaala, pyaare se is jag ki mere swarg balaaen lete thha, vistrit jag mein hai gayi kho, meri nanhi madhushala...*" (There was a time when I was satisfied with a little wine, an innocent beauty served me wine and my cup was a small one / even heavens expressed joy at my state / Alas! my little wine house has disappeared in the expansive world). The pain, the loss, the poignancy of the loss and the irrevocable lost beauty and innocence had been so perfectly expressed by the poet in just four lines! "Where have you gone, my nanhe Dehra Dun?" she asked herself while singing the composition which received a thunderous applause from the audience.

The girls were excited by the success of the show and the forthcoming Diwali holidays, too. The junior school was already closed while the senior school closed that day. Roop was in Class Four and was taught music by Miss Shweta Sarin who was an old student of the school.

Sunaina had been offered a job at her alma mater but she could not bear all the lovely memories it would evoke so had decided to work in another Convent. Her addiction to the past would make the line between the past and present disappear. She would be totally lost.

Mrs. Jasjeet Sandhu, her English teacher and role model in her schooldays, had tried to convince her but when Sunaina explained the problem, she understood. "But do come to school to meet us whenever you have time," she had said in her well-modulated soft voice, clear as the sound of the water of a hill spring on a winter afternoon. Mrs. Sandhu was still her role model!

She was there for the concert and met Sunaina during high tea afterwards. "We are so proud of you, Sunaina!" she said while holding her hand and pressing it warmly to convey the happiness she felt. Sunaina felt her eyes suddenly fill with tears. She was surprised and also relieved to discover that she could still cry. When her father had passed away, for days on end, she wept. And then, it seemed her tears had dried up forever, as if nothing would again move her to tears.

She had not after all turned into stone. "Thanks, Ma'am," she said as she hugged her old teacher who had seen her grow into a dedicated teacher. "I wish I was a teacher like Mrs. Sandhu who has stayed in my heart throughout these years like an anchor, even in my memories," she thought to herself as she drove home that evening.

Prashant was in a hurry to go back, as usual. They went to Tanu's place for a meal, saw a film and shopped for some woolens. He seemed very cheerful and relaxed. Tanu and Sumeet were happy to see him after such a long time. "You must come and join all of us here in Doon," said Tanu. "Well, let's see. I am thinking of getting myself a more peaceful life too!" said Prashant, with a laugh.

"Well, you'll have to come here soon as we are not going to send Sunaina to Delhi," said Tanu with a smile.

Sunaina felt apprehensive about how Prashant would react to all this. He wouldn't say anything here but would demand to know from her later why her friend said all that. She hoped Tanu would close the topic. Fortunately, Tanu did.

He left after staying two nights and a day telling Sunaina he would join them for Holi in Doon. Roop was thrilled to hear that. "But I may have exams around Holi," she said after realizing that Holi was in March. "Don't you worry! We'll celebrate Holi, exams or no exams!" her dad said, giving her a hug.

It was a holiday and Sunaina had taken her mother and Roop shopping that morning. It was the first week of December and Dehra looked quite blissful despite the fact that trees in the town were being cut mercilessly to make way for more houses and flats, the freeflowing cool canals along the main roads were being covered with concrete and the traffic had become extremely chaotic.

Yet Dehra looked lovely that cosy winter morning and Sunaina felt warmth creeping into her heart to have been a part of this town's glorious past and its charm which had captivated many outsiders who had made it their home after having stayed for a few years. There was a feeling of calm about the town. Mornings were slow-paced and serene. Nobody seemed to be in a hurry in those days. There were very few cars in the town then. The horsedrawn tongas trotted leisurely through the streets of Dalanwala and Race Course. She remembered going to the railway station in a tonga. There was no trouble with the traffic at all! Sometimes, she wondered whether things now appeared different to her as she was no longer a child. The world always appeared something else through a child's eyes. But she had enough evidence that this was not the only reason the place looked changed now. The changes were so glaring and loud that they were there for all to see and feel.

No longer could one see the azure blue skies which had been one of the most beautiful experiences of her childhood. She would stare at the sky, while sitting in the lawn with a book, and would not be able to take her eyes off it. The deep and bright blue hues captured her soul and she would drown herself in their striking beauty. Her eyes would then begin to move downwards towards the tall and imposing trees that lined the streets and dotted their garden too.

The scenic beauty had faded. It had been once so pronounced that any visitor to the valley would be enamored of it and would want to stay on longer. That was how her father had made Dehra the family's home.

"Ma, let's go to the music shop," said Roop who wanted to buy cassettes for her friend Divya's birthday. Sunaina bought some Sufi albums including one of Hansraj Hans with her favorite number "*Nit khair manga soneya main teri, dua na koi hor mangdi*". She wanted to learn Sufi music from a Guru but, until she found a teacher, Sunaina tried learning by listening to famous Sufi singers like Abida Parveen, Wadali Brothers and Hansraj Hans. "*Chhaap tilak sab chheenee, mose naina milayeke*," Amir Khusro's composition, she had heard from her parents. She had once sung it at an inter-college competition before she had met Ranvir. He had told her later that he had been ill while that competition was held. Why did everything remind her of Ranvir even today?

7

Winter had arrived in earnest and Dehra was quite cold, though not quite so cold as ten years ago. It had not snowed yet in Mussoorie even though it was late December. Every day trees were being felled. Apartments were being built with a swiftness never dreamt of in the old sleepy days. What hurt Sunaina was that even some of the old resident families did not express any shock or unhappiness at the rapid changes for the worse around them.

Why must she feel such pain at the changes she saw every day? she asked herself and the answer she got was that the town was part of her personality, part of her golden days and she could not bear to see it disappearing before her eyes, vanishing into history!

Old, cosy restaurants which she and Ishaan had spent many an evening during their schooldays, had now been changed into mechanical looking Pizza joints. Newcomers to the city felt that this gave it a smart look. They had no memories to lose, no time to hear the town's story. They would never know how the town had been a haven of tranquility and greenery, surrounded by lovely, thick sal forests and laden with sprawling fruit orchards.

The nehars, the open canals that gurgled their way across the various parts of the town had been like silver ribbons criss-crossing each on the face of the valley. Dhobis used to wash clothes on the banks of the canals and water from here reached the lovely litchi orchards of Dalanwala to irrigate them. Now the canals all ran underground. They had all been covered to widen the roads. Sunaina and Ishaan had often played near the canal that flowed past their home, fascinated by the snow-white froth they could see on the water surface. But their mother would bring them back from there, afraid that they may fall into the nehar. The nehars had been like necklaces of fresh water and gave joy to humans, animals and birds.

There was nothing which had stayed the same for her in her life which, for some years, had been like a roller-coaster ride. The town where she had spent so many years of her life was her anchor, her haven where she could find herself once again after losing a part of herself in each of life's battles. And now that was changing too! Would anyone understand her agony?

Her life had been like a fairy tale as long as she had been at school here. Sheltered by her parents' devoted love and dreaming of a rosy world ahead which would be an extension of her little home in the foothills of the Himalayas. How naïve she had been! And if Tanu was to be believed, she still was, despite all the shocks life had given her, all the rough and tumble she had been through in the last twenty years or so. "Well, you are just a wee bit wiser now than you were in school," she would say. And then they would both laugh aloud.

Her father, having assessed her naiveté at an early stage, had asked her to leave her world of "romantic novels" and relate with the outside world. She did not want to do that and had paid for it heavily. Many incidents, after she left for the University in Delhi, brought her in touch with this harsh real world in a way which made her grow up, but gradually. Rude shocks awaited her at several steps and she wept bitterly in the first few years when all her romantic illusions came crashing down. First, it had been Ranvir who made her go through the trauma of being suddenly left in the lurch at the peak of their closeness. Most of her illusions had been destroyed by his going away. But she had, after coming out of the initial shock, still believed that all people one met in life would not be like him. that he had been just one those few who could not stand up for their beliefs or rights or to decide about their lives. With time, she had recovered hope of meeting good people who would behave honorably and keep some of her illusions alive.

Living in the hostel at the university, she realized that her room-mate and other girls too were far wiser and soon understood that she had been living in a world of her own, a world of poetry and music.

While in college, Sunaina greatly missed Tanuja who was studying at Lucknow University. In the classroom, during lectures, she would think of the fun they had at school. Waiting for the classes to get over so that they could go to their favorite stairs behind the old building which was hardly used by anyone. Sharing their tiffins and letting each other know of all that happened at home the previous evening. It seemed as if incidents and episodes were not complete for them till they shared every bit of them with each other.

During their college days, they would write letters to each other as often as possible and sometimes talk over the phone. Tanu had wanted to come to Delhi but her mother was not comfortable with the idea. Tanu's mausi lived in Lucknow and this made her mother feel safer. Though Naina's mausi lived in Delhi, her parents believed it was better for her to stay in the hostel. Her college was quite far from mausi's house. Later, when she had begun working, she had shifted to mausi's place. She met Prashant there, after Ranvir had walked out of her life to become the good boy of his family. She had terrible memories of their break up. Everyone in the house knew about it as Ranvir had been a regular visitor for years.

Hurt by his decision, her uncle and aunt had wanted to talk to Ranvir's parents and to him, too. But Sunaina would have nothing of that. She had too much self-respect They understood and helped her get over the pain. Even Sunaina's parents decided to let Ranvir be part of the past.

Prashant had been Aditya's classmate at the School of Planning and Architecture and Adi, Sudha mausi's son, had called him for the New Year Eve party that year, along with other college friends. Sunaina had sung at that party. She could remember the details clearly. Mrs. Guha had taught her a ghazal in Raga Yaman. It was Mirza Ghalib's "*Har ek baat pe kehte ho tum ke tu kya hai, tumhi kaho ke yeh andaaz-e-guftagu kya hai*". Prashant had listened carefully, though he later told her that he had great difficulty following Urdu poetry.

She had also sung one of her favorite Lata Mangeshkar songs from the film *Anupama*. "*Kuchh dil ne kaha, kuchh bhi nahin ... aisi bhi baatein hoti hain, aisi bhi baatein hoti hain*". This was understood easily and greatly applauded. Sunaina still had a photograph of that party, where she looked extremely pretty in her blue and white churidar, kameez and flowing white dupatta with her hair done up in a long, loose plait.

Prashant had told Adi that he wanted to meet Sunaina again. And Adi, like a keen Cupid, had made every possible effort for them to meet often and become serious about each other.

Prashant was serious first and Sunaina was swept off her feet by his charming ways of showing that he cared. It had been more than a year since Ranvir had walked off, leaving her feeling absolutely lost and hurt. She had thought that she would never again be able to believe in any kind of affection or tender feelings. To an extent, this was true. There was a deep core in her heart forever locked and it was only on the surface that she now reacted to anything or anyone.

She herself did not venture into that locked corner as she knew that, once opened, a torrent of pain would flow out and drown her very existence. She held so much of herself inside, yet nobody knew because even the space outside the locked area did justice to any relationship. As she was over emotional in the first place.

Her parents had come and met Prashant's parents who specially flew in from Manila where Prashant's father worked as a Biotechnology Consultant. He had taken up the job after teaching at an Agricultural University in India for several years. Prashant's mother was the principal of an International School in Manila.

The engagement ceremony had been a simple one with a few friends and relatives present including Tanu who had come from Dehra Dun. She was already working in a bank in Doon and her wedding had been fixed for next year. Sumeet belonged to Doon too. It was an arranged match.

Prashant's parents were simply wonderful. Tanu was greatly taken by their warmth and so was Sunaina. "It's good that Ranvir did not have the courage to go against his parents. They were such ogres, anyway," said Tanu. It was wonderful how she could make anyone laugh with just one word of hers!

After the engagement, a year passed before the marriage. She met Prashant often but what she noticed about the meetings was that they did not bring her the spontaneous joy which she had felt when she had been with Ranvir. She did not feel like moving out too much and most of the times, Prashant came over for a meal to her aunt's house. Much of the conversation would be formal. She noticed that Prashant loved to talk about his work. He was not much interested in music but tried to show interest when she spoke about her passion. Sometimes, they would go for morning shows of old Hindi films which ran at *Uphaar Cinema*. He enjoyed them as much as she did.

Even during that time, Sunaina yearned to go back to her hometown. And she had told Prashant often about this. He didn't take her seriously and considered it a whim which she would soon get over. But she had been totally serious about it. Always. She described the town to him in detail. And wanted him to share her love for her hometown with her. Prashant did pay attention to what she told him but was confident that he would be able to convince her not to think of going back. Often, this point of conflict assumed dangerous proportions and he would simply shout at her and leave.

However, she had not wanted to depart from Delhi amid conflict though that was how it had happened ultimately. The distance between Prashant and her had grown by the day and she felt absolutely lonely and discarded. She drifted away from her music and even from Roop. She had stopped teaching at the school and had abandoned training for music in the evenings. Awfully depressed and defeated by her condition, she blamed everyone for it without having the courage to see where she herself had gone wrong.

Prashant's work had hugely expanded, leaving him with no spare time. With each passing day, he seemed to be pulled deeper into the quicksand of meetings and work schedules.

8

Sunaina's father had met with an accident on the Doon-Delhi National Highway. He was driving back to Doon when his car was hit by a bus somewhere near Meerut. He had been killed on the spot.

Had it been just a little more than a year ago? She felt it had been a day in another life of hers. A past life, millions of years ago. That Black Day, the blackest in her life so far! The day her father, her life force, her entire world, had passed away into nothingness, leaving her alone forever to fight the world and its idiosyncrasies.

His sudden death had devastated her. She had stayed in his study for several days just to be near him, his things, his books and his warmth which could be felt in the house even now. Even now, she would sit and do her riyaz in his cosy study where he had spent hours everyday reading the great masters of English Literature. It was in this room that she heard him recite "Ode to Autumn" of John Keats which was one of his favorite poems. It was here that she had sung to him the ghazals he had been so fond of. The room was special for Sunaina, the "sanctum sanctorum" of their house. The solace she found in it was something she could not describe.

"Hi Sunu, where are you? Are you still living in this city or not?" It was Tanu calling on her cell phone. It was rarely that anyone called her Sunu.

Sumeet was going to Dubai for a week and Tanu wanted to know whether Sunaina wanted anything from there. "Thanks Tanu but really, I do not want anything," she said.

"Okay, I'll tell him what to get besides chocolates for Roop and Shashank," she replied.

"Tanu, if you have time, please come over tomorrow evening and we'll sit and talk," she requested. As usual, Tanu readily agreed.

School was carrying on well. The girls were back after a short winter break and with the final examinations approaching, music practice as well as theory was being taught and learnt at a heightened pace. Though Sunaina had hardly any time to feel down and out, there were some problems which she found difficult to deal with.

Her mother hardly ever discussed anything about Prashant for she knew that this upset Sunaina greatly. She avoided talking about her future plans as well. She let things be and spoke only about the day-to-day affairs of home and school. She talked mostly about music, her favorite subject. Regarding the relationship between Prashant and Sunaina, Mrs. Bakshi was at a loss as to what could be done and she often wished she could have had her husband to guide her about her daughter's future.

Mrs. Bakshi was preparing to perform at a concert in the Ladies Club next week on Basant Panchami. She would sing a "Thhumri" in Raga Basant Bahaar and Ustad Saàb had made sure that she had perfected it.

When Tanu came over, Sunaina was teaching Roop who was busy preparing for her finals. Roop liked studying English with her mom and often told her that she was her best teacher. "Mom, you should become our teacher too," she said. "When I join senior school, will you teach me music?" she would ask. "We'll see," Sunaina would reply, wondering where she would be after two years and what she would be doing.

"Go and learn this chapter while I speak to Tanu Mausi," she told Roop and began making tea. When they sat down to tea in Sunaina's room, Tanu watched her friend closely. She could read her face like a book. "Why do you think so much about the future? Who knows about it?" she said, concern echoing in her soft voice.

"Tell me Tanu, is it wrong to want to be totally without any bondage. Without any kind of accountability to another person?" she asked. "I do not feel anything for Prashant and sometimes, even for other people."

"It's a phase that will end soon," Tanu consoled. "Don't be so sad. Things will turn out all right."

This was what Sunaina had wanted to hear. Tanu's words of comfort always worked wonders. Even though things remained the same, they began to look easier. Why could she not see things like Tanu could?

They talked of this and that and had their tea leisurely. "We still have to go to Mussoorie. Let's go on Saturday," said Tanu.

9

Ranvir was not happy. He was in Delhi for a holiday and often thought of Sunaina. Everywhere he went – alone or with Megha, memories of the years spent with Sunaina overtook him and he felt haunted by her presence.

He had been married to Megha for nearly eleven years but had never stopped missing Sunaina. He felt ashamed of the way he had treated Sunaina. His keen desire to be the ideal son had placed him in a situation with which he could never be comfortable. He had walked into the trap of emotional blackmail laid out by his parents. And had done so knowingly. He was amazed that Sunaina had not even once tried to contact him since he had told her that he would be marrying Megha, after all. In a way, he felt proud of her behavior. The fact was that he still loved her and often pined for her. But there was nobody with whom he could share this.

Megha was a total contrast to Sunaina. And also to him. They had hardly anything in common and seemed to be living their own different lives under the same roof. In the beginning of their life together, he had told her everything about Sunaina and also the fact that he had backed out of marrying her. Megha seemed to gloat over this and feel superior to Sunaina. But sometimes she would get jealous and Ranvir felt that he had made a great mistake, telling her anything at all.

"Do you still miss her," she would ask him, during these times.

"Not at all. Never," Ranvir would try to convince. But she would not believe him and he would just fall silent. How could he lie to another when he could not lie to himself? How could she believe his denial? It was one he himself could not believe in. But it was evident to him that he had committed a blunder in marrying someone whom he had known nothing about. Within the marriage, he was living a solitary life, hardly communicating with his wife.

Ranvir was keen to know whether Sunaina had forgiven him or had just forgotten him. He had not forgotten the tall and lovely girl he had met as a youngster in college and with whom he had shared all his youthful dreams and interests, his apprehensions and his joys. No one could take her place in his heart. He had often thought of contacting Sunaina but had decided against it. But he was sure in his heart that one day, he would meet her, or at least, hear from her.

He remembered Sunaina's passionate love for Doon and Mussoorie, recalling his own visit during their university days. Doon had been a quiet little town then and had not even dreamed of growing up overnight into a noisy commercial capital. Some other college friends had also been with them and they roamed all around the valley, enjoying its joyful sights and sounds and the unpolluted air which made them feel like little children, running in the lush green grounds of the cantonment area.

His eyes filled with tears as he looked back on those miraculous years when all they could ever want had been theirs for the asking. Those dream days would never come back and nor would they ever walk together on tree-lined drives into the mountain sunset. He had no one to blame but himself. And he never stopped blaming himself for his lack of moral courage. He had never realized at that time that Sunaina was part of his heart, his soul, his very existence. By shying away from making her a part of his life, he had forfeited beauty and happiness forever. His life with Megha had been nothing but a compromise. His lack of decisiveness had prevented him from taking any step which would allow him to be free of this life of mere adjustments.

He had stopped singing at concerts. He sang for himself sometimes, at home – in the car. But Megha had little interest in music except present-day film songs. Ranvir often felt like talking about music to someone, but classical music was not to Megha's taste. He could not remember even one conversation between Megha and himself which he could call "heart-to heart".

He had ten days before returning to Jammu where he was posted. He had often thought of going to Mussoorie alone. Sapan, who was their good friend, had once told him that Sunaina was living with her mother in Doon. This time, his plan materialized as Megha, with their daughter Saloni, was going to stay with her parents in Jaipur for three days. He would go to Mussoorie and look for his lost world, to have just a glimpse of the beauty his soul had been hankering after for years. He would go ... he had to go.

It was a beautiful winter morning in the hills! The warmth of the early morning sun was not effective. It was only by noon that the winter sun brought comfort to the shivering town of Mussoorie.

This was the Saturday chosen by Tanu, Sunaina and Roop to visit the hill town, just an hour's drive up from the valley. It was the girls' day out and a lot of excitement had preceded the trip. Shashank didn't want to go and was with Tanu's Dad at home.

It was around mid-February. Doon was quite cold too. All of them were well packed in their woolens.

Chewing gum, chooran, imli and Avomine tablets were bought on Friday evening. All these were important for Sunaina whenever she went to the hills as she was always hit by nausea on such trips. Sandwiches were packed and so were mineral water bottles. They took Tanu's car as she was adept at driving upto Mussoorie. Sunaina refrained from driving in the hills and always loved Tanu for taking care of that.

"I'll sit in the front with Tanu Mausi," said Roop when they began their journey. Sunaina was happy about that. "Why did Naani not come? She's always practicing with Ustad Saàb for the Basant program," complained the little girl.

"We'll make sure she comes along next time around," said Tanu, kissing Roop on her dimpled cheek. Roop had got her dimples from her dad. Sunaina had always envied people who had dimpled cheeks. In school, she would feel jealous of girls who had them. She remembered she used to come back from school and sometimes tell her father about it. He would comfort her by saying that she had a beautiful cleft chin which not many girls had in her class. This would make her happy for a while until she was again confronted by a girl with dimpled charm! Perhaps this was God's way of compensating. Prashant's and Roop's dimples were enough to make up for all her lack of them!

When they reached the mid-way point, the "Toll-Tax" point at Kolhukhet, they got down for a cup of tea and some fresh, hot pakoras, which were a favorite with their families and several other people. For years, they had all stopped at Amir Chand's little Pakora and Tea shop. Sunaina remembered him as a not so young man when she had been Roop's age. He must be ancient, she often thought. She saw him as timeless, ageless. Always working alone at making those tiny pakoras which she had never found elsewhere. The onions and potatoes in his pakoras would be visible here and there, looking out of the besan. And the chutney he made was a special secret formula which he had once shared with Sunaina some years ago. But she was sure he had left out an ingredient or two as it never tasted so good when she made it. Rock salt was an important ingredient in this magic chutney.

"Beta, you have come after a very long time," Amir Chand remarked.

"Yes, we have been a bit busy but will come more often now," said Tanu who always called Amir Chand "Rip Van Winkle," though not to his face.

Having had their fill of pakoras and elaichi tea, they drove on. "Why don't you sing?" Tanu asked Sunaina.

Tanu's favorite song was Kishore Kumar's "*Bekaraar dil, tu gaaye ja, khushiyon se bhare wo taraane*" and Sunaina sang it often, at her request.

However, today she sang one of her own Kishore Kumar favorites from the crazy comedy *Padosan* ... "*Kehna hai, Kehna hai, aaj tumse yeh pehli baar*". And after that she sang "*Woh Shaam kuchh ajeeb thhi*" from *Khamoshi*. She really enjoyed singing these golden oldies of her growing years, which had a special meaning for her as they had seemed so apt. This was true for Tanu, Shridhar, Ishaan, and Ranvir and for Sunaina's mom too. About Prashant, Sunaina could say that the songs had never entered his soul. They had stopped in his mind somewhere and rushed out.

All other people to whom she had spoken about this agreed with her. These old Hindi film songs, with their depth of thought, amazing music and comforting words, were a part of nearly everyone's life.

Reaching Kincraig, they decided to go up to Library Point. There were two ways to enter Mussoorie – one was Library Point while the other was the Picture Palace point. When they had been children and came up with Dad and Mom, Sunaina always used to want Library Point first while her brother Ishaan wanted Picture Palace side. So Dad sometimes bowed to her and sometimes to Ishaan. Roop, like her mother, also liked Library Point better. Tanu liked both.

Walking in the winter sun through the crisp mountain air was a feeling which Sunaina could never describe in words. It was an amazing experience and every time she felt it anew, from the first time she had come here as a little girl in a blue jacket and white woolen cap knitted by her mother. Seeing Roop running along the Mall Road railing, she could picture herself doing that and wondered at how life was miraculously repeated.

They walked for an hour and then sat down for a cup of coffee at "Jhoolaghar". Not many people were around and most shops were closed as it was "off-season". Some shopkeepers were listening to the radio while others were playing a game of cards on the steps of the shop. The atmosphere was one of complete leisure. But in these days of leisure, one could clearly read in the faces of the traders an expression of hopeful waiting for a good season ahead. They could barely make ends meet during the long winter months. Sunaina marveled at the spirit which kept them patiently waiting for summer.

"Let alone Dehra, even Mussoorie has changed. Look at those sky-touching hotels on the hills!" exclaimed Tanu while they were having coffee. Sunaina sat quietly, drinking in each moment. It was after so very long that she had come up to this wonderful town. Nodding in agreement, she told Tanu that she wanted to go to the public library near Picture Palace. "Come on, don't be such a bore!" said Tanu. Roop joined her. It was decided that Sunaina would go to the library for an hour while Roop and Tanu would visit the few shops which were open. They would meet at *Kwality's* for lunch at 1:30. Roop also had plans to meet the Englishman on the horse who asked for his cigar to be lit. "But he might only appear at night," she said. "Let's see," said Tanu.

Sitting in the library, Sunaina looked around and remembered how she and Ishaan had come here to borrow story books when they used to stay all summer at the government guest house where Dad booked rooms for the family. She used to have a tough time keeping Ishaan quiet in the library and many an elderly person would glare at both of them as Ishaan spoke loudly and sometimes even shouted, scampering around the reading space.

She ran her eyes over the day's newspaper. Looking up, her eyes suddenly went towards the gentleman who entered the library right then. For a while, her mind did not register anything. The vision remained merely with her mesmerized eyes. The moment seemed endless. Then, in a flash, as it were, Sunaina realized that she was now face to face with her past. As close as it could ever get. After eleven long years, she and Ranvir were in the same room. In the same town. He did not see her at first as he stood near a rack, glancing over the books, picking up one or two, placing them back. When he turned from the rack, his eyes met hers.

10

It was a bright Saturday afternoon and, for a change, Prashant was relaxing at home that day. He had worked in the morning leaving a few precious hours for himself.

Prashant was more than six foot tall and well-built. He wore spectacles and often sported stubble. His dark hair was thick, curly and worn long. He was fair and with his rare smile, his dimples were enchanting.

He was not a very artistic person, more matter-of-fact. It was this streak in him which troubled Sunaina most. And he realized it. But this was something inherent which he did not wish to change. His habit of calling a spade a spade interfered with Sunaina's rich imagination and she soon switched off after making some effort to get him on her wavelength.

Prashant knew by now that he was a workaholic and hardly had a thought about anything unrelated to his work. As long as there was work to do, he was happy. He had completely lost touch with his family and friends. Even as a student, he was always immersed in his studies. Not for him any bunking of lectures for picnics. He hadn't watched more than three movies during college time. He had spent most of his studying years in the hostel and hardly had an idea what a typical family routine was like.

When Sunaina had felt, after they married, that he should be like others and come home every evening to join her for dinner, he knew she was right but gradually, all her efforts had made him even more stubborn about his habits and he simply had refused to listen to it anymore. "That's it!" he had told her clearly. "Take it or leave it."

He could never be subtle about anything. He was blunt and sometimes quite rude. His words felt like hammer-blows on Sunaina's heart given her soft nature and she used to squirm and wish that the earth would open up and swallow her. She was not used to hearing harsh words. Whatever Ranvir had decided for their relationship ultimately, he had never once raised his voice to Sunaina. Neither had her parents.

She and Ranvir had both been like two children, having fun, laughing and singing. They had no ego issues with each other. In fact, she would sometimes throw tantrums and Ranvir would go to any extent to pacify her. He pampered her and made her feel like a little girl. But Prashant, in his gruff and down-to-earth manner, had, on many occasions, hurt her sensibilities. He was self-centered and inconsiderate to an extreme. While they had been engaged, he had made her feel very special and cared for. This had given her a reassuring feeling that she could be loved by another good looking man even after Ranvir had left her for a stranger. It nursed her wound to quite an extent.

But she had seen some glimpses of his mood swings even during their courtship. Once they had been shopping for books in Janpath when she met Parag, one of her college friends who was also from Dehra Dun. She introduced him and Prashant to each other. Parag and Sunaina spoke to each other for a while about their hometown. Once Parag left, she could see that Prashant had a look of anger about him. Moving on to a coffee house, she walked quietly beside him. When they were sipping coffee, he began his tirade. He actually expressed resentment that she had spoken to her old friend for so long. She was quite taken aback and tried to explain herself, feeling terrible. She could feel that he was demeaning her by implying that she had been close to Parag at one time. She found it very strange and shocking but after a few days, she forgot about the ugly incident. Little did she know then that her married life would be replete with such episodes.

Over the years, Prashant had realized where he had been wrong, unreasonable. While it had all been happening, he had not cared to think about it though he was subconsciously aware of it. In retrospect, things always appeared clearly but then it was too late to make amends. When he remembered how he had behaved towards Sunaina on many occasions, he would sometimes try to justify his conduct to himself. But later, the feeling that he had been atrocious prevailed.

He knew he was different from the people he worked with. His outlook on life was far removed from theirs and though he missed Sunaina at times, he was quite comfortable by himself and with his work. He too dreaded the conflict surrounding them when they had lived together in this house. He could make out that Sunaina would never hold him in the esteem she once did and this made him feel worse and he would again jump into a kind of war with her and her silence. It had become a vicious circle!

Roop was Prashant's weakness but knowing that she was happy with her grandmother and mom in Doon was a big comfort to him. Seeing her during vacations was something he looked forward to besides his work assignments. She was his baby and would always be close to his heart. He smiled to himself, thinking about Sunaina's accusation that he had no heart to begin with. Their differences apart, he could not help being fascinated by the strength of Sunaina's personality and strongly-held values which her parents had taught her during her sheltered upbringing.

He got up for some water and, suddenly, his cell phone rang. It was Roop, calling him from Tanu's phone. "Guess where I am, Dad! In Mussoorie, having a softy ice cream," she said excitedly.

"And you know what, we are also trying to find that Englishman I told you about – the one who rides a horse and asks for a light for his cigar."

"That's great! Please tell me if you find him and say I said Hello to him," said Prashant, Roop's infectious excitement rubbing off on him and making him feel almost like a little boy. "I'll talk to you again," said Roop and ended the call. He wondered why she wasn't calling from her mother's phone.

That was the moment when Ranvir had entered the Mussoorie Public Library.

This was something time had not prepared Sunaina for. She was greatly disturbed by the sight of the man who had made a decision, all on his own, to change her entire life. She had never thought she would ever come across him again. She had no idea what to do and how to deal with the sudden upsurge of resentment and regret she felt at that moment. Resentment at how he had left her when she was closest to him and regret at the loss of years which they could have happily spent with each other. By the time she and Ranvir could collect their wits, they were out of the library and standing near its gate without having said a word to each other. They had realized, even in the dazed state, that they could not remain in the library, among several people. They needed to be out of that room and alone. So they walked out, Ranvir behind Sunaina.

"How have you been?" Ranvir asked her, as if he had met her a week ago. He looked the same but for the few strands of grey near his temple and the weight he had put on. Dressed in black trousers with a brownish pullover, he looked almost as boyish as Sunaina remembered him. And she couldn't help staring at the longlashes covering his brown eyes.

"I've been okay," she said, totally at a loss for words. She was still shocked to meet him after eleven years and didn't know how to react to this moment, to his reappearance as if from nowhere, on this beautiful winter afternoon. She was not sure whether to express her anger which she had kept locked up in her heart all these years.

"How's your music? Sapan told me you are teaching in Doon," he said, as if informing her.

"Yes," she said tersely as they began walking towards the Mall. Sunaina, in her light pink salwar and kurta and short black coat, her hair tied in a long, loose ponytail, looking more like a student than a teacher, walked, as if in a dream, slowly. "My daughter and my friend Tanu are with me. Let's join them," was all she could think of saying.

Conflicting feelings clashed with each other in her mind and heart. One moment, she felt all the years melting away. Felt as if she and Ranvir were walking along the Mall road near the University. The next moment she thought why was she not showing him her anger and hurt. Was it because the years had dimmed the anger, killed the resentment and healed the hurt? She wasn't even sure of that.

When she and Ishaan used to spend their summer vacations in Mussoorie, they often visited this library. There was an old world charm about the wooden roofed library with large wooden cupboards full of rare and classic literature. Little did Sunaina know in those days of childhood that one day, the Mussoorie Public Library would witness such a dramatic moment of her life!

"What brings you to Mussoorie?" she asked him.

"Something was pulling me here, so I came and found it," he replied with the gentle smile which lit up his face. Sunaina could not smile. "I find all this rather difficult to believe," she said scornfully. Her voice was wet with her unshed tears. He did not know what to say to this, as if admitting the huge blunder he had committed, greatly changing both their lives. They didn't ask each other anything about their spouses or parents or jobs. This was not that kind of meeting. It was one of those encounters which is on an extremely different plane. Totally out of context with sharp reality … the moment where all logic fails, all reason vanishes. The moment of truth. And yet a dream.

Tanu and Roop were most surprised when they saw Sunaina with Ranvir. Tanu knew him from college days and had been fond of him too. But since she learned of his dilemma, she was not willing to forgive or forget. How dare he do that to her Naina, she always thought. She couldn't even forgive Sunaina for having forgiven him! When she saw him with Sunaina, she was greatly put off but was careful not to show her feelings due to the presence of Roop. But her expression was enough to let Ranvir know what she thought of him and always would.

Roop was seeing him for the first time. When Sunaina told her that they had studied together, Roop was all excitement. "Was Mamma naughty?" "Was she always in the library, as Naani tells me?" and several such questions she hurled at Ranvir Uncle. Tanu was not too happy at the prospect of having lunch with Ranvir and making small talk, but she knew that she would have to do so, for her friend's sake. Had Roop not been here, she would have really given a piece of her mind to this man who had given deep pain to her dearest friend and led her to marry a man who was so tough with her. With great difficulty, she held back her fiery words. But her eyes said it all.

Roop took a liking to this new Uncle and Ranvir was charmed by her. She was a real sweetheart and he was busy talking to her while Sunaina and Tanu looked at each other and communicated as they had done ever since they could remember.

They had lunch, followed by coffee. Roop had another icecream. The conversation was limited to questions and answers, mostly oneliners among the three adults, interspersed by Roop's comments on Mussoorie, on Shashank's school and on her own approaching examinations. Sunaina tried her best to keep the conversation on a level of politeness as Tanu made no such effort. "Tanuja, it's good to see you and Sunaina together after such a long time," said Ranvir.

"Well, everyone is not as ruthless as some people can be! Some of us are quite boring and stay the same throughout our lives," said Tanu. The sharp sarcasm was not wasted on him.

Ranvir excused himself after lunch. He had exchanged phone numbers and email IDs with Sunaina and promised to be in touch. For Sunaina, it was a bit of a relief that he parted from them. She was wondering how their day would turn out if he stayed with them until evening. She did not invite him to Doon on his way back to Delhi. She didn't even ask him how long he would be here. Something inside stopped her. Even she didn't know what.

Too much had happened and she could handle no more today, thought Sunaina.

Seeing Ranvir walking away, she felt that she was leaving her dream and waking up, aware of the sights and sounds around her. Roop wanted to go on the Giant Wheel at Jhoolaghar and Tanu wanted to sit near the railing and enjoy the amazing view of the Doon valley. Putting Roop on the Giant Wheel, they both sat on the bench near it and began talking.

Tanu gave vent to her feelings, chiding Sunaina about her silence. "You should have told him all you have kept inside you all these years!" she said, quite worked up. "How could you treat him so cordially?"

Sunaina caught hold of her friend's hand and tried to calm her down. "Tanu, I know I should not be saying this, but I was really happy to see him after so long. It was as if I suddenly went back in time when life was a celebration, a constant joy and there were no harsh problems to be dealt with at every turn."

"I know what you mean," said Tanu, "But..," she stopped herself. She suddenly understood that this was Sunaina's moment and didn't want to spoil it by saying too much.

"We shared a lot, Tanu, and today I felt that I suddenly met a part of myself which I had forgotten all about, a part which was close to the real me and extremely important to me," said Sunaina, her eyes filling up.

Tanu, now calm, put a hand on her arm and gave her a look which said she understood. That was enough for Sunaina. She collected herself and called for Roop to come down from the Giant Wheel.

By the time they all got back home, it was almost dinner time. The temperature had suddenly dropped and clouds gathered in the sky as they were driving down to Doon. "Is it going to snow?" Roop wanted to know. "It might, by tomorrow," said Sunaina, while lost in deep thought.

"Mom, I have to tell Dad that I didn't meet the Englishman on his horse," said Roop.

11

Ishaan had not been able to get leave in January and would be coming home for Holi. Prashant was coming for Holi too. There was still a month to go before Holi and Sunaina didn't want to think about it. She had never been fond of it. She had never played it even as a child.

Holi heralded summer through which she lived waiting for autumn which bathed the valley in its orange, brown and russet hues making the hills look as if they were waiting for the pure and lovely snow after having borne the torture of the heat in summer.

She was busy preparing the eleven girls for the board music examinations. Besides Smriti and Rewa, Ankita, Bakul, Neeti, Muskaan and Suhaana were also good while Deviyani, Sunanda and Pia needed extra attention. Extra classes were required and Sunaina was completely lost in her music. She had also asked the students to feel free to come over to her place in the evenings if they needed to. Roop was also preparing for her examinations. The days were short and the cold was extreme at times. It was a severe winter and with exams around the corner, teachers, students and parents were all part of a drill which happened every year.

Mrs. Bakshi's *Basant* concert was a welcome break for Sunaina and Roop. It was from four to six in the evening at the Rangers' College Grounds. Sunaina wrapped Roop in two jackets. They would be sitting in the open. She herself wore two sweaters and a shawl and felt like an Eskimo which she often did in Doon winters.

"It seems we are going for an Eskimo concert," said Roop with such a straight face that all of them burst out laughing. Tanu was also with them. She brought the chocolates, dates and perfumes which Sumeet had bought in Dubai. Roop was more excited about the goodies than about the concert. "Naani, don't be nervous," she told her grandmother while they were on their way to the concert. "Okay darling, I will try not to be," said Bhairavi, giving her a kiss on the forehead.

Sunaina, as well as Roop, had told Bhairavi about meeting Ranvir. She spoke to Sunaina about it and asked her about him. Sunaina did not have much to say and told her the facts and how he had lunch with them and went away. Sunaina knew that her mother had been quite fond of him and had been disappointed when they had parted. His love for music had won Bhairavi over. During his visit to Doon, they had had a kind of a mini-mehfil where *ragas* had flowed and *taraanas* had reigned.

In her heart, Sunaina now felt new stirrings for a past love. Stirrings which told her that it had perhaps never become a past love for her all these years. Had she been lying to herself all this while? She could no longer deny that her feelings for Ranvir had not changed. She still loved him. Her innermost being had not forgotten this love even for a moment! Ever since she had come back from Mussoorie, her thoughts had been wandering towards Ranvir and many things which she had forgotten about their time together suddenly came out from under the several layers her mind had placed over them. Much as she would like to believe that she had now become devoid of all emotion, she could not escape the fact that Ranvir had once again succeeded in making her forget all logic and reality. Just as he had done in the college days. She was amazed at the way she again felt like a college student who had fallen newly in love!

Somewhere, deep inside her, her saner mind cautioned her that this perhaps was not the right way for her long buried emotions to resurface. But the deep-rooted love for Ranvir she held in the deep recesses of her heart and her gypsy like spirit, quelled this thought and put a lid on all doubts, urging her to live for the present and forget all else!

The concert was going well. Mrs. Deshpande, her mother's friend, sang a ghazal based on Raga Yaman, an evening raga which scintillated with joy. After that, her mother went on stage. Roop and Sunaina clapped and so did Tanu. She was very fond of Sunaina's mom. She had lost her own mother a few years ago whom she missed every day of her life.

"*Vasant hai aaya, rangeela*" were the words of the bandish on which Bhairavi Bakshi had worked so hard with Ustad Saab who was sitting with her on stage with his taanpura, looking extremely serious.

Sunaina always thought her mother sang better than she did. Their voices were similar but the polish which comes with experience was evident in Bhairavi's singing. Sunaina felt really proud when she heard the loud applause as her mother ended the song. There was also a performance by Ronjana Bhattacharya who sang Raga Bhairavi with a bandish which went "*Tesu khile, aaj mann mor.*"

All three singers were honored by the club with floral garlands and bright yellow shawls as mementoes.

It was dark by the time they reached home. Roop was studying while Sunaina fixed a quick dinner of fried eggs and paranthas with ginger tea to wash it down. She sang to herself while cooking. And suddenly she remembered how she used to sit with her dad, waiting for dinner as her mother sang in the kitchen. A strong feeling of "deja vu" came over her. How beautifully life sometimes repeated its special moments!

12

Tanu was sitting alone and thinking about her problems. Her dad was unwell of late and she had been worried about him. Now there was the nagging feeling that all was not well between her and Sumeet.

He had been paying absolutely no attention to her and Shashank, let alone her dad. Tanu's in-laws also lived in Doon. She had a mother-in-law, a brother-in-law and his wife. Sumeet's sister, Sameera, lived in Lucknow teaching history in a women's college. She was older than Sumeet and single. Tanu got along really well with her.

After her mother's death, Tanu and Sumeet had shifted into a house on her father's residential campus. There were two independent houses in the compound and Tanu's dad lived in one while she and Sumeet lived in the other. They had their meals together. Her in-laws and their relatives complained about this decision but Sumeet had been with her totally. "We are in the same town and will always be dropping in," he told his mother who was quite upset with this arrangement. Even several years later, Tanu was not comfortable at her in-laws' place. And there was no question of their visiting her father's house!

But she had noticed that Sumeet was now a little antagonistic towards her, as if wanting her to show how grateful she was to him for having supported her. Perhaps it was his male ego which was now coming to the fore and which made him feel restless, living at her parents' home. There was a strange feeling of guilt that was gripping him for having lived away from his own people while being in the same city. He threw his weight around quite a bit these days. Tanu was not happy at the way things were between them.

Despite all this, Tanu had never regretted her decision to be with her father. Shridhar was always away so her father had no one else in the whole world! Tanu had promised her mom, during her mom's illness, that she would always be there for her dad. She had been a wonderful daughter. Even the meaning of her name, Tanuja, was, amazingly "daughter" and she lived up to it!

She did not usually discuss Sumeet's behavior with Sunaina. This was a major difference between the two friends. While Sunaina always poured out all her grief in Tanu's presence, Tanu had always been the pillar of strength who rarely spoke of her own troubles and always tried to cheer Sunaina up whenever she was down, which was quite often!

Sumeet drove in just then and she brought out another cup of coffee. He seemed quite tired and a bit off-color.

"Shashank called up today and said his exams are going well and he has to get back here next week," said Tanu.

"You can fetch him back, I'm sure!" he said.

Tanu didn't say anything just then. She thought there was still time before the school closed and she would talk about it later.

"Tanu, my work is not going on well and there seems to be a real slump in the market," said Sumeet.

But Tanu felt that this was not all. There was something else which was troubling him and which he did not wish to share with her. He had coffee and then went for a bath.

Tanu sat thinking, having yet another cup of coffee. She often wondered whether Sumeet had ever loved her. She had got married to him immediately after completing her Post Graduation. She had been in a girls' school and also in a girls' college. She had hardly met any boys during her adolescence and had always missed having a "crush". She had never experienced that heady feeling of adolescent love which other girls used to describe. The only person she had ever had a crush on was Vinod Khanna, the famous actor who was extremely popular when she was in Class Six or Seven. He was a joint crush of Tanu and Sunaina for a couple of years.

They even used to watch those of his films which didn't do well at the box office. When they had seen his film *Imtihaan*, in which he played the role of a suave teacher, how they had wished and prayed that they could get a teacher like him in their school. "Thank God that didn't happen or both of you would have stopped studying and would have always been looking at him." Sunaina's mother used to say.

Tanu smiled as she remembered those crazy days of innocence when she and Sunaina actually fought over Vinod Khanna and used to have a competition going in the number of photos they used to cut out of film magazines and paste in a scrap book. How funny it sounded now! Well, that was the beauty of innocence. It was so artless.

"Well, Tanu, I met Vinod Khanna at a music function in Delhi," Sunaina had told Tanu last year. "You should have told him about his two great fans from Doon," she had told Sunaina.

"I almost would have if Prashant had not stopped me," said Sunaina.

It was unusual for Tanu to think too much of the past. But she was feeling really nostalgic today. Things had not been going on well with her and she was forced to take refuge in memories of her "golden days" as she often called them.

She wondered why and how things had changed so very much. Something precious had been lost. She could not describe it in words but could feel it strongly all the time. Though she tried her best to remain cheerful and cheer others up all the time, there were times she too needed to be cheered up. All those close to her seemed to have forgotten that, somehow. She wondered how and why that had happened. She was always expected to be the strong one. Tanu, the dependable, Tanu, the comforter, Tanu, the pillar of strength. She was tired of living up to this image.

When her mother had been alive, she was the one who understood that Tanu was actually quite vulnerable. But her father had always looked to her for strength and comfort. And to keep her promise to her mother, Tanu carried on with the image and felt that she would never be allowed to leave it.

Her son was also quite practical and had always wanted to be in a boarding school. He loved to play various games and had become quite independent. In a way, it was good for him, she thought. But she missed him. Though he was just an hour's drive away. Well, that was why she had agreed to send him. She wouldn't have sent him further than Mussoorie. And the fact that he was doing well and was happy at school was a great consolation to her.

Tanu was not as emotional as Sunaina though. Sunaina's feelings always came first and thinking later. This had caused her misery on several occasions. But when it came to losing temper, Tanu was quicker to do so. Her anger would vanish equally fast though. It was like a flash during which she would not see any sense. But these were rare occasions and related to specific matters.

In all these years, there had not been even one confrontation between Tanu and Sunaina. They had had misunderstandings but managed to iron them out quickly and simply, by telling each other what they had felt and when. With Tanu, Sunaina could be expressive about misunderstandings but with others, she found it almost impossible to be open. Luckily, the differences between her and Tanu had never been too serious! They could not afford major differences as they would not be able to do without each other at all. They were like each other's "other self". This term had been evolved by Tanu and Sunaina had found it apt. They were like soulmates. Some people even went to the extent of calling them twins! But Tanu felt that they were too different from each other to be that. But despite their differences, they were as close to each other as twins are.

13

Holi was close and only a few examinations remained. Sunaina and Roop had been extremely busy. Just a day before Holi, Prashant and Ishaan were expected. Roop was very excited and so was her grandmother but Sunaina did not know what to feel. She had hardly any time to make preparations for the festival. Gujias were prepared by her mother with other sweets and savories too. Roop had begun collecting her pichkaaris and balloons and had also asked her dad for more supplies.

Prashant was coming for just two days while Ishaan would stay for two weeks. It had been quite a long time since he had come home.

Ranvir had called Sunaina a few days ago and had asked her how she was doing. They had spoken for around four minutes, quite formally. She told him about Prashant's Holi visit and also asked him where he was spending Holi. He replied that he would spend it in Delhi and return to Jammu. He sounded a bit nervous, as if he was speaking to her for the first time. She was not nervous but was at a loss as to what to say to him, He didn't mention their meeting in Mussoorie and neither did she. But she was very happy to get a call from him.

Sunaina had been feeling for quite a few months now that she was not doing justice to her music. She believed that she could touch greater heights in music and wanted to take steps in that direction. But there were some constraints as she was not ready to go to big cities and perform there and did not have the resources to cut an album of her own. She often dreamt of starting a unique music school in Doon. There was no good music school in her beloved city. But she had not been able to decide clearly as to which was the best possibility for her to achieve. Considering that she would like to stay in Doon, she felt the idea of a school most viable for realizing her dreams of being a well-known name in music some day.

"Mom, please help me learn this chapter," Roop said interrupting her thoughts as she brought her English text book.

While teaching Roop, she always remembered how her father had taught her religiously, from Class Two onwards. She loved the time when they sat together to study. He easily came down to her level and she now wondered how he could do so, being such a serious and well-known professor of English Literature.

She missed her father every single day. His death had been so sudden that she had not even had a chance to talk to him beforehand. She had never really overcome the feeling that something had been left incomplete, like a story without a conclusion, a raga without its detailed rendering, left suspended midway.

There were so many things she wanted to discuss with her father. Sometimes, she would talk to him when she was alone. And she really felt that he was listening to her, somewhere. It gave her great satisfaction to share her thoughts and problems with him. With him around, she had always felt secure, without a single care in the world. He took away all her troubles, just by placing his gentle hand on her head. She remembered how he would pat her on the back every time she came home, even with the smallest achievement. He had made her believe that she was the best.

She wanted her father to explain more about life. What he had told her was not enough to tackle today's situations. Her mother's advice was never as balanced, as viable as her father's. Even her mother was often at a loss now and she asked Sunaina how to deal with some situations!

It always came to her mind, when she thought of her dad, that she was somewhere responsible for depriving her little Roop of one of the most precious relationships in the world – that between a father and a daughter. This thought she usually dismissed quickly, as it disturbed her greatly. But deep in her heart, she knew that in this context, she was a culprit.

Ishaan arrived in the afternoon and Prashant in the evening. Roop's excitement knew no end.

Ishaan was still sleeping when Prashant arrived. Roop woke up her maamu and they all sat down to tea. All the goodies prepared for Holi were brought out and enjoyed. Sunaina had made fresh paapri chaat and aloo tikkis which both her brother and her husband relished. She packed some for Tanu and Sumeet as they would go and meet them later in the evening.

Prashant sounded extremely relaxed and light-hearted which relieved Sunaina as she was always wary of his changing moods.

Both Ishaan and Sunaina discussed how Doon had changed for the worse so fast. "Some of the old houses which I remember from my schooldays were looking so uncomfortable sandwiched between those luxury apartments which have come up all over Doon," said Ishaan.

"Didi, do you remember the famous Woodland Cottage on Eucalyptus Road? I saw it today. It looked so strange amid those ugly new buildings. And Eucalyptus Road no longer has any eucalyptus trees!"

"I know, Ishaan, I have seen all these changes come about every day and they are now irreversible," she replied while pouring tea into the cups.

"My friend Nitin's old house in Race Course has been sold to a builder and is being demolished. What lovely plum trees it had. I can't forget the tangy taste of the raw, green plums we used to feast on!", said Ishaan.

"And once when you had an overdose of them, you went green in the face and vomited all evening!", Sunaina reminded him, laughing like a little girl.

Prashant could understand what the old Doonites must be feeling but he could not see why so much discussion was needed on the subject. He had always lived in huge cities where all roads and all houses looked the same.

"I just cannot think of any city which ever made me so nostalgic. I wonder what such a feeling must be," he remarked.

"I think it happens only when one stays in a small town for many years in one's growing up years," Ishaan replied.

When Ishaan asked Sunaina what she and Prashant were planning for their future, there was an uncomfortable silence in the room.

And then Prashant came out with a statement which took all of them by surprise.

"We are all looking for a life of our own. I seem to be searching for it in Delhi while Sunaina is seeking it here. Let us complete our search. Then we'll see."

It struck Sunaina as a perfect description of what they had been doing. Looking for a life of one's own! Of course, that's what she was doing. Would she succeed? Or would she keep looking all her life?

Ishaan laughed. "That's what we all keep looking for, don't we?" he said. "But most of us do not find it."

Roop could not sit still any longer. "Let's go to Tanu Mausi's house, Shashank must have come back by now. His school has closed," she said. "Please, please, please get up. Let's go."

Ishaan was meeting Tanu after a long gap and somehow, he had never met Sumeet until now. And even today, Tanu had said that Sumeet was out.

Tanu's dad sat down with Ishaan and asked him about his various army postings. He himself was a retired Lieutenant Colonel and was pleased to meet an army man.

Prashant, Tanu and Sunaina sat at another table while Roop and Shashank played on the lawn. Tanu and her dad enjoyed the chaat while the others had Nimbu Paani made from fresh lemons from Tanu's lovely garden.

"Tanu's famous squashes, pickles and jams just can't be matched," Sunaina said, while enjoying the fresh lime.

Tanu was in the habit of keeping awake half the night, as late as 1:00 or 2:00 preparing these magical potions and pickles, and then sharing them with her friends. It gave her great joy to do this and the praise that was showered on her for them often embarrassed her.

Roop would tell her mom to learn from her friend. "Well, dear, she has been trying for years to teach me but I am a bad student in this case," Sunaina would tell her daughter.

Holi came and went, with much excitement for Roop. A bit of gulaal, a bit of socializing and lots of gujias was what it finally amounted to. As usual, Sunaina waited for it to end peacefully.

Sunaina remembered how when she was in Class Twelve Holi had come in the midst of the board exams. She had locked the gate of her house from the outside and jumped back in early in the morning.

One of her neighbors, Vanya, had seen her do that and she went and told the entire neighborhood gang that Sunaina must be attacked and taught a lesson.

Vanya or Vanu, as she was lovingly called by her parents and friends, was a typical tomboy who would be often found on trees, sitting there and eating guavas or mangoes. Sunaina was, in fact, quite fascinated by all that Vanu could do. And while Vanu's mother always scolded her daughter and gave her the example of Sunaina's excellence in studies, Sunaina would in turn marvel at Vanu's accomplishments like carrying small puppies and cats, bathing them under the garden tap, cycling while keeping both hands off the handlebars, playing football with the guys and always climbing fences and trees. Sunaina, inspired by her, had tried some of these things but had given up, finding her limitations.

Vanu was not at Sunaina's school, though she was in the same year. Her school was a co-ed one and Sunaina often wondered whether that was the reason why she was so accomplished! Vanu often reminded Sunaina of the William gang in Richmal Crompton books.

It was this tomboy who had seen Sunaina locking the gate. Though it was her own board exam too the very next day, Vanu was not at all bothered.

By eleven o'clock, Sunaina had studied quite a bit and got up to make herself some tea. It was then that she got a shock. Totally colored in all hues of Holi were all her neighbors and friends, dancing and singing in her garden, some carrying buckets of colored water.

She was terrified, as they shouted her name and demanded that she come out immediately. She ran to her dad and begged him to rescue her from them. He readily agreed and told the motley group, from the covered verandah, that Sunaina had a cold and would not be able to come out and play with them. Luckily, they didn't create a fuss and left, as they had come, jumping over the gate.

These were the feelings she had always associated with this festival. But she could understand Roop's thrill and also Ishaan's happiness at spending Holi at home with his mother after so many years.

Prashant sat with her in the afternoon and talked about this and that. He told her that he was trying to place a limit on the number of hours he worked. "Don't do things which are not in your nature," she told him.

"So you also really believe that each of us must find a life of his own," he asked. Sunaina smiled and he smiled too, showing his dimples. Sunaina wondered how her fascination for dimples had not lessened since her childhood.

"I really don't know but I have yet to find my answers to many questions and will certainly try my best to do so. I want to give myself a fair chance of exploring my abilities," said Sunaina, very confidentially. But was also quick to add, "The feeling of detachment is growing within me every day and it scares me sometimes."

"I think it's just a phase," he said, with a faraway look in his eyes. "Don't think so much about it. One day, very soon, both of us will be together and will be happy too."

She wondered how that would happen but didn't contradict him.

14

With the children enjoying the ten day break after examinations, Sunaina and Tanu also felt relaxed. Though Tanu was free only at weekends, they managed to go out quite a bit. The weather was really pleasant. In earlier days, Doon in April had been like a bride bedecked with spring blossoms. Sweet, hopeful scents were in the air and the lanes and bylanes of the city were a riot of blooms. The mango and the litchi flowers filled the atmosphere with an indescribably exhilarating, intoxicating fragrance. It could only be called a divine experience! Now, there were just a few areas in Dalanwala, Race Course and Rajpur where one could enjoy the real beauty of spring in Doon.

In these scents and sights of the spring in the valley, Sunaina found a peace which the best ashram in the world could not give. Seasons were an obsession with her. She had studied the smells and sounds of seasons all her life and, like a true artist, thrived on their beauty and mystery. They always brought back such sweet memories.

She often wondered whether others, besides her mother, were so close to the changing seasons. Prashant was not at all bothered about such things. She had come to the conclusion that women were more sensitive to changes in the weather. But then she would remember how her father used to enjoy these beautiful shades and hues of every season. She was really glad that she had this sensitivity to such changes.

She had had a friend in school who had simply loved the monsoons. Cathy Peters. She had come to the school after having studied at a Convent in Kanpur.

Cathy had joined Sunaina's school in Class Eleven and they had taken a great liking to each other from the first day they met. Cathy was extremely jovial and merry and always had a joke or anecdote ready for Sunaina while they waited for the next teacher after a period ended. Cathy would bring a quick-fix tiffin with a jam sandwich or an apple and banana. Sunaina, however, brought paranthas and achaar, packed lovingly by her mother. Cathy relished these as they were not made in her home. They were from Kerala and mostly ate rice and fish. It was rarely that Sunaina ate her own tiffin. Cathy would, in fact, finish it up before the interval.

Cathy's life was totally different from Sunaina's. She was independent and strong, even at that age. She looked after herself, and also her mother, at times. She would tell Sunaina how she cooked, washed her own uniform and even ironed it. Sunaina was full of admiration for her. However, most of the teachers were a bit upset that the two girls sat together in class and appeared really close to each other. While Cathy was quite naughty, Sunaina was considered the sober one by teachers. They had even hinted at this to Sunaina but she was unconcerned. Cathy was her friend and that was everything to the emotional Sunaina. Tanu was in the Commerce section while Sunaina and Cathy were in the Arts section.

Cathy was always full of beans, always smiling, even in the face of difficulties. Her father had died many years ago and her mother was not well off. She used to stitch clothes to make a living. The nuns at school helped the family. She spent her evenings reading romantic novels which she borrowed from the nearby bazaar. She would narrate some of the highly dramatic love stories from these books to Sunaina who would admire her striking narrative powers.

Sometimes Sunaina would feel really guilty for having a family and parents who pampered her and never let her do any housework. She loved to listen to Cathy's stories about her parrot who woke her up every morning for school and spoke to her both in Hindi and English. She had never seen the parrot as she had never been to Cathy's home in the two years that they were together. Sometimes, Sunaina felt that perhaps the parrot was a figment of her friend's fertile imagination.

Cathy didn't mind getting drenched whereas Sunaina always caught a cold and fever if she did so and had strict instructions to avoid rain as far as possible. And how it used to rain in Dehra those days! The "Four o' clock rain" of the valley was famous and usually occurred in summer after two or three days of heat. The dark clouds began gathering at around three and by four, the downpour would begin and at night, blankets would come out, even in June.

What lovely, carefree days those had been! There were times when, during the monsoons, they had a tough time reaching school when it was raining all night till the morning. On such rainy days, Sunaina's school used to declare a holiday. Most schools did that. Sunaina, Tanu and Shri were some of the students who managed to reach the school gate where dear old Sister Rosa stood under a huge umbrella waiting to give them the good news that it was a holiday. Shridhar would know that his school was closed too as it was the brother school of this school.

The sheer joy of knowing that they could now get back home, and read story books while their mothers made hot pakoras was so extreme that they didn't mind cycling back through the large puddles.

That was heaven! Sunaina could not remember anything else which had given them so much happiness except for the day when the examinations used to end and they all went to the movies.

She had lost touch, somehow, with Cathy. She had even been to the Old Cantonment Bazaar where Cathy had lived. But no one seemed to have any clue about her. All she had was fond memories of a loving, cheerful girl who had taught her how to laugh in the face of problems, a valuable lesson she had always cherished.

"Where are you, Cathy?" she often said to herself. Losing touch with Cathy, she had somehow lost touch with an important part of herself. She had, however, still not given up hope of meeting her again in life. One day, she might just turn up and ask her for a tiffin – full of paranthas and yummy mango pickle!

15

Ishaan had been with them for almost ten days and would soon be leaving for Meerut where Neera and his son were waiting for him. Sunaina and Ishaan had refreshed their memories by talking about various people they used to know and friends whom they had lost touch with. Ishaan also liked Sunaina's idea of starting a music school and so did her mother. Sunaina had been toying with the idea for several months and knowing that her brother and mother approved of it made her feel good. She would first start it at home and then gradually move it out to another place.

"Will Ustaadji and Naani also be teachers in your school?" Roop was ready with her questions.

"Yes, why not?" said Sunaina, excited at the prospect of opening a little music school where different voices would learn the essence of goodness, the soul of life, the beauty of pure sound!

Roop said she would also learn at the "Home School", the name she had given to it.

Ishaan had taken them out for dinner to one of the older hotels of the city, with which he was still familiar. It had opened when they were in school and, at that time, people talked about it a lot. What Sunaina remembered was that it was far out of the city. And true, it was. But that was then! Now, it was in the very heart of the city. The city had changed its heart and had expanded beyond anyone's wildest expectations. Did it have a heart any longer? She hoped it did.

The hotel which was really classy and had maintained its good standard over the decades served "Sunset", a mocktail made from Pineapple, Orange and Mango juices. It was one of the most delicious drinks Sunaina had ever tasted and was a favorite with the entire family. They had made it at home, too, and it had turned out really well.

She had met the Sufi singer Manas Kaul at the hotel while they were waiting to be served dinner. It was their third meeting. She had met him at the Ghazal concert at the Indian Military Academy in October and then at her own school, at the Dussehra program.

They had spoken a little and she gathered that he was now in Doon where his parents lived. He was an only child and his mother was unwell. His father had called him back from Mumbai last September and he had been here since then. In December, he had cut an album of Sufi songs in Delhi and promised to give her a copy.

Sunaina had been taken aback when she had first seen Manas. He was so much like Ranvir! The physical resemblance had been so striking that she could not hide the amazement in her eyes when she had first been introduced to him by a common acquaintance at the IMA auditorium during the tea preceding the ghazal concert. She had, in fact, forgotten to say anything at all to him, in her amazement. Later, she had wondered what he must have thought about her quaint behavior. But when she met him at her school, they spoke a few words.

When they met at the hotel, Sunaina asked him to have dinner with them but he said he was in a bit of a hurry and would meet her later. They exchanged phone numbers.

Sunaina really hoped that he would teach her the sufiyana style of singing. When they spoke next, she would ask him. Sufi music was the ultimate form of yearning and spiritual seeking. The Kaafis of Bulle Shah had always left her spellbound. When she had heard for the first time "*Nahi Bolna Jaa, Dholna, main nahi bolna*" sung by Narendra Chanchal from the superhit film *Bobby*, she had wanted to know everything about that kind of singing. She found interesting the story of Raj Kapoor having spotted him while singing at a "Baisakhi Mela" in Punjab and giving him this song to sing in the film. The song catapulted him to fame. At that age, such things sounded to her like fairy tales!

It was then that her father had explained to little Sunaina the background of Sufism, the philosophy, the poetry, the music, the soul-stirring ideas.

She had been really fascinated and had read Amir Khusro and heard all possible Sufi "Kalaams". Her dad had even taught her some. He had studied Sufi philosophy closely and could explain everything she wanted to know.

Yes, she would learn from Manas, she decided. And she would also talk to him about the school she wanted to start. Perhaps, he could give her some useful tips.

Ishaan would be going to Meerut and Roop wanted to go with him to Meerut and then to Delhi for a weekend before the schools reopened. Sunaina thought she would go, too. But there was still a week before they would leave. She would finalize her plans for the school before that. This gave her a joy she had not known for a long time.

A library of music related books and journals and musical instruments would be needed for the school. She had quite a few books and would buy more in Delhi. The instruments were available in Doon. A medium sized room in their home was occupied by old furniture and some other oddments. That could be emptied and cleaned and the old things could be placed elsewhere. Darris, mats and Diwans could be setup in the room to give it an easy, casual look. She would tell Maaliji to help her with all this work, thought Sunaina excitedly. Little Somu, Maaliji's son, would gladly come and help, too.

Suddenly, Sunaina remembered how she had wanted to set up such a school at their home in Delhi. Prashant had taken strong objection to it and found it a tacky idea. She had been really hurt and had given up the idea completely. She had hated him for his insensitivity. In fact, it had always been her major grudge against him.

"He does not understand my soul and now I do not want to explain anymore. I am tired and want to be on my own," she thought, Ishaan's words echoing in her mind, "We are all looking for a life of our own, are we not?" Sunaina knew that she definitely was, even if she had to take some tough, unpleasant decisions to find it.

Music was her life, her very soul and she lived to sing and to listen to singing. To the extent that despite what Ranvir had decided about her in life, she still respected him for his musical talent and the sensitivity he had towards music.

She thought it was high time she took control of her life. She would start the school, carry on with her job and also work towards giving regular performances in town and in nearby cities. That would be the right beginning towards her goal of surrounding herself with music every minute. Having decided her course in the immediate future, she felt much better. If Prashant was happy living alone in Delhi and working, she too would make herself happy and content staying in her father's home, looking after her mother and Roop and immersing herself totally in her musical pursuits.

Was it Ranvir who had said once that artists should never marry? Well, she felt that to a great extent he had been right. But he had married and so had she. There was no going back on that now! And it was also Ranvir who had said that she was married to music. Well, there too, he had been right.

16

Sunaina went to Meerut and Delhi with interest as she wanted to buy books for the library of her new school. The weather was pleasant for shopping and roaming around happily and she bought a lot of music books, some in English and others in Hindi. She met her mausi and Aditya. Aditya's wife, Surbhi, was a doctor and practiced at Green Park. They had a three year old daughter who was Mausi's little darling, The center of her life.

Prashant, when he heard of the school she was planning to start, did not say much but she could see that he felt she had no plans to return to Delhi and to the life she had one day suddenly left.

The ugly incidents that had made Sunaina ultimately decide that she would take no more of nonsense were unpleasant memories. But they were there, etched in her mind and soul. She could never get over them completely and had closed her heart to Prashant and also to the years they had lived together in Delhi.

After one of his fits of rage during which he had abused her without any fault of hers, it was a flash decision which she took and then there was no desire to go back. Over the years, his angry outbursts on minor issues had pushed her gradually into a stony silence. When she finally reached her own little room in Doon, she broke down in her dad's arms. She was glad she was home, secure and protected from the strange ways of the world, its weird idiosyncrasies!

Within three months, Sunaina had begun working and things appeared to be somewhat normal. But that was only on the surface. She tried her best to hide her pain and disillusionment from her parents. She had lost all her vibrancy and her parents could feel her silent pain. Dad was sorry to see her without her dreams. Earlier, he was the one who had urged her to be practical and realistic. But when he saw her trying to become that, it broke his heart. "I wish I could have given you a world which would match all your illusions and dreams," he had said, stroking her head and feeling sad. "I feel that somewhere, I have failed," he said.

"Please, Dad, don't say that!" said Sunaina," It's because of you that I can again find my inner strength and start life with complete dependence on myself," she had said, trying to appear strong and happy, though she felt really eaten up inside.

Deena had recently come back from her in-laws' place at Saharanpur to her parental home in the outhouse of Sunaina's home in Doon. Maaliji, who lived in the outhouse, had lost his wife three years ago and had a little son who studied in the nearby government school. Deena had been married five years ago and had two little girls by now. She had been coming back many times, even when her mother, Bimli, had been living. Sunaina had heard of a wicked mother-in-law who beat the little girls and cursed Deena for having produced them.

Many a time, Deena had decided not go back. Sometimes, her mother had persuaded her to return and at other times, her drunkard husband had taken her back to Saharanpur after making false promises to the trusting Deena.

But last month, around Basant Panchami, Deena had come back with only one of the girls. She had been in a dreadful state! Bruised and beaten up, tattered clothes and a look of grief and shock in her eyes.

She had been thrown out of the house with one of her daughters. They had kept the elder daughter to learn housework and serve them. That's what Deena told Sunaina and her mom. Sunaina was full of grief and anger at Deena's condition and gave her as much consolation as she could. Maaliji was absolutely shattered at his daughter's plight and Sunaina saw the tears shining in his old eyes. He had been with them for the past thirty years now and had seen Sunaina grow up. He was part of her family and Roop now played with him as Sunaina once had.

"But how will you get your little one back?" Sunaina asked Deena who was now quite calm and collected after crying for two days.

"Didi, I will think of something. But I thank God that I am out of there. It was such a hell."

Sunaina could now see Deena, who must be around twenty five years old, settling down into a routine at the outhouse. She would cook and clean, wash clothes, look after her father and brother while also keeping an eye on her two year old all the time. The little girl, called Noni, would walk into their verandah many times and Roop would enjoy playing with her.

The rhythm of life had a way of diminishing even the worst of crises, Sunaina thought when she saw Deena these days. Somehow, she could not help comparing Deena's condition to her own although Deena was illiterate and ignorant while Sunaina was highly educated and from a different social environment. But when it came to basics, there was not much difference between their fates!

In fact, Sunaina sometimes noticed that Deena was more mature and confident. She was more worldly wise and had a native practical knowledge which Sunaina had not been able to acquire even now despite all her reading and experience.

Had Sunaina undergone a situation where her child was taken away from her, she would have died a hundred deaths. But Deena had taken the better course. She had decided that looking after herself, her old father and little brother and daughter was more important than sitting and weeping over the loss of her elder child.

Deena's presence had changed the entire scene at the Outhouse. It had earlier been so quiet that Sunaina often forgot that it was Maaliji's house. The little boy was in school or studying at home. He was not a naughty fellow and made no noise at all. Maaliji was also a quiet and sober old man.

Her dad had been very fond of Maaliji and called him by his name, Samar Singh. Maaliji's friends called him Samru. Samar Singh would be ever ready to look after the smallest needs of Sahib as he called her dad. Samar Singh and his wife had come to Doon along with Dad and Mom from Lucknow. As a child, Sunaina had begun calling him Maaliji and still did.

Sunaina had been taught by her dad to pay respect to everyone who worked for them. And she had always remembered this. "Their dignity is all they have and respect is all they desire," he had explained to her and she had understood. In the Bakshi household, the word "servant " was never mentioned.

Deena was very good at stitching so Mrs. Bakshi gave her paid stitching work to do. This made Deena feel extremely happy and useful. Some of Mrs. Bakshi's friends also gave her stitching and embroidery work which she finished neatly and on time. She had not had any formal training but was self-taught. It was inborn.

Samru and his family seemed more comfortable and well nourished now and in that, Deena had played a crucial role. Sunaina often admired the serene calm look Deena took with her wherever she went.

"This is a gift of God to enable her to withstand the terrible shocks in store for her," Sunaina's mom once said when they had been remarking that the girl was ever-smiling.

17

Manas was a tremendous singer. He had visited Sunaina last evening and had sung a composition of Amir Khusro. Both Sunaina and her mother were highly impressed with his musical caliber. Tanu had also been at their place and she too appreciated his singing. He was an extremely gentle person and despite the fact that he was forced to come back from Mumbai against his wishes, he did not appear to hold any anger or resentment.

Mrs. Bakshi asked him to spare time for the school they were planning and he gladly agreed. "I can come thrice a week for two hours," he said.

There had been much singing and laughing in the usually quiet household the previous evening. Sunaina suddenly felt light-hearted and younger than she had felt for years.

She had also sung "*Chhaap Tilak Sab Chheenee*" last evening and Manas had said that she had a flair for the Sufi style. This had made her quite happy and she knew that she would be able to realize her dream of singing Sufi Kalaams better. Manas kept reminding Sunaina of Ranvir, though she did not want to admit this even to herself. But Tanu had also noticed the resemblance and had mentioned it to her. "Are you sure you are not going back in time and trying to revive some happy memories?" she asked her.

Well even if she was, Sunaina did not care. She would not let even Tanu talk about this. "As long as you are happy, it's fine with me," said Tanu with a smile. It was true that there were certain things about her which Tanu sensed even before she herself became aware of them. Wasn't that strange? Sunaina thought. How truly Tanu had described herself as Sunaina's "other self"!

Mrs. Bakshi did not remark on the resemblance. Sunaina was thankful for that!

Maaliji, Somu and Deena all came to her help when she began cleaning and organizing the room for the school she had decided to call "*Sarang Sangeetalaya*".

For two days, they kept cleaning and airing the room and disposing off the old things. Some old chairs went to Maaliji's house while the moth-eaten carpets were thrown away. The old, dusty books were cleaned and put in the bookshelves in Sunaina's room and the old table was polished and kept in a corner of the music room. It would house the taanpuras and tablas.

Sunaina planned to start the school by mid-April when all schools would have finished exams and the new session would have started. She had also decided not to have any age barrier for enrolment in her school. Anyone and everyone who wished to learn music would be welcome to join the "*Sarang*" family.

Manas came after four days and Sunaina showed him the room. Some of the instruments she had ordered had arrived and the room looked attractive and serene. A diwan and colorful darris gave it a cheerful look.

"It looks really lovely, just the place I would love to sing in," said Manas and promised to bring a few books from his own collection for the library. Mrs. Bakshi came and sat with the two of them and a mini-mehfil was held to inaugurate the school informally. Coffee and biscuits made the mehfil more lively and Roop brought her guitar and played a tune or two to make her mark on the homely inaugural. They kept talking for more than two hours and it was almost dinner time when Manas suddenly remembered he had a meeting with one of the sponsors of a show which was being planned for July.

He told Sunaina that he would teach her too on the days when he came to the school. "Although I wonder whether I can teach anything to such an experienced teacher and singer," he said. Sunaina laughed and suddenly her laughter sounded strange to her ears as it was such a long time since she had actually laughed like this, in such a carefree manner. She felt grand about it.

Classes had started in *Sarang*. Schools would reopen only in mid-July and Sunaina felt that two and a half months would be time enough for her to establish a routine in her own school.

Most of those who joined the classes were boys and girls between eight and eighteen. There were two middleaged ladies and also a man who was in his mid-seventies and had been keen on classical music for many years. He had a wonderful voice but no formal training. Sunaina was highly impressed by the reverberating quality of his voice. His name was Raj Singh Mehta and he lived with his son and daughter-in-law near Tanu's house. In fact, it was Tanu who had told him about Sunaina's school.

Mrs. Bakshi was teaching the little ones while Manas had begun taking classes for the young girls and boys and Sunaina was teaching the two ladies and Mr. Mehta. However, a little time was also spent by each teacher on all three groups. The time table was flexible and sometimes, in the evenings, classes were held informally on the lawn. Two tabla players accompanied the classes. They also taught the tabla to some of the children.

Roop was still as excited about this venture as she had been in the beginning. She felt responsible and grown up and helped in her own small ways. She dusted the taanpuras and tablas, kept the books in order and also sang with the little ones. Ustad Saab was still away at his village near Varanasi for a family wedding. He would join them at the beginning of July.

18

Summers in Doon were hotter with the growing deforestation and the increasing pollution in the city.

The litchi and mango trees, which had once been abundant had been shrinking quite fast as people were building houses by cutting down orchards. No doubt the Dehra of the past would soon be forgotten. Dust storms, which never used to occur so frequently, had become a normal feature in summer. It was May now and most of the ripening litchis on the trees were blown away by strong storms.

However, there was still some consolation in that it had rained on many a May evening this year. Last year, there had been no summer rain. Sunaina thought it had gone away forever, like all the other good things of Doon. This May, she was thrilled to enjoy the downpour which always made summer evenings so wonderful in the valley.

"Manas, you haven't seen the real rains of summer here. You were in Jammu then," she told her new teacher as they sat on the lawn one evening after classes at *Sarang*.

"But I have heard about them from neighbors and friends, all the old Doonites," he said.

"Hearing is not the same as experiencing. That rain is more enchanting than all the music in the world," she said.

"Well, I am having a taste of it this year," he said, smiling at her passionate feelings about Doon.

Manas was four years younger than Sunaina. He had not thought of marriage yet, so involved was he with his music. His parents had been insisting for a few years but were not saying anything now as he was happy and doing well. They thought that once he was settled, they would broach the topic again.

Sunaina had noticed that Manas had the same long, curling eyelashes which had made Ranvir's face so special. His voice also bore some resemblance to Ranvir's. Ranvir's voice had, however, not had the slight nasal tinge which was the unique quality of Manas's voice.

His longish hair also made him look like Ranvir. Sunaina stopped herself from dwelling too much on this resemblance. Pointless anyway! A resemblance to someone who was remote from her life. Why did she even notice it? These questions haunted her but she pushed them out of her mind. They would, however, keep sneaking back.

But Manas had a temperament different from Ranvir's. He was clear about everything including himself. He knew what he wanted to do and have. He was not impulsive as Ranvir had been. She had greatly liked his impulsiveness. In that, they had been two of a kind!

She sometimes felt that Manas was too mature. He would think hard before taking any step or making any decision. He was not like artistes usually were – reckless, impulsive, over-emotional and soft. Perhaps that was good for him. Sunaina had seen the problems which could occur from an obsession with either emotions or practicality. Experience had taught her that fine balance was needed for a smooth life.

"I wish I had as much sense as you. Things might have been different for me in life," she said to Manas.

"But then you would not have been you," said Manas in his controlled, resounding voice, smiling slightly at her desire to be like him.

"I guess you are right," she replied cheerfully. She was getting really fond of him and was not yet sure whether this was due to his likeness to Ranvir or due to his own charming personality. And she was not ready to think of the reasons why she was becoming fond of him.

His lessons were very interesting. He also told her a great deal about the background of Sufi music. Most of it she had known but it all sounded new and different from the viewpoint of a Sufi singer and musician. His study had been in-depth to Degree standard. Sunaina was thrilled as she had yearned for a deeper knowledge of this subject.

He had even told her to practice some film songs based on the Sufi style. One of them was a recent song "*Maahi ve, mohabbatan sachiyan ne, mangda naseeba kuch hor hal*." The freedom and elation singing such songs gave had made her want to learn more of such music.

Suddenly Sunaina realized how things were changing within her, after years of having stood still.

Earlier, only time had been moving. Now, she was also moving along with time, at her own pace though.

For a long time, she had not even been aware of her own thoughts, as if in a slumber. Nothing had affected her or made a difference to her inner being.

It was high time she woke up, she thought, feeling a strange joy at her moving in the world which she had created for herself and not the world at large.

She realized that the recent meeting with Ranvir after so many years and her friendship with Manas had somehow made her reconnect with her lost self.

Tanu had often visited her these days but Sunaina noticed that she was not her usual self. Once, she had tried asking her but amid all the classes and settling down the new students, she had not really had the time to have a hearty talk with her friend.

Hearty Talk was a term coined by Sunaina in their school years to describe their long conversations with their hearts open to each other. They would discuss everything – from clothes to books, from movies to neighbors, from headaches to recipes. In school, they often used to tell stories to each other.

These stories were either of books which one of them had read or of films which one had seen.

Remembering those story-telling sessions, Sunaina would always smile to herself and even laugh out aloud. How naïve they had been, how innocent!

Tanu had seen a film called *Chiragh Kahaan*, *Raushni Kahaan* which had Meena Kumari and Rajendra Kumar in the lead. There was a child, too, who was the centre of attention in the film. "You must hear this, Sunaina," Tanu had begun narrating the tale one sunny winter forenoon in school when there had been a free period with the teacher absent and no substitute to take the class.

The film was an old classic and Tanu had seen it at a morning rerun one Sunday with her parents and Shridhar. Sunaina was all ears. The story, however, seemed to have no end. It was a tale of misery and tears, with songs that tore at one's heart.

In the narrations, songs also had to be reproduced by the storyteller. Clothes also had to be described and so had the settings of each scene. It was not an easy task and needed sharp observation, Sunaina realized now.

"But you have already told me about this scene," she told Tanu almost a week after the narrative had begun. "Oh, no! That was another scene. In that one too, she had been crying in front of the hero," Tanu cleared the misunderstanding and happily continued recounting the travails of Meena Kumari and the chiragh. "Oh, Tanu, please try to remember whether this movie has any end," said Sunaina, almost in tears.

And they had laughed throughout that day over this. They still did. Those were the days! Golden mornings, pink evenings and nights that sang with the joys of life in all its varied hues! Everything seemed like a beautiful dream. The world was at their feet and they had just to raise the little finger to get all the things they could ask for. This had been the feeling which had made those times so magical.

Sunaina thought she would go over to Tanu's place and ask her what was troubling her, or she would speak to her on the phone when she was alone for a while.

The holidays had become really busy for the household with the music school running for four hours and housework and shopping to be done. Roop had plenty of holiday homework to complete and Sunaina helped her. Her father was out traveling and Roop was spending her vacation in Doon.

Manas had come once with his parents and Sunaina wanted to return the visit. His mother looked quite ill and she had to be taken home after half an hour as she felt tired. They talked about Kashmir and the tragedy that had marred the natural way of life of the people there. They had first come to Jammu and then to Dehra Dun as some of their relatives were settled there.

Manas had taken after his father but was a bit taller. He was around five foot nine and extremely fair. His eyes and hair were absolutely black and he had a mole on his chin. And though he may not have had the typical artistic temperament, he had the perfect looks of an artist.

19

One Thursday evening Sunaina heard loud noises from the Outhouse and ran out immediately to see what was happening. She was aghast when she saw Deena's husband, Ramesh, pulling her by the hair while she screamed in pain. The little girl was crying and Somu was shouting and crying too. Maaliji was not at home.

After Sunaina had managed to rescue Deena from his clutches, she asked Ramesh why he exhibited such beastly behavior.

She gathered that he had suddenly barged into the house wanting Deena immediately to go back with him to Saharanpur. She had refused and asked him to wait for her father to come home. That had been all.

"Sit down and calm down, all of you," she said, sending Somu for some glasses of water.

Ramesh was in a foul mood and kept murmuring to himself, scowling all the time, looking fierce and belligerent.

Deena said she would not go back to his house. "Didi, even if I do not get my daughter, I will never step into a house where that witch of a woman lives. I'd rather die than go back to that hell," she said, her eyes red with pain and tears.

"It's fine, Deena, no one can force you to go back. Don't get so upset, please."

"She will have to come back. All our relatives are saying that we have thrown her out of the house. We have been painted black by the Biradari. She has to return and tell everyone that she went away on her own," said Ramesh in his high pitched, sickening voice.

"You should have thought of all this before throwing her out," said Sunaina trying to sound as stern as was possible. "And Deena, please do stop crying now or your daughter will keep on crying too."

By this time, Maaliji had come back. Somu had gone out and found him at a neighborhood shop.

Sunaina felt a bit awkward now, sitting like a judge amid the family and wanted to go back home. At the same time, she was apprehensive about the situation if she left. She was thinking what to do when Mrs. Bakshi came to the Outhouse. Somu had told her that things were amiss.

Sunaina was glad to see her mother and felt more confident that things would work out better. Ramesh looked a bit scared now and felt he had bitten off a bit more than he could chew. He started saying that his mother was too dominating and he had no say in front of her. Within minutes, he had gone away, leaving Deena for a few days. Her yearning for her daughter had been refreshed and she was miserable.

Everyone tried to comfort her and assure her that one day she would get her daughter back. "Mem Sahib, they must be treating her like a slave, what should I do?" Deena broke down before Mrs. Bakshi.

Sunaina told her that they would all visit her in-laws' place one day soon and talk to them about Deena's daughter. This placated her and she looked gratefully at her "Didi", trying to smile amid her tears.

Such events strengthened Sunaina's belief that marital relationships were often the cause of the worst possible torment and tragedy.

But when she looked around her, there were so many happy marriages where husband and wife worked in tandem to make life smooth. She wondered how this was possible. Even her parents, who were so much in love with each other, had had difficult moments between them. They both had strong personalities but having spent such a long part of their lives with each other had made them comfortable in each other's company.

But some other couples she had met were carrying on a routine life and that itself seemed a great achievement to Sunaina.

"Perhaps they are all too good and I am a failure or maybe they are better pretenders than I am," she would think. She would feel really inadequate when she saw all these "sugar and honey" married people but, at the same time, she also felt a sense of relief that she could just be at one with herself rather than playing out various roles for the benefit of different people.

Deena was soon normal and went about her work singing to herself. "Music is a part of everyone's life in this household," thought Sunaina as she heard Deena hum a folk song and smiled. "How little it takes to make some folks happy and how difficult some people are to please. That's life!" she told herself.

Listening to Tanu that evening, Sunaina felt really sad. Sumeet had always looked so considerate and gentle. If he was behaving roughly with Tanu, she could imagine how much Tanu would be hurt by his behavior.

"Should I talk to him?" she asked.

"I don't think that would help. Let me see how things carry on for a few more days. It's his mother. He told me that his parents feel bad when people ask them why we have been staying with my dad for so many years," Tanu replied, looking really downcast.

"Oh God, why are things so strange in our society?" Sunaina said telling Tanu about what had happened at the Outhouse the other day. Tanu listened to her story and marveled at how Deena was coping.

While they were having coffee with Tanu's dad, Tanu asked her about Prashant.

"He calls up just twice a week. He seems to have no time even to think of Roop now," said Sunaina. "But Roop calls him up often."

"I do not think that he will ever leave Delhi and come here to stay," Tanu said.

"Even I know that and am prepared for anything. After what happened between us, things could never be the same. When I go to Delhi, I try that I should forget that he is a person different from me, totally unrelated to me in his soul. But it's impossible to do that."

"Beta, if a person is not worth giving up your happiness for, one should not do that. There's just one life for everyone. Why give it up for someone who doesn't even realize its value?" said Tanu's dad, Lt. Col Ajendra Srivastava. He spoke rarely when the two friends were talking to each other. Even when Sunaina used to cycle down to Tanu's house during her school years, Tanu's parents used to leave the two girls alone in the room to gossip, giggle and talk about their teachers and schoolmates. Sunaina remembered how Uncle used to bring them orange squash and namkeen while they talked nineteen to a dozen. Her mother used to sit near them sometimes, busy with her endless knitting.

"Aunty, you seem to be knitting caps and mufflers for the entire town," Sunaina told her often.

Aunty loved to knit. It was like a form of meditation for her. In a world of her own, she would knit on and listen to people talking. Sometimes she would put down the knitting and go and inspect the cooking but would soon be back on her favorite sofa with her needles held lovingly in hand. Sunaina missed Aunty whose benign presence could even now be felt in the house. Both she and Tanu were really lucky to get a wonderful set of parents, Sunaina thought. All through their growing years, their parents had nourished and cherished them, giving them the freedom and independence to make their choices and learn from their mistakes. But she and Tanu both knew that their parents were always there in the background, to lend support and encouragement, and give the much needed advice, just as Uncle had done now, when she was discussing her confusions with Tanu.

Tanu and Naina had also tried their hands at knitting when they were in Class Four. Sister Grace, who taught needlework, encouraged them and they managed to make some kind of mufflers and socks. But unlike Aunty they did not have a real passion or love for the skill and after the initial flush, that had been the end of their knitting ambitions.

20

When Shashank went with Sunaina to spend the night at her house he took along his story books and a small gift for Roop whom he treated like the sister he did not have. Sunaina was very fond of Shashank. The boy bore a great resemblance to his mother, with a wheatish complexion and large black eyes, an oval shaped face with a wide forehead. His eyes always reminded Sunaina of Tanu, innocent but with a touch of mischief.

"Maasi, you spend so much time with music. Don't you get bored sometimes?" he asked her on the way back.

Smiling at the rather serious question from the eleven year old, Sunaina replied that one could never get bored with work which one loved more than anything else in the world.

"Is music your work?" he asked her, wide-eyed.

"Yes, darling, it is. Am I not lucky?"

He nodded wisely as he fiddled with the audio-cassettes which were lying around in the car.

Sunaina's car was like a mini-room. She had all sorts of unexpected things in it which were not usually found in peoples' cars. Manas thought her car was very comfortable as it had all one could need. Spoken with a straight face but she knew he was amused at finding biscuits, combs, small towels, a packet of saunf and some books lying on the backseat.

Like a gypsy she enjoyed these things around her to make her feel at home. Diaries, lots of pens, a perfume or two and a couple of books of poems – all of these were in Sunaina's car on any given day.

She had chosen all her favorite old melodies from Hindi films, especially from the golden 1960s and recorded them on audio cassettes which she kept with her while driving. Lyrics and tunes of these songs were so much a part of her that she needed to hear them often. They haunted her all the time.

She knew that they were part of her sub-conscious as well as conscious mind. Memories of her kindergarten days came alive in songs like "*Badi mastaani hai, meri mehbooba*" from the Jitendra hit movie *Jeeney Ki Raah* and "*Teri aankhon ke siwaa duniya mein rakha kya hai*" from *Chirag* starring Sunil Dutt and Asha Parekh, both her favorites. Some songs which had been close to her dad's heart were also in Sunaina's collection. When she heard these, she thought of her dad talking about their finer points and their flawless beauty. Songs like "*Aji Roothh Kar ab kahan jaaeeaiga*" from *Arzoo* and "*Chhod de saari duniya kissi ke liye, yeh munasib nahin aadmi ke liye*" from *Saraswati Chandra* were two of the songs which her dad had often hummed while he worked. These songs had created an entire world of beauty, poetry and melody for Sunaina from her childhood and often she liked to walk into this little world which resounded with notes dear to her heart ... a little world of soulful, sweet memories that echoed in her very being.

She had sent emails to Ishaan, Ranvir and Aditya and all three of them had congratulated her for her efforts in the new school. Ishaan, Adi and Sunaina had spent many vacations together during schooldays and had common memories. There was a code language, which only the three of them could understand. They also used to write letters to each other when they were in school in the "Tic Tac Toe" code which Sunaina taught Ishaan and Adi.

She had also taught the code to a thrilled Roop who had passed it on to Pihu and Saima, two of her close friends.

Reading Enid Blyton and Richmal Crompton, writing letters to one another and watching evening film shows were the important activities for them in the long summer holidays. Homework was done, too, but they had not bothered as much about it as children these days did. Chilled Mango Milkshakes, Kulfis and Golas made of grated ice and luscious colors made summers a great time. Sunaina often talked to Tanu about how simple their childhood and even their college days had been. "Thank God, we were born when we were. I would not have wanted such jazzy schooldays with those gadgets around me," Tanu had said.

In a game they had often played they used the pebbles of varied hues spread all around the gardens in Doon as jewels. One would become the jeweler and others would get pebbles and ask him to make rings or necklaces out of them. The orders were taken seriously by the jeweler, who was Adi most of the time, and string, sticks and paint were used to make the "jewellery".

Ranvir knew all these childhood secrets of Sunaina and her group of cousins and friends. She had told him and bared her soul to him, in all innocence. They were like kindred spirits who knew each other inside out. That was why she had found herself a different person after Ranvir's decision not to include her forever in his life. It was as if part of her life had been snatched away from her suddenly, leaving her poorer. She had wanted to cry and plead before Ranvir but something had stopped her. She had felt terribly injured in spirit which had made her reclusive and isolated. She found it difficult to let Ranvir know what she was going through. If he did not know that himself, it was no use telling him.

She had never wanted to bear again the pain which she had been through all those years ago due to Ranvir. But there were moments when an intense and sharp feeling of loss flashed through her heart and she knew that she would never love anyone else the way she had loved Ranvir. That love had stayed in a corner of her heart – sometimes ignored, sometimes suppressed ... but always there, like a tiny little bag of soft velvet and gold carrying all the precious moments they had spent with each other and the feelings evoked.

But today's reality scared her. She could no longer see Ranvir as she had for years. He was too far removed spiritually from her. She was part of his past which she was not sure he cherished as she had done. Though when she had met him in Mussoorie, she could see in his eyes that he still held her dear.

However, though the past could never repeat itself, the feelings related to the past could be held in one's soul forever. That is what Sunaina had discovered. She had never let go of memories that had made her happy at some time or the other, like her dad. He had carried all memories in his heart all the time and would share them with his daughter every day. Memories of his school teachers, his parents, his childhood friends, his college mates and even of his students. That was a treasure for him and Sunaina had inherited this love for the past, for the good times and people and things that had been.

"Dad, you have told me hundreds of times about the little boy who used to leave his school bag somewhere in the village after school and kept looking for it at night throughout the entire village. But I enjoy it more every time you narrate it." said Sunaina whenever she heard from her dad the story of Sain, a playful fellow who had no interest in his studies and used to throw his bag down just anywhere after classes and play around in the village until night. He would then roam around the village, looking for his bag, asking everyone if they had seen it anywhere.

"That's because I have let this true little tale stay in my heart so long that it's become a classic," her dad said. Even Mom knew all these anecdotes by heart as she had shared them with her husband long before Sunaina had come into the world one stormy October evening.

In one of the songs which were close to her heart, there was a line which always brought tears to her eyes. It evoked a feeling of irrevocable loss ... a feeling of yearning for people who would never return in one's life, of terms of endearment which no one else could know and about a closeness for which one pined all one's life. The song was one of Gulzar's from the film, *Parichay*. "*Beetee hui batiyan koi dohraaey, bhoole hue naamon se koi toh bulaaye*" was the line which pulled at her heartstrings every time she heard this melody. Nothing could bring back voices from the past and, if they ever returned, they could never sound the same.

21

It was the month of June and the valley was witnessing extreme heat during the day and pleasant weather in the evenings. Sunaina had so often heard eulogies about "Subah-e-Banaras" and "Shaam-e-Awadh" and wondered why no poet had ever written in praise of the beautiful and calm evenings of Doon which made one forget the heat of the day and relax. Banaras must have a wonderful dawn and Lucknow a picturesque evening but in Sunaina's eyes, "Shaam-e-Doon" would leave all these far behind in beauty and tranquility.

Evening was her favorite time of the day. She had never been a "morning person" and remained groggy until almost noon. During the morning music classes she took in school, she was always in a daze, and only after she had had her third cup of coffee did she fully wake up to the day.

All her friends had always teased her about this. She used to study late at night always but could never get up early to study. Once, wanting to experiment, she had woken up at five on the day of her Maths exam in Class Eight. It made her feel so sick that she spoilt her paper and learnt the valuable lesson of not trying to go against nature. Her father had not known of this experiment and was very upset with her when her mom told him. "You should know that everyone has been made differently by God, each of us is unique in his or her own ways. Don't ever try to become like someone else. Be yourself and follow your nature," he had advised.

Sunaina often wondered how and when her father had become her friend, philosopher and guide and then thought that all daughters looked up to their fathers. But she would rather believe that her relationship with her dad was also unique as her dad had said she was. Again the thought of Roop and Prashant crossed her mind. If things had been normal between Prashant and Sunaina, would Roop have been able to experience the same kind of relationship with her father? That would always, in her mind, remain a question, the way things were going on, she thought. Or would she be able to see the two together in a closeness that she had shared with her own father? She pushed the thought to the back of her mind as it disturbed her.

These days, her evening classes at *Sarang* kept her busy. At dusk, she liked being outdoors instead of sitting inside. Once it was dark, she didn't mind being inside the house. The fragrances and colors of the evening had a wonderful effect on her mind and heart, making her a better person.

"Let's have coffee and then we can begin our Sufi class." It was Manas who had walked into the lawn unseen through the open gate.

"Oh! I was lost in my thoughts and didn't see you," she said, giving him a smile.

"I have seen you lost many times earlier, too. Seems you live in a world of your own most of the time," he replied, taking a chair near her.

"Yes, that's right. It is a world of my dreams, my memories and my emotions," she said. "Have you read Faiz? He says in one of his nazms, '*Hamne dil mein sajaa liye gulshan, jab bahaaron ne berukhi ki hai*.' I always follow that."

"Yes, I have read Faiz, though I do not remember having read those lines," said Manas. "Each one of us has an inner world but many never experience it."

"I have lived more in that world than in the outside one," she said, realizing that she had not spoken to anyone about herself like this since her dad had passed away. How had she begun trusting Manas so soon and how had she become so comfortable with him? These were questions she didn't want to bother about. But she was happy that she still had the ability to express herself in words. There was a time, not too long ago, when she had started thinking that she had closed herself totally to people and feelings.

But at the same time, she did not want to get too close to anyone. She had been hurt so badly by relationships that she was extremely wary of emotional and physical closeness to a man. And she knew that she always would. That was the price she had paid for her experiences. Such "normal" things were not for her and the sooner she realized it, the better it would be for her, she knew.

Manas had requested her to try taking part in the concert they were organizing. He had spoken to the organizers and they were keen that she perform at the show. She was a little hesitant but had almost made up her mind to perform after having a talk with her principal. It would give her experience and a new dimension to her art.

She handed over a cheque to Manas for his contribution to the school. Though he felt quite strange taking it, she insisted that she would not turn his music into social service. "As it is, this is far less than your due," she said.

Sunaina had received a phone call last night from Prashant who was now toying with the idea of going abroad and working there for some years. It seemed that he had got a lucrative offer from a firm in Muscat and he had almost made up his mind to accept it.

She was not really surprised as this was something quite in keeping with the way things had been going on in Prashant's mind. She always knew that if he ever had a chance, he would leave his country at once, without giving a thought to anything. She was lost in thought over this when Manas arrived.

Prashant's parents were already abroad and she had known about his penchant for working and living abroad, though he never admitted it to anyone.

But, somehow, nothing he did or said affected her much now. In fact, she felt like a spectator in most situations. When and how this had happened, even she did not know.

"Life is really strange," said Manas, having his second cup of coffee. "I never thought of living in Doon and even following my musical ambitions here but I am teaching, performing, cutting albums … all in Doon."

"Life takes us wherever it has to but at times, one has to keep an eye on it to avoid being dragged into a mess," she replied, calmly.

"Sunainaji, I have never asked you anything personal and will not do so again but what makes you come and settle down here with your mother? If ever there is anything you would like to tell me as a friend, you can always do so."

At these words of Manas, Sunaina realized that there were some things which sensitive persons knew without being told. "Humko kiske gham ne maara, yeh kahaani phir sahi", she said, laughing. It was a tinkling carefree laughter, which had always been appreciated by her mother. "Even if you laugh once a day in the house, the house keeps echoing with joy the whole day," her mother would say. "It sounds like ghungroos".

Sunaina often, marveled at the sincerity of parental love – the only selfless love in her life. The joy parents found in their children and the unconditional love they showered on them was a divine experience and could not be matched in intensity and purity by any other relationship in this world. Even the children's love for their parents was sometimes marred by worldly factors but never had she come across parents who would put anything in life before their children.

And she felt particularly indebted to her parents who had sheltered and pampered her in her growing up years; had provided a safe harbour when her ship of life coursed through stormy seas and choppy waves; had installed value systems and beliefs that sustained her throughout her life. The debt she owed them was infinite and could never be cancelled out. Her return to life, especially to music, had been possible only because of their constant, unstinted support. Was she depriving Roop of such a treasure and pleasure by choosing to stay apart from Prashant was a question that haunted her subconscious. But she quickly pushed the thought aside, given the trauma she had faced, wanting to rediscover her self and her music.

While singing along with her Sufi teacher, Sunaina again thought of the spiritual ecstasy which this music brought to the singer. It was as if the singer became an instrument for a divine message, a yearning for the ultimate sanctity in life and beyond.

22

Tanu was quite surprised when Sunaina told her about Prashant's phone call. "Do you think he will stay back if you insist," she asked her.

"No, I do not think so and I do not wish to insist anyway," she replied. "For me, it's the same if he is in Delhi or in Muscat. It will make a difference to Roop but what can be done? He called me up after making up his mind. And he also spoke to Roop about it."

Roop was at first thrilled to know that her dad would work in another country but when she realized that he would not meet her often, she felt a little sad. But it did not put her down for long. Her dad had told her that the new job began after three or four months.

"Will I be able to come and see you there?" Roop asked him. "Yes, in your vacations, and I will visit you when possible." Roop was very close to her naani and loved her home in Doon. When she stayed with her dad, she used to be happy and excited but coming back to Naani, she felt she was back home, secure in her little world. Even when Sunaina had been in Delhi, she would bring Roop to Doon in the holidays. Roop missed her naanaji a lot now and often Sunaina found her in his study, opening his books and notebooks and touching the pages. She would then hug her little one who had no words to express the feeling of loss.

Driving towards Paonta Sahib on a June Sunday morning, Manas was humming an interesting tune based on the notes of Raga Bhopali. Sunaina, who was accompanying him to meet the concert organizers at Nahan, not far from the Doon valley, asked him to sing the words. "I am still working on it to be part of my performance at the concert," he replied.

"It sounds really melodious. Somehow, I have never been good at composing music," she said.

"But you have so much music in you that you do not need to compose any more," he replied, turning to look at her.

"I would love to believe what you say but don't feel that I deserve such a profound compliment," Sunaina smiled as she told him.

"Why have you stopped believing in all good things?" he asked. "Life cannot carry on well like this, with all our positive beliefs being eroded."

Sunaina realized that he had asked her an important question. Without having understood why she had become like this, she had continued to prevent good things and good people from affecting her. She had kept herself aloof from the bad as well as the good for a long time. Tanu had warned her many times not to close her heart to all the beautiful things in life but it had been difficult for Sunaina to emerge from the vacuum she had created within.

She was trying not to behave in a guarded manner with Manas as she realized that he was a kindred spirit. But was there also, at the same time, a fear that she may get too close to him?

"Manas, I am trying to reconnect with the happy things. I am sure you can see that," she said to him with a gentle smile.

As they reached Paonta, she first wanted to pay homage at the Gurudwara which she had been visiting since childhood and which was one of the places where she could drink in the tranquility and joy of the site. For years, Guru Gobind had meditated here on the banks of the Yamuna and had written "Baani". His "Kavi Darbar" where several poets met the Guru and recited their verses was preserved for posterity.

Sitting in the Gurudwara and listening to keertan, she recollected her daadi's love for shabads which her father had imbibed and she too had inherited. Sung in the ragas mentioned in the holy Granth Sahib, Sunaina felt that these shabads were like the word which had been there before the creation of the world and which would be there as long as the world existed and long after that. Classical music was strongly linked to Gurbaani and this she explained to her students when teaching them compositions from the Granth Sahib.

After taking the prashad of black channas and the delicious kadhaa cooked in pure ghee, they carried on to Nahan for their meeting with the concert organizers. One organizer was from Nahan while another was from Paonta. The concert would be held at Nahan, a quiet sleepy little town which had not changed in the last thirty years. "Lucky Nahan!" she thought. "No builders and developers to kill its spirit as Doon".

"Dear Old Nahan, it's good that you were not made the capital city of any new state," she wanted to tell the tranquil hill town.

It was decided that the concert would be held on July 20 at the Pavilion Ground of Nahan. A couple of Himachali artistes would participate in it besides Manas, Sunaina and Sukriti, another classical singer from Doon. The theme of the concert would be "Saawan" with compositions based on Raga Megh Malhar. "We shall feature light classical music besides pure classical," said Jatin Sood, the organizer from Nahan.

He said that they would come down to Doon in early July and would finalize everything then.

After lunch, Manas and Sunaina drove around Nahan. They went to the Circuit House where Sunaina and her family had stayed one summer many years ago. Things had not changed much and Sunaina made a special request for the delicious tea made with powdered milk which she enjoyed in that summer vacation. It was still available and tasted similar enough to bring back sweet memories.

"Nahan seems to be a younger cousin of Shimla and Mussoorie, doesn't it?" said Sunaina seriously. The way she had asked the question made Manas laugh and marvel at her childlike quality.

Most people he had met in life, especially in Mumbai, had worn masks making him forget that a person free of all pretences existed. Sunaina had that quality and he admired her for it. And what made it even more precious was that she was unconscious of it. He did not want to bring this to her notice and wanted to witness many more spontaneous statements and actions from her.

By the time, they reached Doon, Sunaina was very tired. It was after a long time that she had traveled to that area and walked in Paonta and Nahan. She was tired but happy, aware of her accomplishment by meeting the organizers and ensuring her participation in the concert. At the same time, the outing had been a change after a month at *Sarang*. As she had not gone out in the heat she felt especially good about the visit.

Manas told her his mother was improving now, making him feel much better. She had been ailing for long and he believed that his presence had surely helped her fight the illness. Though his mother always told him to go wherever his music took him, he did not have the heart to leave her and work in the big cities. He had opted for the middle path making short visits to other places with Doon as his work base. That way, he could spend more time with his parents. He had realized sooner than Sunaina had that there is no one else in the world more worthy of one's love than one's parents. He often talked of this to her and she was glad that they both felt this. "There are some people who never realize it," she told Manas, thinking of the stories she had heard about people who ill-treated their parents or ignored them to live their own lives.

"Parents never dominate you or suppress you as some others do. They want to see you grow and blossom," she said, hoping that her views would not sound too biased to him.

Her experiences had shaped her views and built her conclusions about life, and she did feel that Manas agreed with her wholeheartedly. She felt that he had perhaps been in a relationship which had broken due to his decision to come to Doon and look after his parents. He had hinted towards that once or twice. Sunaina knew that she had become too biased against love relationships but chose to diligently believe the lessons life had taught her, though she knew that this was not true for everyone.

23

Deena's husband, Ramesh, turned up one Sunday morning with her elder daughter. He had brought two suitcases with him containing all his worldly belongings. At first, Deena thought that he had come to take her back forcibly to Saharanpur. She panicked and ran to Sunaina. But it soon became clear that Ramesh had other intentions.

"My mother was ill treating my daughter day in and day out. I was not able to take it any longer and protested. She abused me and Deena and my children. I could not bear it and packed my bags and came here," he explained, looking absolutely woebegone.

The daughter's joy knew no bounds at seeing her mother after so many months. She laughed and cried at the same time, and so did Deena and Mrs. Bakshi at the emotional reunion.

Sunaina was happy for Deena and surprised at the decision Ramesh had taken. She appreciated him for his action and knew that Deena's days of misery had ended. Good for the gentle girl who had been pining inside for her daughter but had always put up a brave front. She knew that the family would work together to make a life free of abuse and ugliness. For there could be no ugliness where Deena, with her benign and sweet presence, was.

Sunaina asked Deena to come to the house and take some rice, daal, vegetables and lassi for Ramesh and her daughter who had come by bus in the noon heat. She knew that Deena had not yet cooked the afternoon meal.

Sunaina and Mrs. Bakshi felt very happy for Maaliji's family. Such days were so satisfying and always remembered.

"Ramesh will look around for some work here, Maaliji was telling me," said Mrs. Bakshi.

"Now that he knows clearly what he wants in life, all their problems are over," replied Sunaina. "It's only when one does not know what one wants in life that problems arise," she said to herself.

Mrs. Bakshi knew her daughter was thinking of her own situation, the uncertainty of her future, and her disappointments in relationships.

"How right you are," she said. "But there are people who spend their entire lives without knowing what they want from life."

"That's a scary thought!" said Sunaina. "I do not want to be one of those people."

She knew that it was high time she decided what she wanted to do, anyway!

She did not want her happiness, like Deena's, to depend on anyone's returning to her. That was something she would never want. She had prepared herself for Prashant never being an important part of her life. He had charted a different way for himself and so would she. In fact, she had begun doing that.

"Everyone must find happiness within themselves," she said aloud. Her mother, who was making coffee, heard her and felt disturbed at the fact that Sunaina had, so early in her life, realized a truth which she herself had not yet fully understood. But at the same time, she felt that her daughter could now face anything in life and that was good.

"How strange life is!" she thought. Her little daughter, about whom her father had been so protective even when she was in college, had reached a stage of spiritual strength where she did not need protection any longer. She remembered thc time when Professor Bakshi was not even confident that Sunaina would be able to cross the crowded Delhi roads safely! She realized that there was a limit to how much parents could protect their children from the storms of fate. Sunaina's life had gone beyond that limit long ago. But she knew that she would stand by her daughter at every step of her life while she was alive. She did not need to know any more.

Ranvir was now in Jammu, working. He spent most of his time in office or on tour. But he was in a kind of a trance all the time. Ever since he had returned from Mussoorie, life had not been the same for him. It was as if he had been close to a dream once again in life and had been rudely awoken to carry on, out of touch with himself, with his innermost being and emotions.

He had not mentioned to anyone about his meeting with Sunaina, the days of joy and fondest memories. There was no person with whom he could share what the meeting had meant to him.

Again and again, he relived every second of that beautiful winter afternoon in the hills. Had it actually happened? he would ask himself. It seemed to be like a perfect painting, a lovely scene on the canvas of life, to remain etched on his heart for as long as he lived. Even the pain he felt was far better than the life he had been living with Megha all these years. A life empty of all emotion and warmth!

He felt that he had got a lifetime of happiness from that one meeting. He did not want to analyze why. It was enough that it had come his way. He suddenly felt fortunate and rich.

Ranvir had suffered enough for the one wrong decision in his life when he was in his twenties. He knew he would never have taken such a step if he had been a little more mature. Wasn't it sad that the wisdom which came with years of experience was sometimes desperately needed in the early years! He felt that "wisdom delayed is wisdom denied" was as apt as "justice delayed is justice denied".

With wisdom came regrets at not having been wise enough when young. And how painful these regrets were Ranvir knew only too well.

"Is it possible that we become good friends and be in touch with each other once again, even if it is just through emails?" he had written to Sunaina in his latest email to her.

"We have so many years to catch up on," he had added, feeling anxious about the reply he would get.

He felt that after he had seen Sunaina and talked to her, things had suddenly fallen into place in his life. For years, he had felt lost and disoriented. Whether his sense of guilt had been reduced by Sunaina's behavior or his soul had been refreshed and made to come alive by this meeting, he could not explain. But whatever the reason, he felt complete again.

It's not that he had not tried to understand Megha and feel close to her but he had discovered over the years that the there was hardly anything in common between them. She was totally different. More interested in jewelry and saris, in doing up the house or calling on colleagues and talking late into the night, focused on the latest films, gossip revolving around the film industry and the neighborhood and sales in the town's various departmental stores.

There was simply no comfort for him in such a scene. He maintained a silence on these issues at the centre of Megha's life. She understood that his interests were far removed from hers and this made her irritable and sometimes jealous of the "other world" which he inhabited and which she believed Sunaina had once shared with him. There were other women who could take an interest in art and music as well as saris, talk about history as well as shopping. But Megha did not belong to that category, he knew too well by now.

This led him to loneliness over the years, looking always inwards and living in a world of his work, his memories and his unfulfilled wishes.

But now he would not let anyone stop him from communicating with Sunaina. She was the only one in this world who really knew him. It was this level of comfort and openness he yearned for most. What more could one ask for in this wicked world than a friend who would understand exactly what you meant, exactly how you felt and thought? He would not disturb Megha's world of glitter and chatter but he would not let her deprive him of what his spirit longed for. Though he had been rudely awakened from the dream when he had returned to work and home, he was now resolved to enjoy the feeling of completeness and elation. He had called Sunaina just once since he had come back from Mussoorie and hesitated to call again. But he had sent her two messages on email. Her reply to his last message had not come in yet. But the prospect of regaining some kind of closeness to her was enough to lighten the burden he had been carrying all these long years.

24

Prashant was preparing for his new job. Most formalities were complete and he had begun winding up his work in India. It was late June and he would be leaving by the end of September. There was a lot to be done before that. He was thinking of going over to Doon in July and spend time with Sunaina and Roop. He was a bit nervous as to how they would behave now when they knew that instead of planning a shift to Dehra Dun, he was on his way to leaving the country. He knew he must follow his secret dream.

"I want to discuss many things with you when we meet next month," he told Sunaina on the phone. How Sunaina hated that tone! She had heard it so many times. It had always brought unhappiness and confusion for her. She had come to dread those words, so she did not reply when he said them this time. But they did not have much effect on her and she almost managed to ignore them.

When Sunaina had married him, she had been quite vulnerable and, within a few months, he had managed to get the upper hand in the relationship. It was most unequal and made her feel like an inmate of a reform home. He would not tolerate anything which was not to his liking.

Gradually, the terror took hold over her sensitive mind and she developed a deep-rooted fear of him which killed love. She knew very well that she would not be able to love someone who had, though unintentionally, drilled such fear into her over the years.

The physical assault, along with words of abuse which she had been victim of were the last straw, and she then realized to what extent the relationship had deteriorated. After that, though she had tried her best to put up some appearance of normality it was, in many ways, a finished story for her. Sometimes for Roop, sometimes for her dad and sometimes for the world, she had put up a show. But in her heart of hearts, she knew that even Prashant had no longer any hopes from her. She often wondered who would finally be honest and face the truth. When she was honest with herself, she knew that it wasn't so much her love for her city or her mother that was keeping her away from Prashant as it was her fear of living with him forever. "Forever", in this context, was a terrifying word!

Meeting Tanu after receiving this phone call from Prashant, Sunaina told her that she had finally prepared herself for the ultimate separation from Prashant. Surprisingly, Tanu was not shocked. She had been with Sunaina through so much that nothing about her dear friend shocked her. Tanu believed wholeheartedly in Sunaina's goodness and honesty and would not hear a word against her. She was very protective of her and did not care even if she had to be rude to someone who tried to do or say anything against her.

"How's your Sufi singing going on?" asked Tanu, with a smile which Sunaina understood to indicate the similarity between Ranvir and Manas which both she and Tanu had noticed and admitted to each other.

"Come on Tanu, when I did not try or bother that day to be with Ranvir for a longer while, why do you think I should be fascinated with someone who resembles him?" said Sunaina.

"I never even said a word about Ranvir or Manas," said Tanu, with an even wider smile. Sunaina knew that Tanu was in the mood to tease her. And she also knew why she was pulling her leg ... to make her feel better and forget the unpleasantness which always surrounded her after she spoke to Prashant. The memories associated with him were so bitter that she could never feel good about talking to him.

Tanu's dad had not been well and Raj Singh Mehta, Sunaina's oldest student at *Sarang*, had come to be with him for a while. Sunaina greatly admired the way he had followed his love for music and religiously done riyaz even when he had no guru except *All India Radio* to which he always expressed gratitude.

Sunaina and Tanu had been talking in the kitchen while Tanu made elaichi flavored tea. It was evening and Sunaina had taken an hour off after her classes to be with Tanu and Uncle. She had made dhoklas and carried some for them. Uncle was extremely fond of dhoklas and imli ki chutney which was prepared with gur (jaggery) and roasted cumin seeds and was a great favorite of Sunaina and Mrs. Bakshi.

The four of them had tea and dhoklas in the garden. Raj Singhji was, as usual, in a jolly frame of mind and sang a very old film song to cheer up his friend and also to tell all of them how he was benefiting from his classes at the school. The song was one which Sunaina had heard about from her mother. The words were "*Bahaarein Phir Bhi Aayengi, magar ham tum judaa honge.*" It was a sweet, melodious song – liltingly sad. It created a spell of its own. Sunaina felt like singing, too, and sang one of Uncle's favorites "*Geet Gaaya Pathharon Ne*" from the old film of that name. It was based on raga Durga of Bilawal Thhaat and was one of the rare film songs based on this peace-evoking raga.

Going back to *Sarang*, she took a class of little ones that evening and this made her feel really alive as she heard their sincere, soulful voices maneuvering themselves around the complexities of classical notes. Sunaina spoke to Manas for a while. He was feeling glad that his mother was improving. He said he had met Tanu the other day. "She seems to know you very well," he said.

"She knows me better than I know myself, sometimes," she replied, thinking of what Tanu had hinted at about Manas and smiling to herself.

"I have never had such a close friend and envy you for having one," he said.

"These friendships just happen in childhood. They are not conscious decisions and choices like later in life. That's why they remain so unsullied and natural," she answered softly.

"I agree with you on that. Too much effort goes into most relationships and they become strained and forced."

"But we must thank God for those bonds which are unconditional and which nurture one's soul," she said.

Manas was quiet for a while and then asked her about her preparation for the concert. "I am carrying on with the riyaz and expect to be quite fine by next month," she answered.

"Good," he said. "I will be going to Jammu for a week," he added.

Suddenly it occurred to her that Ranvir was also in Jammu. "One of my old friends is in Jammu now," she said, before she could stop herself.

"Who is that?" he asked, showing great interest.

"We were at the university together. He is now posted there in the government. He's Ranvir Mallik."

"That's great," said Manas. "Would you like me to meet him?"

Sunaina kept quiet and then asked, "When are you leaving?"

He was leaving in four days. She said she would let him know about Ranvir's phone numbers before that. All the time, she tried her best to show that there had not been anything more than friendship between her and Ranvir.

25

Roop had finished her holiday homework and was mighty pleased about that. She had gone to watch a film with her naani and some friends. Sunaina had stayed in as she had a touch of fever. Deena had come over to be with her that afternoon. Ramesh was assisting Maaliji with gardening work these days and learning the trade. Maaliji found it tough to complete the work at three or four houses as he was quite old. By training Ramesh, he thought he would hand over his work to him.

As long as there were gardens in the world gardeners like him would be needed to weed, prune, water, plant, save the seeds and to move about like a benign presence among the trees and flowers. Ramesh would soon learn and then there would be nothing to worry about. Deena and Ramesh would bring up their daughters and manage to live through their industriousness. Maaliji's bad days seemed to be over.

Deena made wonderful tulsi tea and whenever Sunaina felt feverish, she was sure to have some as they had plenty of tulsi in the garden. Both of them were having tea and talking. Sunaina was extremely fond of Deena and found her a reliable and comforting presence, teaching her to be content with whatever was available, to smile in the face of problems and to look after others.

There was a song which Deena often used to sing which Sunaina had picked up. It was a folk song of Uttar Pradesh which said "*Nimbua Taley Dola rakh Dai Musafir, Aaayi Saawan ki bahaar re*", and spoke of the emotions which a girl felt at leaving her maternal home and going over to her in-laws place. The tune was haunting and often brought tears to the listener's eye. The tune had been used in a song from the film *Bandini* which had the words "*Ab ke baras bhej bhaiya ko babul, saawan mein leejo bulaaye.*" Both songs were very moving and had made Sunaina realize the beauty of the folk music of Uttar Pradesh where there were endless Kajris and Birhas sung on various occasions.

"Didiji, we will all live in your house forever and wish that no more troubles come upon any of us. We always pray for the happiness of you all who have been like our guardian angels for so many years," Deena said to Sunaina who was taken aback by this expression of gratitude. Usually, Deena was a little shy in expressing her feelings. Sunaina was touched by her honesty and simplicity and wondered how much Deena would have achieved if she had had a decent education.

"Didi, can you come with me to get my daughter admitted to the school after the holidays?" Deena asked, a bit hesitatingly.

"Why not? Of course, we'll get her to school very soon. Don't you worry about that," Sunaina reassured her warmly, appreciating Deena's concern for her daughter's education.

The two cups of tea did her a world of good and she slept for a while after Deena left. She was woken by a phone call. It was Ranvir. She was surprised and taken unawares.

But soon, the conversation went smoothly but for a few pauses. Sunaina suddenly found herself sharing with Ranvir all that had happened in her life recently. She had not thought she would do so but it just happened naturally – about Prashant and his decision, about Manas and his planned visit to Jammu, about her fever, about the happenings at *Sarang* and her nervousness about the forthcoming concert.

He kept listening and by saying "Okay" or "Wonderful" or "That's great", he expressed his understanding even of that which she was not saying. Sympathy, appreciation, encouragement, joy and sadness were all expressed by him at the right moments in the conversation making Sunaina realize that all these long years apart had not succeeded in decreasing the comfort level between them. She could simply be herself with him and say whatever she felt without fear of being misunderstood. What a wonderful feeling that was!

"I hope I have not talked too much," she said after she had told him all she wanted.

"Not at all. I think you'll have to talk a lot more to make up for the decade-long silence," he replied in his warm, resonant voice which had always been a source of comfort to Sunaina.

"It's impossible to put that silence into words now," she answered.

Ranvir asked her to tell Manas to come and see him. "Let me see this look-alike of mine!" he said jokingly.

"I'm not sure whether you'll be able to see the similarity," she said. "But he is quite different from you in character."

After talking to Ranvir, Sunaina realized that life had taught her to look at the gray shades instead of always focusing on black and white. She had learnt that nobody was entirely good or bad and that destiny and character together made people take steps or act in ways for which they were not totally responsible. Life was like a collage and not a neat avenue with clear cut divisions and shining milestones at equal distance. Things had become so much easier for Sunaina when she understood that life was a complex entity and nothing or no one could stay in the same part of the web forever. In its complexity lay the beauty of life.

One of Sunaina's favorite compositions was the one sung by ghazal maestro Mehdi Hassan in Raga Bhimpalasi, "*Zindagi mein toh sabhi pyaar kiya karte hain, main toh mar kar bhi meri jaan tujhe chaahunga*". She was listening to it this morning, wondering yet again at its freshness and innocence. She found it the ultimate expression of romance and a poignant rendering of emotions so delicate that one was scared even to imagine them. She had practiced it many times with Manas who was equally fond of it. There seemed to be no end to the people who loved this nazm. It began with her dad, her mom, her brother, Ranvir, Tanu … a universal hit! And had been for decades. She had grown up listening to it and it was part of her treasure of melodies and memories, of old associations and cherished moments.

She was writing emails to some of her friends. She had been lucky with friends. It was only in her relationships with the two men who had come into her life that she had not been able to get her bearings. She often thought perhaps God had not meant her to live the life of a typical family person. There was always a gypsy-like quality about her life and now she even enjoyed it. She had learned to take everything in her stride living a day at a time and not making long-term plans. Sometimes she would suddenly get ambitious about her music and think of what she could achieve. But that was not the real Sunaina.

"Which compositions are you preparing for the Saawan Concert?" her mother asked when she heard Sunaina humming in the morning.

"Well, this is not one of them, Mom," she said, smiling, as she knew that her mother recognized this bandish in Bhimpalasi very well.

"Don't you tease me about the ragas. I knew them long before you had even dreamt of being born," said her mother, who seemed to be in an especially good mood that day.

"Roop is having a small picnic for the *Sarang* students in the garden this evening and we are busy cooking for that," she told Sunaina.

"That's a great idea. What are you making?"

"We are going to have poha, dhokla and rasgullas," her mother replied.

"I'll make the dhokla," Sunaina said. "And the chutneys." She was not too fond of cooking everyday food but loved to make dishes which were special including idlis, dhokla, tikkis, paapri chaat, gaajar ka halwa, green mango chutney and sambhar.

"It's a pity Manas is away and will miss the picnic party," she said. Manas had left for Jammu with Ranvir's phone number and his office address. She could have gone with Manas but she knew she would not have felt comfortable.

She believed more in life happening to her rather than trying to force it. Good things in her life had all come to her unexpectedly. If ever she had tried to get something into her life, things had gone wrong.

She often wondered how some people planned their future in such great detail. Her wonder grew when she saw some of them actually succeeding in realizing all those plans. She put this down to destiny, too. As for herself, she believed that if one ran after a wish, it flew away like a butterfly and if one just forgot about it, it came quietly looking for you.

26

The concert was just a few days away and Sunaina had prepared herself well. With Manas returning the next day they could practice together – then meet the organizers who would be coming to Doon.

Classes were fine at her school. Ustad Saab had returned and had been surprised and delighted to see the school. He immediately took to teaching. The students were, at first, a little nervous to see him, with his long freshly hennaed orange colored beard and his stern countenance. But they soon took to him. It gave Sunaina immense satisfaction to see the little ones singing away earnestly during class. It made her feel a strong link in a greatly revered tradition – of Indian Classical Music – which was held in awe by people the world over. She felt happy that she had gone ahead with her idea of starting the school, keeping it open for all irrespective of age. She felt that this way she had done her little bit, had contributed her share, and thereby kept alive the great tradition.

"Mom, school will also reopen in a few days. How will you manage the home school then?" asked Roop while they sat in the garden after the picnic-party was over.

"While I'm at school, Naani and Ustad Saab will manage. The little ones will come only in the evenings now as their schools will also reopen," she replied.

"Will Manno also go to school?" asked Roop.

Manno was Deena's elder daughter. "Yes, I'll get her admitted soon."

"Manas Uncle said he would take me to Rishikesh one day as he has some work there. Will you let me go with him? Roop's questions went on. "Yes, baby, we will all go. Naanu will also go and so will Tanu Mausi."

Roop was thrilled. She loved such outings.

"But, first, we are all going to Nahan for the concert."

Roop had not seen Nahan and wanted to know more about the kind of place it was. "It's really like a little fairy town," Sunaina told her.

"Then the ghost of Mussoorie will not be there. Fairies drive away ghosts," said Roop, making her mother smile at her fascination for the Mussoorie ghost.

The picnic had been a great success where students and teachers had sung and played together. A game of Antakshari was also part of the evening and it was great to see the kids belt out the latest filmy disco numbers though this came as a bit of a shock for Ustadji. But he took it in his stride. Tanu had joined in with Shashank who was now preparing to go back to school.

Tanu told Sunaina that Sumeet had been spending quite a lot of time at his mother's place and had even begun staying overnight. "But is he unpleasant with you?" Sunaina asked.

"Not exactly, but things are definitely not the same. It has been driven into his mind that I am governing his choices in life, and he has now begun reacting to it. But I just cannot leave Dad alone," said Tanu with a strange look of helplessness on her face.

"I think you should talk to him some day when he is calm and happy and find out what is bothering him" said Naina. "Give it a try."

Tanu nodded and looked a little better.

Prashant and Manas came to Doon the same day. By the same train. In fact, Prashant had not informed them that he was coming over. He just arrived. Sunaina was shocked that for the first time, no long-term planning had gone into his visit.

The monsoon had also arrived and the valley was looking fresh and charming. Nature's bounty was so vast and immeasurable that despite the extremes to which man went to disturb it, it managed to bounce back somehow. The torrential rain in the valley was abundant enough to blur all its marred parts. Rejuvenation had come to Doon as a gift of God in the form of rain and for the time being, it didn't matter what plans were being cooked up to destroy its spirit further.

Sometimes it rained through the night so that by morning, every leaf and flower looked as if granted a new lease of life by the rain gods. The rain-soaked air had a chill in it which Sunaina always associated with the times they came back to Doon from Mussoorie before the schools reopened after the summer vacation.

"I don't want to go back," was Sunaina's plea every year to her dad. "I want to live in the hills. Please leave me here. Let me go to school here."

It broke her heart to leave the hills and go back to school. She always made friends in the summer holidays in Mussoorie whom she missed afterwards. Most of them also went back to their respective cities. Letters were exchanged for a few months and if they happened to come back to the hill station again next year, they would all meet. But most families did not choose Mussoorie every year as Sunaina's family did.

There were a few local kids also whom she had befriended and how she envied them for staying in Mussoorie once the rains set in and schools reopened. They were the ones who had taught her to find kaphal and walnut trees. Juicy, red kaphals, something like the faalsas one got in Delhi, were really wonderful. More than eating them, Sunaina loved to gather them in her little white handkerchief where they left wet, pink marks.

Jhimli and Birju were sister and brother – children of an old Garhwali caretaker at the Guest House where they stayed, who were extremely close to Sunaina and Ishaan. Adi would also join them for a few days at Mussoorie and this group of five would roam the hillsides and the narrow streets of the town. Sometimes they would make friends with tourists on the Mall Road and at other times they would play Video Games for hours in the popular stalls on the Mall.

When Prashant arrived suddenly, Roop was really excited and gave him all the latest news about Doon. She wanted to show him the music school immediately but he said he would see it after he had freshened up and had tea. It was at this time that Manas called up Sunaina to inform her of his return. She mentioned that Prashant had arrived. He said he would come over in the evening.

Mrs. Bakshi asked Prashant about his plans. He looked a little embarrassed while he discussed his new job with them. He was definitely uncomfortable. When Sunaina sensed this, she went out of her way to put him at ease. She wanted him to realize that his decision had not exactly spelled the end of the world for her!

She behaved so normally that Prashant was actually at a loss how to react. He was quiet most of the time.

"Manas Uncle is coming in the evening," Roop informed her father.

Prashant knew about Manas and his role in the newly set up school, though he wasn't particularly looking forward to meeting anyone at all that day. He was tired and a little put out at Sunaina's cheerful and breezy behavior, something he knew was not part of her nature and was being put on specially for him!

"It took me a lot of thinking before I agreed to the Muscat job," he told Sunaina.

"I realize that. It is the best thing for you – something you had always wanted and dreamt of," she said.

"My parents are planning to come to Muscat for a month when I join," he said. "Would you like to join us?"

"We will come there when the school is closed, during the summer or winter vacations," she replied, sounding vague.

"You must come as soon as you can," he said. Sunaina nodded and gave directions to Deena about the evening tea.

When Manas arrived, Prashant was on the lawn with Roop. They met before anyone could introduce them to each other and began talking.

Hearing voices from the lawn through the kitchen window, Sunaina looked out and saw them. She saw Manas and Prashant in conversation and told Deena to keep a watch on the tea, which was about to boil, and went out on the lawn. Roop had introduced them after they had begun talking to each other, Manas told Sunaina.

The conversation was about Prashant's new job. Manas didn't say much about his trip to Jammu except that the weather was similar to Doon and that Jammu always reminded him of Doon.

"I've never been there," said Prashant. Sunaina was thankful that Manas did not say anything about Ranvir. Prashant had always held a grudge against Sunaina about him. Sunaina had told him about herself and Ranvir. He even knew about their recent meeting in Mussoorie. Though Prashant had never been gentle towards her or able to understand her priorities, he somehow could not tolerate the mention of Ranvir.

He had been really upset when informed that after all these years, the two had met again. He knew that it was a formal meeting and Roop and Tanuja had been with her. Yet he felt he had always taken second place in Sunaina's affections. But at the same time, somewhere inside him, he also knew that he had not exactly done his best to win over her love. He was really confused. Sometimes he felt he had taken her for granted while at others he thought that she was taking him for granted. Of course, most of the time he did not think of all these things, he was busily engrossed in work.

But whenever he met Sunaina, especially in Doon, he felt left out of her world … the little world she had created around her with her warmth and her unique outlook on life. But when he was away, he would forget about that and be happy in his world of work, competition and official parties.

"Prashantji, will you stay for the concert?" asked Manas.

"No, there is still a week before that and I have to be back in the office day after tomorrow," he said.

Manas asked Sunaina about the school. "Ustaadji is now settled in with the students; his favorite is Mrs. Sinha whose voice he greatly admires," she said with a laugh.

"To please him is quite a job. Lucky Mrs. Sinha!" said Mrs. Bakshi who had joined them. It had been raining in the afternoon but was now clear and very pleasant. With stars shining, it was heavenly sitting out with a cool breeze wafting, bringing to them the amazing scent of the flowers of the "Raat Ki Raani".

After Manas left, Sunaina was expecting the unpleasantness of a talk with Prashant about which he had been warning her for so many days. She seriously prayed that the "talk" would be over soon and she could go back to her world of music. She had no desire to discuss matters which she had risen above. Internally, she had withdrawn from such conflict-ridden relationships.

She was now back to her childhood habit of wishing away things she did not like or understand. While studying, she would tell her dad how she wished that there was no Maths to do, only English and Hindi Literature to study.

"It's always the pleasant and unpleasant which make up life. One has to go through one to reach the other," he would patiently explain. "Oh God! Why did not the unpleasant things in life end with Maths?" she wondered now. "Even Maths was better than this relationship called marriage."

"Had it not been for Roop, I should be glad to be out of this legal bond," Sunaina had said to Tanu a few days ago.

"Just let it be. Unless you are interested in marrying someone else or Prashant wishes to do that, there is simply no point in breaking the marriage legally," her friend had advised. Sunaina fully agreed with Tanu.

However, there was no talk between them that night. Roop slept with her mother in a big room. Sometimes, she would go over to her naani's room to sleep but stayed mostly with her mother.

Prashant was busy talking shop on his cell phone until almost midnight, by which time both Roop and Sunaina were fast asleep.

27

Prashant left the next afternoon. He had spoken for a while to Sunaina, deciding that before he left Delhi, she and Roop would come and see him off. He looked disturbed but Sunaina did not feel like asking him why. Nor did he say anything about it.

"Sometimes I feel more like an acquaintance of yours than your husband," he said.

"Is that my fault?" she asked.

"I am not blaming you. It is just that I feel that both of us are too passionate about our own selves to fit into a typical family framework."

"Please see how irrationally you behaved in the early years of marriage. I am not mad to have taken the decision of not staying together literally," she said softly but firmly.

"I realize the mistakes we both made. But for Roop's sake and for the sake of my parents, I do not wish to disturb this state of affairs," he said.

"Do I not figure anywhere in the picture?"

"Of course you do. I realize your strength of character and admire you for your principles. It's not just to meet Roop that I come here," said Prashant, with a strange look in his eyes.

"We'll meet you in Delhi when you leave. And I hope, for Roop's sake, that you will be coming to India often," she replied, suddenly feeling really sad about the way they had both failed to give Roop a normal childhood. Would Roop forgive them for it when she grew up? Sunaina was scared to think.

It was raining heavily when Prashant left. That evening, when the rain stopped, the students began coming in and later, Manas walked in with a gift-wrapped packet in hand. He gave it to Sunaina who looked at him questioningly.

"It's not my gift. I am only the courier," said he. "I should have brought it for you yesterday but it slipped my mind. Sorry!"

Mystified, she slowly opened the packet and found two thick volumes. One was *The History of Indian Classical Music* while the other was *A History of Urdu Literature*.

"Mr. Mallik has sent these," said Manas.

She was taken by surprise; after a long time such a prettily wrapped surprise gift had come her way. She felt like a little girl opening birthday gifts. That feeling of excitement and wonder could not be matched by any other. But at the same time, she did not want her expression to give her away in front of Manas who had, however, already sensed her joy and felt fascinated by her expression when she saw the books. He was happy for his friend. It took so little to make her feel thrilled. In so many ways, she was just like Roop, he thought.

"He told me to come along with him to the bookshop and then carefully selected these books for you," said Manas.

"How is he doing?" she asked.

"I met him for half an hour and had coffee with him. He had to leave for an urgent meeting just after we bought the books."

"Did you notice that he looks like you," she asked Manas, almost blushing.

"Of course I did and he also mentioned that you had already told him. You should have told me too," Manas said, in a complaining tone which made her laugh.

"Well, that was my surprise for you!" she answered suddenly, feeling like a college fresher and behaving like one. They talked about Ranvir. Manas told her that Ranvir had shown great interest in Sufi music as well as *Sarang* and the Saawan Concert.

"He knows a lot about music but seems to have lost himself too much in every day affairs," he observed.

"We met first at a university music fest," she said. Suddenly, she wanted to tell Manas all about her days spent with Ranvir. Even Manas was waiting for her to say more. Roop and Mrs. Bakshi were at *Sarang* when they both sat and talked. In fact, only Sunaina talked and Manas listened. Each word held so much pain and joy, so much of feeling and intensity that Manas wondered how Sunaina had kept such emotions and memories within her heart for so long.

"Manas, I have seen really terrible times. The person for whom I could have even laid down my life showed me that he had simply no value for my life. It was the worst wound I could have ever received."

It was as if she had fallen under a spell. Without realizing what she was saying, she kept speaking for almost an hour, expressing all the trauma she went through when Ranvir rejected her. And then she went on to talk about the nightmare which the early years of her marriage to Prashant had been. She looked at Manas and saw that he too appeared hypnotized … by the intensity of her narration and expressions. His eyes were wet, she noticed. This made her realize her relived pain so strongly that her voice began to shake a bit and she stopped, finally telling him about the chance meeting in Mussoorie.

All that she told him made Manas realize what she must have felt when she met him as now, he had met Ranvir and seen for himself how much Ranvir resembled him.

He also knew what rejection could do to a person. He too had been rejected by a woman who was once ready to spend her life with him. However, Manas realized that the relationship which Sunaina had shared with Ranvir was far more intense than his had been with Natasha. Natasha had not been half as emotional or sensitive as Sunaina.

"I always knew that there was something very precious which you had lost. Now I understand what it was," said Manas, quietly holding her hand and pressing it to convey that what she had said in confidence to him would remain with him and that he could relate to her pain and regret at having lost something so valuable.

"Thanks, Manas, for listening. I haven't spoken about this to anyone else at such length, not even Ranvir," she said, looking into his eyes. And the irony was that even when she looked there, what she could think of was how much his eyes looked like Ranvir's!

They both got up as Manas had to leave. Keeping the books safely in her bookshelf, she walked with him to the gate and then went to the school to call her mother for dinner.

Uncle told Sunaina that Tanu and Shashank had gone over to Sumeet's parents' place for a few days. Tanu had taken leave from the bank as her mother-in-law was not too well and Sumeet had taken them there to stay. Sunaina had gone to Tanu's house one evening and when she found Uncle, sitting alone and looking quite sad, she thought Tanu had gone to the market. But when Uncle told her that she would not be back soon, she was quite shocked. Tanu had spoken to her two days ago but had not mentioned anything about all this.

"It was suddenly decided yesterday and she applied for leave and went there," said Uncle, slowly, looking older than he used to. Or perhaps, it was Sunaina's imagination. The house wore such a deserted look today that she just wanted to get up and leave. But she stopped herself and sat for a while.

"When will they be back?" she asked him.

"Tanu called up a while ago and told me that Shashank would come back and leave for school from here. She has arranged that. But she didn't say anything about herself and Sumeet," he replied. It seemed to her that he would start crying if she asked him anything about Tanu.

She warmed up his dinner and had some salad with him. After making some coffee, she left, telling him to call her whenever anything was needed. Though Hari, a young boy from the hills, was looking after Uncle, he had gone to a relative's wedding. "Tell Hari not to go out much till Tanu gets back," she said before leaving.

On her way home, she kept thinking of this sudden development. She knew that there had been a build-up to it. For months, Tanu had not been herself. Her light heartedness and characteristic exuberance had been missing and, though Sunaina had been really busy with her musical activities, she could immediately sense the change in Tanu.

She would speak to Tanu in the morning and find out what was happening, telling her not to worry about her dad.

As she drove back, it began to rain once again, making her suddenly feel better. In one's worst moments, Nature always came to cheer one up, if one just noticed this. As usual, the music system in her car was playing one of her favorite songs "*Aji Rooth kar ab kahaan jaaeeaiga*," Lata's masterpiece in Raga Desh. Desh was a raga on which few film songs were based, thought Sunaina. "Perhaps that's what is behind the magic of this melody," she thought. Rain and music seemed to calm her troubled soul, and she felt quite at peace with the world by the time she reached home.

Roop was waiting for her for dinner. She and Mrs. Bakshi were watching one of their favorite TV serials and enjoying it thoroughly. Sunaina usually watched only music-based shows and news on TV. She was a keen radio listener, though. Nowadays, her favorite was FM Gold which played all the golden oldies. As a child she had always been fond of Hindi film songs and listened to *Vividh Bharti*, *Radio Ceylon* and *All India Radio's Urdu Service*. Wednesday nights would see her huddled in bed, all ears for the *Binaca Geetmala* presented in a unique manner by the famous Amin Sayani.

She wouldn't miss it for the world. Her parents also heard it with her and even now whenever she remembered those magical Wednesday nights, she felt cosy and wonderful inside.

The only thing about *Radio Ceylon* she didn't like was that at eight o'clock every morning, they played a song of Kundan Lal Saigal, after which she had to rush to school which started at half past eight in winter. She would listen to the song happily but would not like to leave her dad and go to school. Her dad would be sitting in his armchair, having his second cup of tea, glancing through the newspaper headlines, and when the radio would say, "Loma Time! Eight a.m. Use *Loma Hair Oil*!" Sunaina knew that she must leave for school.

All the Saigal songs she knew had been heard courtesy *Loma Hair Oil*! These included "*Jaadu hai, Jaadu hai, un do matwaare nainon mein*", "*Jab Dil hi toot gaya*" and "*Baalam Aan Baso More Mann mein*". Her father described Saigal's voice as "liquid gold", a phrase she just loved!

She told her mom about Tanu. Mrs. Bakshi was extremely concerned and asked her to call up Tanu. "It's quite late. Let's wait until morning," she said.

"Deena had gone for admission form for Manno and the school people have called them all on Monday. You must go with them and get the admission done," her mother said.

Sunaina nodded as she took out the two books which Ranvir had sent her. She had been too busy to look through them. She would read them a little tonight. Both books were about subjects close to her heart. Ranvir still knew what would make her happy.

28

All of them, including the *Sarang* students, went together in the hired bus to Nahan for the concert. It was like a great picnic. They left in the morning to return the next afternoon, staying at Nahan overnight.

Sunaina felt awful that Tanu was not able to make it due to her mother-in-law, who had suddenly begun to assert herself over Tanu and Sumeet. Tanu had told her that she would return home as soon as possible to her dad but she could not go to Nahan.

Sunaina found it a slightly unnatural situation but she could not say anything. Half her joy was gone. But, when she looked at the excitement in her mother's and Roop's eyes, she felt much better and decided that she must make them proud by performing to the best of her ability.

The atmosphere of Nahan was extremely tranquil and a great change from the now noisy Doon. They all rested in the afternoon in the government guest house and then went to the concert venue, a sprawling ground. It was a fine evening, with no sign of rain, much to the relief of the organizers, participants and audience.

Sunaina was performing on stage after a very long gap. Besides the college festivals, she had sung twice at concerts in Delhi and once, two years ago, in Doon. Her performance at the school function, she considered a homely affair.

She was more excited than nervous and hoped that she would measure up to everyone's expectations – most of all, her own.

The opening recital was by a Nahan-based artiste, Sanjay Mahajan, who played the Santoor. Raga Pahaadi sounded enchanting on the Santoor and so did the next raga, Raga Megh Malhar. Sunaina was listening in a trance. After him, Manas took over the stage and sang a Sufi composition, "*Meri bukkal de vich chor ni*" of Bulleh Shah. There was thunderous applause amid which Sunaina prepared herself to go on stage. She met Manas backstage and he wished her all the best. She could see the bright and eager faces of her students, Roop's the brightest of them all, and also her mother, who was sitting in the front row.

Her Alaap was a short one and then started the slow bandish which gave her time to settle well into the Raga, Miyan Ki Malhar. The words were "*Nainon mein hai saawan, sakhi ri, bairi nainon mein hai saawan*". As soon as she began singing, Sunaina was in a world of her own ... a timeless, faceless world where melody was queen and swara was king. Everything else just melted away and she was one with her song. The place resounded with her soulful singing which seemed to have a life of its own. The composition and the music mingled so well that what remained was a heart-stirring sound which had no beginning and no end.

After she finished, she heard the applause and also a request for another song. What came to her mind was "*Zindagi Mein Toh Sabhi Pyaar Kiya Karte Hain*" and she went ahead and sang it. Softly, "*Main Toh Mar ke bhi meri jaan tujhe chaahunga*." It was a fitting icing on the cake, and she felt ecstatic at the way the entire ground resounded with applause. She bowed her head before the audience, kissed her hand after touching the stage and came down.

Manas sang again after Sunaina and brought the concert to a wonderful close with his rendering of Malhar. Sunaina had still not come out of her reverie; people came and met her, congratulated her, thanked her. She thanked them, smiled, laughed, talked, had her dinner but as if in a dream. Roop kept hugging her and so did Mrs. Bakshi. She had truly made them proud! The little students as well as the grown-ups were all around her and Raj Singhji kept blessing her.

She had not experienced this kind of elation for years. How she wished her dad had been here to listen to her singing, to share this happiness with her ... to bless her and hug her. Somewhere, she could feel him with her. She was sure he could see her and bless her.

The next morning saw them all at the Paonta Sahib Gurudwara. A guide who was part of the Gurudwara went round with the children, telling them the history of the place and the sites in and around the shrine. They were amazed to see the massive length, breadth and weight of Guru Gobind Singhji's weapons. "He must have been really tall and strong to have used these swords," said Roop, placing her hand on her mouth in amazement.

"He was more than seven foot tall," said the guide and they all looked at him in awe. They didn't know how far he was right but wanted to believe him. Looking at the size of the weapons, they did believe his word. It was a beautiful morning with a slight drizzle carrying on since the early hours.

After spending two hours at the gurudwara, they started back for Doon. The organizers who had come to see them from Paonta were very pleased with the concert's response. Promising to be in touch with them and thanking them, Sunaina and Manas took their leave.

Tired but happy, Sunaina sat on a window seat in the bus. Raj Singhji sat with her and they talked for a while. He began singing a bhajan which sounded familiar to Sunaina. "*Ghoonghat ke pat khol re, tohe piya milenge*." She remembered soon that it was from the old Nargis-Dilip Kumar film *Jogan* which she had seen some years ago on *Doordarshan*. Mrs. Bakshi joined in and the two sang the bhajan together while the entire group listened spellbound. It was such a magical rendering! Soon, one or the other was singing his or her favorite song and they reached Doon in no time at all, or so it seemed.

Back home, there was much activity as schools were reopening the next day. Out came uniforms, raincoats, umbrellas, water bottles and tiffin boxes. Books, bags and papers found and arranged.

29

Tanu soon returned from her in-laws place and came over to meet Sunaina and her mother. She had so much to say, but looked happy and relaxed, after months of conflict and tension. She and Sumeet had finally talked things over and managed to come to an equable decision. Tanu was to go over to his mother's place more often and even stay on for weekends and other holidays. He would also go to his mother, with Tanu and alone as well. This would make sure that both her father and his mother would not have any complaints. It had taken Tanu a long time to come to this agreement but she had realized that there was no other way.

"I feel so much better after agreeing to this plan. Sumeet is really happy and has arranged for a housemaid who will look after both houses in Dad's compound," she told them.

Sunaina was happy for her but found it difficult to believe that her friend, Tanu, the great advocate for personal liberty and individual freedom, had given in to an arrangement which would take away from her, her own way of living. But she didn't say anything, realizing that sometimes compromises had to be made in life. They had coffee together and talked about the concert which Tanu had missed. "When the VCD comes, we'll watch it together," said Tanu and Sunaina nodded. Manas had made sure that the VCD was made professionally. These were the things which Sunaina could never plan and she realized how Manas was different from her. He had a mission in life – to be a very well-known musician one day. And he was moving, step by planned step, towards this goal.

Sunaina was very fond of Manas but was not able yet to distance him from Ranvir and memories associated with him. She could not stop thinking of Ranvir when she was with him. Perhaps, after some time, she would be able to look upon him as her friend, Manas, and not a reflection of Ranvir.

He had been telling her to concentrate on her Sufi singing and also plan to bring out a music album by next year. She knew that this was possible and also tried to work for it but she found herself not as steadfast as Manas was. She was given to daydreaming and getting distracted. All this took her away from riyaz often. But she was trying her best.

Tanu had been promoted and was in a mood to celebrate. She wanted Sunaina to bring all her friends and students to her party where there would be a small "mehfil" on the occasion. "You plan the day and time and we'll get organized," said Sunaina. "But make it on a Sunday as schools are opening tomorrow."

Sunaina walked to Tanu's house, a distance of about a kilometer and a half. It was a long time since they had walked together. When they were in school, this used to be a normal routine. At times, they would cycle together on this route while at others, they would walk from one home to the other in the evenings. It was not raining this evening, though both were carrying their umbrellas. One never knew when it would begin pouring! Most people could be seen carrying umbrellas. It was part of the monsoon gear.

"See how bad the traffic has become even in this area. It's tough to drive and tougher to walk," said Tanu who often discussed the deteriorating condition of the valley with great passion. She was always more vocal about things than Sunaina who kept her feelings within or expressed them through her music.

But she loved to hear Tanu talk. It made her feel as if she was still in her childhood world, the world of a green, clean Doon where tongas trotted from one street to another and people greeted each other at every corner, where life was extremely simple and calm and summer meant just a week of tolerable heat, where "development" was unheard of and every place was within walking distance. All this and much more could Sunaina feel through Tanu's voice which had been with her ever since she could remember. This voice was so much a part of her consciousness.

"The other day, an old family friend of ours came from Lucknow. She came here after ten years and could just not find our house," said Tanu. "She was looking for a house in the wilderness!"

That's what Tanu's house had been when it was built – a lone house in the wilderness! Sunaina clearly remembered that they had been in Class Nine when the house was being built. She used to cycle down with Tanu sometimes to look at it. Uncle or Aunty would be present there, giving instructions to the contractor and labor.

She and Tanu would do a round of the incomplete rooms and decide which room would be whose. They would have luscious red litchis and unripe green mangoes from the trees in the compound and thoroughly enjoy themselves.

"Why can't people leave good things of the earth alone?" Sunaina's heart would cry whenever she saw an old landmark of Doon vanish before her eyes. The gushing East Canal after which the E. C. Road had been named by the British had been covered up when the road was expanded and rebuilt two years ago and now the canal was nowhere to be seen – it was just the East Canal Road sans the Canal.

The same went for Eucalyptus Road. She had often cycled through it as a young girl, imbibing the fresh and invigorating scent of the tall white Eucalyptus trees that stood as guardian angels all along the scenic road once upon a time. Were all beautiful and special things in life meant to wither away like those majestic trees had done? It just wasn't fair! The litchi and mango trees that had lined the Chakrata Road beyond the Bindal Bridge had been ruthlessly felled to widen the road. There was hardly any shade left in the valley which had been shaded by massive trees at almost every step. She had always associated this with comfort and security and the bright, strong sun with the problems of this world. All the gracious, benign presences were going away from the valley which was invaded by the representatives of the so-called "modern" life and culture which believed in leaving no place for shade in the long, hot sunny day called life.

30

It was grand to meet all the students and teachers at school after the long summer vacation. There was a great deal of news to be exchanged and much work to be done in the new academic year.

The results had been encouraging with most of Sunaina's students faring well in the Board Examinations.

The first day's assembly included, "*Where the mind is without fear and the head is held high*" from Tagore's *Gitanjali* and a shabad of Guru Gobind Singh, "*Deh Shiva var mohe ehe, shubh karman te kabhun na darun*". Both of them gave the message of fearlessness and Sunaina experienced a wonderful feeling of being absolutely free of fear while she led the singing of these two great works. If they could inspire her so much at this stage of her life, she could well imagine their impact on the impressionable minds of the young students.

The rhythm of the school routine was refreshing after the languor of the summer break. Though she had done a lot of work during the holidays, it had been a bit haphazard and not regular as her day was when she was at school.

The women students were coming to *Sarang* in the mornings while the children came in the evenings now. Her mother and Ustadji saw to the morning classes while Manas and she taught the youngsters and also those senior students who wanted some special coaching in the evening. Sunaina's day was full of music – what she had always wanted. She had decided that she would not teach any girl from her school at *Sarang*. One or two students had asked her and she refused, making her position clear. "You can learn all you need in school if you pay attention and grasp the lesson," she told them.

She had spoken to Ranvir over the phone and thanked him for the books. He was really happy to get her call. "I was waiting for your call ever since Manas reached Doon," he said. "I was very busy with the concert and then the school reopened," she said. "Thanks for remembering what I like to read."

"How could I forget after years of listening to you talk about music and Urdu poetry? They became so much a part of me because of you," he said.

They spoke about the concert and he was excited at her success. "Manas is a really dedicated musician. It seems his professionalism has rubbed off on you too."

"Not yet, but I have begun thinking in a more organized manner, no doubt."

She asked him what he thought of the resemblance between the two of them. "It is there but he looks more like I once did. I have changed quite a bit now. My hair is quite short now and I have put on weight."

"When I saw you in Mussoorie, you looked hardly any different from the college days," she said.

"You were looking at me with eyes of the past which do not notice flaws," he said and laughed. His laughter had always been endearing and one of the reasons she was attracted to him.

Somehow, within her heart, Sunaina was never ashamed of the feelings she had for Ranvir. Neither before he ended the relationship nor afterwards. Nor before nor after her marriage. These were heartfelt feelings as natural as flying to a bird, as scent to a flower. No worldly factor had a role to play and that was why despite all these years having passed, the comfort-level between the two of them had not been affected, not even by the fact that Ranvir had himself decided to marry another woman. But now, things could not be felt in that purity and innocence, she knew only too well. But she was trying to relive those days of unsullied romance and beauty.

Having met Ranvir when she was nineteen she had hardly known the world outside. Straight out of a Convent in a small town, she was like a child. Sometimes she found that Roop, at the age of nine, was far smarter than she had been at nineteen. Ranvir, who was just a year older, was similar. He was simple and down-to-earth and had never tried to impress her as she had seen other University boys doing. Their relationship had been like a friendship forged in childhood, it was so pure and fresh even today.

"Well, I've always lived in the past more than in the present and I don't regret it," she answered after a long pause.

For the first time, Ranvir spoke to her of Megha. She didn't really want to discuss her but could not say so without being rude about it.

"I am as alone as you are," he said. "She belongs to a different world and is far from the soulmate we used to talk about."

"We used to consider ourselves soulmates," she said, sounding hurt.

"Okay, I'm sorry. Let's not go into that. We are still soulmates and that's why we are talking like this … without formality or inhibition," said Ranvir in a voice which was almost like a caress. Suddenly, Sunaina found that tears were rolling down her face. She had not cried for months so it seemed a luxury. Words from one of her beloved ghazals came to her mind. "*Ik umr se hun lazzat e giriya se bhi mehroom, ae raahat e jaan mujhko rulaane ke liye aa*." They were sweet tears which brought release from regret and yearning, from gloom and pain, hopelessness and despair.

When the conversation was over Sunaina sat down on her bed and cried. Even she didn't know why but she just let the tears come. For years, she had trapped them inside her heart which she refused to open even to herself, let alone anyone else. But now they were finally out and flooding her consciousness.

She didn't know how long she sat weeping. But when she got up, it was almost dinner time. Deena and her daughters were in the house and Manno was full of talk about her new school which amused Roop. Sunaina came and sat with the kids. It made her feel calmer. Roop had taken charge of Manno's studies and Sunaina felt proud of her daughter. She was so considerate and helpful.

"Didi, it's like a dream for me to see Manno in school and living with me. Some months ago, I had given up hope of having her near me," said Deena while laying the table for dinner.

Sunaina smiled at her and forgot all her problems. To her, Deena's words always sounded deeper than they seemed on the surface, like a kind of "guru mantra" to her. Whenever she said anything, it always had a deep meaning and gave Sunaina courage to tread the path she had chosen.

Deena faced life with courage, patience and fortitude, never letting go of faith. She had been put to extreme tests, had faced the trauma of having to desert her daughter, her own flesh and blood, the strain of a conflict ridden relationship, and other vicissitudes of life. But she had carried on, taking tough decisions, abiding by them, never letting darkness enter the core of her heart where the light of hope of a brighter future shone forth. And her faith and hard work were amply rewarded when Ramesh returned to her and all her troubles seemed to end.

"We will not have to buy any vegetables now. The kitchen garden is coming up really well," Mrs. Bakshi said at dinner. "Deena has worked really hard at it to serve everyone," she said. Sunaina nodded. She had seen Deena develop the garden with great devotion. It was now bearing fruit which benefited the perpetrator as well as those around her. It could work wonders.

Ramesh had now started working in five houses while Maaliji did another five. Deena spent time stitching and embroidering for people in the neighborhood besides working with Sunaina in the house. Their needs were few and they had settled down to a frugal lifestyle, comfortable nevertheless. Nobody had come from Ramesh's home to find out about him. Neither had he shown any inclination to go back and meet his family. He seemed to have forgotten about them. Maaliji's training had made Ramesh quite an expert and he was getting well paid well for his work. "It's all Deena's magic," Sunaina told her mother.

31

Everyone sang for hours at Tanu's party. Manas and his parents, plus Raj Singhji and his family were also present. It was quite a festive evening when they were all enjoying themselves. They sat in the huge Gol (circular) Verandah of Tanu's house as it was drizzling and the lawn was wet.

The verandah, with its light maroon and black floor, provided them with a great view of the garden and trees. It was truly a "singing party" where there were so many people ready to put in a song. Tanu was absolutely thrilled. Such days didn't happen often ... when everything seemed to be going well ... nothing out of place ... not a note out of tune.

In fact, a competition took place with Tanu's father and Manas's father as judges. One team had Raj Singhji and Sunaina while Manas and Mrs. Bakshi were on the opposing side. It was great fun! Finally, all of them were declared winners by the benign judges.

By the time the party dispersed, it was almost midnight and everyone was reluctant to leave the gathering. However, there was work to be done the next morning so they all said goodbye to each other.

After many months, Sunaina was seeing Tanu in her element and this gave her a lot of comfort. But she was also thoughtful about the way Tanu had given in to her mother-in-law's whims. Sunaina found it all phoney but as long as Tanu was fine, she was happy.

The monsoon days had a way of taking Sunaina into a world of dreams and beauty which she had inhabited even when she was a young girl .... even when a small child. All she wanted to do then was to look at the rain, have coffee and go into a trance where various beautiful memories and thoughts surrounded her. This was the time she read Urdu poetry, hummed old Hindi film songs or simply absorbed the various sounds and scents of the monsoon while sitting on the verandah steps. The greenery around her entered her spirit and refreshed it.

Even when she was taking classes at school, she would look out of the huge windows of the music room at the rain-soaked beauty of the enormous school lawns with their massive jackfruit and banyan trees.

At the University she and Ranvir had spent many a monsoon day in the Coffee House on the Faculty Lawns, simply staring at the cloudy grey skies or making impractical plans for the future.

She often wondered whether Ranvir also lost touch with the factual world during the rains as she did, even now. She would ask him. The joy of the rain could not leave any artist untouched. In fact, Sunaina had seen it overtake people who had nothing whatsoever to do with art or music.

Suddenly, as she was looking at the rain from the Staff Room window, an old Urdu couplet came to her mind and she said it out aloud, "Gungunaati hui aati hain falak se boondein, koi badli teri paajeb se takraaee hai". "What a beautiful thought! How delicate!" said Mrs. Sahni, who was the English teacher in the junior school and fond of Hindi and Urdu poetry.

"I think this couplet is by Qateel Shifai," said Mrs. Naik, the history teacher.

"You are absolutely right," said Sunaina who was really fond of Surabhi Naik and often talked to her in the staff room. She had visited *Sarang* recently and actually wished to attend some classes. "You can come whenever you wish," Mrs. Bakshi had told her.

The teaching at *Sarang* was quite informal and simple. The idea was not to make it appear like a task to the students. Some new pupils had joined this month and Sunaina realized that she would need more space soon. Perhaps they could renovate the garage. The car was usually parked in the porch as the garage was built at an angle which caused trouble while parking the car.

This house had been bought by her dad from one Mr. Mohanlal Mishra who had been an old, retired forest service officer with another house in Doon. Sunaina's dad had often wondered at the odd manner in which the garage had been built. Mishraji had named the house "Anurag" and this name was still engraved near the gate. It was a well-known landmark for people who lost their way in the area. Mishraji's sons, Abhishek and Anurag, lived in a neighboring colony and Sunaina often came across them.

Mrs. Bakshi had not been well for some days and this worried Sunaina. Her mother had always been healthy. In fact, it was Sunaina who fell ill quite often. Seeing her mom out of sorts was something unusual. "I'll be fine," her mom said. "You just look after yourself and Roop."

"I will look after you too," she said.

Mrs. Bakshi was very close to her daughter but had always known that Sunaina had been closer to her dad. Sunaina had always spent more time with her dad. But ever since Dad left them, the two had come very close.

When they had been kids, Ishaan had been closer to his mom. He was actually scared of Dad who was quite strict. "Why are you scared of Dad?" Sunaina would ask her brother, shocked that anyone could be afraid of her wonderful, super and dear father. She was her dad's blue-eyed girl and could not remember a moment when she had ever feared him.

Tanu had once told her that, in childhood, boys were closer to their moms and girls to their dads. But later things changed and as girls grew up they developed a stronger bond with their mothers. And sons, when they married, often drifted away from their parents and became close only to their wives and kids. "A son is your son till he gets a wife, a daughter is your daughter all her life," was an old saying. Shridhar and Ishaan were examples of this. Not that Ishaan was not bothered about his mother; just that things always changed too much for men when they got married. In fact, it was expected that their mothers, fathers and sisters would now have less importance in their lives. Perhaps it was a natural trait. Tanu often discussed this, and philosophically concluded that all the "joru ka ghulaams" had been born in their families. Sunaina laughed at this and wondered how Shri and Ishaan would react to this description.

Until her college days, Sunaina had taken her mother for granted while working to get her dad's appreciation. But as she grew up, she realized how like her mom she was. And she believed that every daughter was an extension of her mother without the need for everything to be put into words. They seemed to know what the other was thinking, instinctively. Sunaina was glad she had a daughter taking forward a part of her into the future.

When the doctor said that chest congestion caused Mrs. Bakshi's ill-health, Sunaina was at once careful and made sure that all medicines and precautions were taken. She had learned that one must never take one's parents for granted. This was one of the most precious lessons life had taught her and she would never forget it.

32

When Manas came in the evening he brought good but unwelcome news. He would be going to Mumbai for six months very soon. One of the better known music directors of the film industry, whom he had worked with some years ago, had requested him to work with him for some time. When he came to know that his mother was better, he became insistent. Manas had not yet committed himself.

"I wanted to think it over," he said, looking confused, something which was unusual for him.

Sunaina suddenly became quiet and found that she had a lump in her throat. Without her having realized it, Manas had a place in her heart. It took her by surprise. She didn't want him to know that his decision would affect her that much.

But she could see that he knew. She had begun counting on him a lot and at this moment, she came to know just how much. He was a friend, a teacher, a brother, a comrade-in-arms … someone who had put her back in touch with her feelings. He had come into her life when she was leading a totally mechanical existence. And she also knew that Manas liked her very much.

"Though I haven't said 'yes' to him, I will go for around six months. I spoke to my parents and they agree that I can give six months there and then take further decisions," he said.

"But what about the album you are working on?" she asked, in a voice which sounded as if it was coming from far away.

"I will be able to take time and do it from there," he said.

She nodded her head and was afraid that her tears would give her away completely. She could not, however, hold them back and felt like a complete fool, weeping in front of him. Why was she was always left alone by those whom she cared for? It was not fair! First it had been Ranvir, then her dad and now Manas. Prashant had never been with her. He was not a part of her consciousness as all these people were. Tanu was the only one who had never left her side in the last few years. She was always there which made her so precious to Sunaina.

"Don't behave like a child, Sunainaji. I am not going forever ... I will always be in touch with you," he said, feeling quite overwhelmed by her tears. It was a moment of truth between them. No need to pretend that they were mere acquaintances or just casual friends. He was like family to her now and she had a special place in his heart, too.

"It's good that Roop didn't see you behaving like a baby," he laughed, trying to lighten the air. "If you like, I will stop here and continue working along with you," he went on.

"I know that you wouldn't even have mentioned all this if you hadn't wanted to go," she half smiled and half complained.

"Will you come and meet me in Mumbai?" he asked her.

"We'll see about that later," she said, feeling a little better. She knew that nothing was forever and constant change was life. But she still had her childhood habit of trying to make good things permanent while life would move on and so would people.

She was in her study that evening while Manas taught some of his students at *Surany*. He looked in again before leaving and saw her reading one of the books Ranvir had sent for her.

"How is Ranvirji? Did you speak to him?" he asked.

"Ranvir is fine and was very happy to meet you," she said. As Manas sat near her on one of the three blue cushioned chairs in the study, it suddenly occurred to him that Sunaina's fondness for him might be only due to his likeness to Ranvir which saddened him. He said nothing.

"What happened? Did I say something wrong?" asked Sunaina.

Without saying a word, he got up slowly and came near her. "What, Manas?" she asked, her voice shaking a bit.

"Do you look at me as a reflection of your past?" he asked in a voice devoid of any emotion. The tone made her wince. How could she have been so insensitive so as not to know what he must have felt after meeting Ranvir!

She caught hold of his hand and pressed it. Holding on to it, she said, "Manas, I will not deny that your resemblance to Ranvir pulled me towards you. It made me want to know you. But, please believe me Manas that was only in the beginning. After having known you, I now value you for who you are. I no longer identify you with anyone. Please believe me," she pleaded.

He kept his hand on her shoulder, overcome by an emotion which he could not identify. And then he left the room. He thought it would be best to let her be with herself for the moment. He wanted to be alone too. Even before Sunaina had recognized it, much less acknowledged it to herself, Manas had known that he was drawn towards this child-woman and she to him. He knew it was not physical love, but something that went deeper. It was a call from a kindred spirit the other wanted to answer and respond and preserve. It was too sublime to put a name to it. And he knew solitude was the only answer to such riddles life threw at a person in the course of life.

33

It was still July. So much had happened in a few days. Prashant was preparing to leave, Manas would go in another week, classes in school were in full swing and *Sarang* was turning into a popular institution. Tanu had started following the new arrangement. Sunaina was caught up in a web of emotions which she had thought she had overcome long ago.

Strange things were happening to her, for instance more weeping. A word, a thought, a gesture could start her crying. She had begun feeling human and vulnerable again. And the worst part was that she actually liked it. Getting in touch with her inner self of which she had become oblivious. She had created a barrier and had been existing just on the surface of life.

The day she met Ranvir in Mussoorie had been the starting point of this change. It was as if the dam she had built had begun eroding, little by little. The years of negating all tender feelings had changed her personality to some extent. But she had thought that it was better for her like that ... away from emotions which stemmed from close relationships such as she had with Ranvir. It was a strong defense mechanism she had created to protect herself from the shattering experience of Ranvir's leaving her like that.

She now understood that, although there was peace in remoteness from her soul, it was a falsehood. She had thought that, over the years, she had gained the emotional immunity and great strength which would see her through life. She now knew how mistaken she was.

Her cocoon had shielded her but had also kept her away from the colors of life, from its heat and dust, from its joys and sorrows. She wanted no more of that protection. She would gradually break the cocoon, come out of it and get back in touch with the rhythm of life, the turmoil and the travail she had ignored. Shedding tears recently had given her more joy than anything else for a long time.

Ranvir had mentioned to her in his latest email that he might come to Mussoorie or Doon on deputation. Sunaina felt she would definitely not like to live in the same town as Ranvir and his wife. Even if she didn't meet them, it would make her feel uncomfortable. She hoped and prayed that the possibility never materialized.

Manas would leave the next morning. He had dinner with them that night after the last class, for the time being, at *Sarang*. The students said they would miss him greatly. Roop was particularly upset and said she would not go to *Sarang* after Manas Uncle left for Mumbai.

After that evening, Sunaina and Manas met only now. He had been busy winding up his assignments and packing. Looking at him, Sunaina understood that he had believed her and also that they shared a special bond which could not be categorized as any specific relationship. She knew that he knew that too.

Mrs. Bakshi was better now and as they all sat down to dinner, everyone felt sad. Departures and farewells were so traumatic. Manas said he would call often and keep in touch. "I can come for a day or two anytime. It's not that I can't get away from there," he said when he saw everyone looking so miserable.

Suddenly, Sunaina felt a pang of despair. Would she never be able to stay near people who made her happy, who made her comfortable, feel wanted?

"I am destined to live like this, without any hope and cheer," she said in a tearful manner which sounded like Roop's. "Why did you come and make us so used to your presence?" she complained to Manas.

"Don't talk like this Sunaina. He'll be back soon. One can't stay away from Doon for long," said Mrs. Bakshi.

That night, sleep eluded Sunaina's eyes. Visions, thoughts, waking dreams and strange feelings surrounded her. She sometimes felt she was asleep when she was actually awake. She felt her dad coming and sitting by her side as he always did. He then patted her on her back as he used to.

She often spoke to her dad in her state of half-sleep and could feel his presence in her room. This usually happened when she was disturbed and restless, as tonight.

Prashant also came to her in her dreams several times. Mostly, he appeared quite upset and would complain. He looked so lonely in her dreams. But when she met him, in flesh and blood, he seemed self-sufficient and well-organized.

It was a terrible night when she could catch only a few winks of sleep. The next day, she was not able to go to school. Her head ached badly and she had two cups of coffee before she could get out of bed. Manas came to meet her on his way to the railway station. She had told him she was home when he had called in the morning. She was with Deena. Roop was in school and Mrs. Bakshi was teaching her students.

He was wearing a black Tee Shirt and light blue jeans, a combination he liked. He looked a little tired when he came to her study while Deena was getting breakfast together for her. She asked her to make some tulsi tea for both of them.

"There's just half-an-hour before the train," he said.

"Just a quick cup of tea and you can leave for the wicked city of Mumbai," she replied in a tone which sounded a bit sarcastic, a bit humorous but mostly sad.

"Sunaina, we'll always be friends and work together when I get back," said Manas. "Please don't change towards me just because I'm leaving." It was almost like a plea, an entreaty to understand, to empathize.

She noticed that he had dropped "Ji" from her name. It made her feel good. She smiled. "Take care and be in touch," she said. He put his arm around her, just for a split second and even before she realized it, he put his hand in hers and took leave. He left, taking along, in his mind, a picture of a true friend, a person who held her values dear and who had become very special to him in the last few months. "Sunaina, the one with the beautiful eyes," he said to himself, as he left her home, remembering the story she had told him about her father having said those words when he named her immediately after her birth.

34

With the arrival of August the rains became more aggressive. Sometimes, it would rain only at night while at others the whole morning until noon. Ever since Tanu became involved with her in-laws, she had not been able to meet her friend. Sunaina wondered how she was managing her job as well as two homes. They had spoken on the phone and Tanu realized that with the departure of Manas, Sunaina was lonely.

Sunaina was trying her best not to feel the change and was going about her work with fresh enthusiasm. Ustad Sa'ab was spending an extra hour at *Sarang* in the evenings and classes were continuing though the dynamic presence of Manas was missed by everyone, even Ustaadji.

Sunaina was teaching Raga Jaijaiwanti both at school and at *Sarang* these days. It was a night raga of an extremely serious nature and sounded as if it were delving deep into life's mystery and bounty. An old melody from the film *Seema* in Lataji's voice had immortalized this raga for Sunaina. Even when she had been only five, she used to listen to it as it was in her dad's LP record collection. He heard it almost every evening. The words were "*Manmohana bade jhoothhey ... Haar ke haar nahin maanein ... Mosey beimaani kari, mujhse hi roothhey*".

It was the kind of creation which gave one gooseflesh because of its divine beauty and haunting quality. It was an important part of Sunaina's repertoire and she never forgot to teach it to every one of her students. It was so closely associated with Professor Bakshi that she felt that it was his own creation. It was one of the many precious gifts she had received from him, his love for music, poetry and all the beautiful things of life. After all that he had handed down to her, unconsciously, and sometimes consciously, she felt that she really didn't need more in life now.

The values he held so dear were all that she required to lead a good and honorable life. They were so solid and strong that she could apply them to any situation and feel a sense of satisfaction. He had been proud of his values and so was she. Whenever she met any of his former students and they talked highly of him saying they were proud to be his students, Sunaina's eyes filled with tears and she felt so proud of such a father.

First term examinations at school were around the corner and Sunaina was busier than usual but she felt this was good for her as it would keep her mind off the various confusing thoughts she had started having about her own life. The book which Ranvir had sent was a very detailed account of Hindustani classical music and was a great help for the theory examination. She made special notes for her students from this book which they appreciated.

"Your book has come in really handy for my teaching," she wrote to Ranvir. She had also written about Manas. He had replied that this would increase her work and also interfere with her Sufi training. He was right. But most of all, she missed Manas's comforting presence. And she could not deny it any longer to herself that Manas had been a reflection of Ranvir for her and had always reminded her of him. But after some time, she had come to appreciate him for himself. Somewhere the two personalities had become merged in her consciousness.

And with his going away suddenly like this, she felt that somehow, she had lost Ranvir again. She would never be able to explain all this to anyone, not even to Tanu. In fact, she did not want to do so.

The loss was worse as it spelt separation from a new friend who had kindled memories which she still held dear. This would always remain her secret. She would never be able to express her attraction towards Manas to anyone, least of all to him. But she knew well that Manas was drawn to her too but would never let her know that. The situation in which they met was of a kind where admitting to this attraction would lead to many complications. And both of them were mature enough to realize that. She, however, felt that this added to the beauty of their relationship.

Manas had called up and had sounded a bit disturbed to her. She asked him about it. "I am a bit worried about my parents and also, it's taking me time to adjust to the pace of life here, after Doon."

He always asked her about the school and her riyaz. He said he missed all of them. "It's the first time that it was so difficult for me to make the decision to leave. I have been a gypsy all my life and think nothing of leaving a place and moving ahead," he said.

"Well, gypsies also have hearts and feelings," she said.

"I guess so," he laughed.

"How is your work progressing there," she thought she must ask him that.

"I have met a few of my old colleagues and there are plenty of possibilities to explore," said Manas.

"Please explore them all and then come back to this valley. It misses your music," she told him.

"I hear the call of the valley and will surely answer it," he said.

Prashant had recently begun sending her emails. They were quite matter-of-fact and gave her all the latest news about what he was planning and how he was going about it. She replied sometimes. Roop replied to most of those mails.

Sunaina was thinking of getting enrolled for a doctorate in music and had spoken to many people in the university about it. She was trying to find out who could be her best guide.

Dr. Dinkar Bajpai was the name that arose in most discussions. He lived in Srinagar in the Garhwal Hills near the university headquarters. She had taken his phone numbers from the department and had decided to talk to him one of these days. She already had a post-graduate degree in music and realized that her study of music would progress well by working for a doctorate. It would take time but it would be time well spent and well used. She would register herself in September, she decided. Her mother was very happy about this decision as it had always been her dearest wish to get a PhD in Music. Somehow, life had not given her the opportunity and now she didn't feel up to it. "You can teach at the university after you get the PhD," she said excitedly, proud of her daughter's talent.

"Yes Mom, I can. But I'll have to devote my time to the doctorate. I wonder whether I'll be able to do that," she expressed her doubts.

"Of course you can. Just think how proud your dad would have felt. That will make you work hard," said Mrs. Bakshi who always used Sunaina's father's name to inspire her daughter. She knew it always worked. She herself drew strength from memories of her husband and the ideal life he had lived. He had been like a guru for her who made her understand all the finer things of life. Mrs. Bakshi could see that Sunaina was like her dad. Ishaan was different. He had not inherited the aesthetic qualities of his father and was rather prosaic. She could not relate much to him now. But she loved him all the same.

Deena came in while they were speaking about the doctorate. She wanted to know what that was, wondering how somebody could be a doctor and have nothing to do with medicine and hospitals. Sunaina explained but wasn't sure that she made herself clear.

"I am happy that you will become a doctor, Didi," she said. Deena liked to read and Sunaina encouraged her, giving her some magazines in Hindi which she could read quite fluently. However, with the stitching, housework and her lovely vegetable garden, Deena didn't have too much spare time. She was looking after so many people but Sunaina had never heard her complain.

She had come to watch a serial with Mrs. Bakshi and Roop as her daughters were asleep and Ramesh had not yet come home from work. "Deena Didi, please put some oil in my hair and give it a massage." This was Roop's request. Roop's hair had grown long and she looked after it well. Sunaina had wished all her life to have long hair. But she could never achieve this goal and had to make do with her auburn, wavy, shoulder length hair. Looking at her daughter's silken tresses, she felt a strange happiness well up in her heart.

Roop had taken the best features of both her parents and was a charmer. Sunaina was enjoying seeing her grow up, day by day. Her name "Roopsi" meant "the beautiful one" and suited her perfectly. Sunaina often wondered what Roop would look like when she became a young lady. She tried to picture her as a young woman but gave up. She thought that with the way technology was progressing, there might soon be a gadget invented which would be able to tell one what a person would look like in the future.

Deena massaged coconut oil into Roop's scalp while they all watched the weepy serial which soon put Sunaina off. But she kept sitting there, watching Roop enjoy the massage.

The weather was alternating between stickiness and heavy rain. Before one could begin enjoying the rain, humidity would creep into the atmosphere and give everyone a tough time. One had to bathe twice, and sometimes, even thrice, to keep fresh. This was a new development for Doon which had never been so humid. Sunaina wondered whether it was the deforestation and the growing population in the city.

She called up Srinagar that evening. Dr. Dinkar Bajpai asked her to come to Srinagar whenever she could in the next two months. He said he had heard about her from some friends in Doon and would be glad to be her guide. "It's not often that music teachers are such great singers. I have heard about your singing," he told her. She was surprised. "I didn't know I was so famous," she gave her tinkling laugh.

"I myself do not have a very good singing voice but my love for music helped me greatly in making a career in the subject," he said.

She was impressed by whatever he told her about himself and his students. She looked forward to a wonderful meeting.

Another thing which was making her feel good was that the affiliation for which she had applied for *Sarang* with *Prayag Sangeet Samiti* had finally come through and her students could be given Prayag diplomas. It was a great step forward in her music journey and she felt a sense of achievement. When she had told Manas, he had said that it called for a celebration. "We will celebrate whenever you care to come here," she told him. "That may be on Diwali," he replied.

"We'll have a bigger and grander Diwali celebration then," she said. Manas had helped her so much regarding the affiliation and she felt grateful to him.

Prashant also congratulated her on her success which was something quite unusual. He rarely spoke about her work or her music. It was as if he was jealous of something alien to his lifestyle, something which made him feel a stranger to her universe. But Sunaina had stopped feeling bad about this. She had no expectations from him. And this had given her peace of mind after years of turmoil. Prashant had taught her a lot about life the hard way. And she did not need any such lessons anymore.

35

The *Sarang* students had requested Mrs. Bakshi to let them have a program at the school where they could perform for a small neighborhood audience. Sunaina was too busy and asked her mother to start planning this small concert. "You can take Ustad Saab's help," she said.

"Don't worry, Naina, Raj Singhji is all set to organize it single-handedly," her mother told her, with a smile which was always so reassuring and warm, making Sunaina feel secure. It was a mother's smile. Inimitable, serene, sweet and comforting. There could be nothing in this world as beautiful as that. It was a blessing that Sunaina always had cherished.

It was a Sunday evening when a call came from Ranvir. He was excited as he had been invited to sing at a charity program organized by the state government. "It's a decade since I was on stage. I think it has something to do with your magic," he said, sounding as thrilled as a schoolboy selected for the school cricket team.

"Will you be able to sing after so many years?" she asked, happy for him.

"I'm practicing and it's not that I was not singing all these years, just that it was for myself alone," said Ranvir.

"And whom will you sing for now?" she asked teasingly, feeling as if they were back in the good old college days.

"If you allow me, I will sing for you … *tu kahe agar jeevan bhar main geet sunaata jaaun*," he said, teasing her in return.

"My, my, someone is getting so filmy," she said.

"No, I am just feeling nostalgic. The thought of going on stage has taken me back to university days when the music fest and the inter-college events used to be the high points in our lives," he said, sounding a bit sad.

"I know. Even today those days keep coming back, in my dreams or in my thoughts," she echoed his feelings.

She felt really good about his coming back to music. It had been such an integral part of him that she could not think of Ranvir without his singing. Together with her, he had been part of a universe which everyone did not comprehend. It was the lucky few who lived in this world of melody and rhythm, of raga and rang. She felt fortunate that God had blessed her with the ability to absorb and express the beauty of sangeet, of music and harmony. It was like understanding the rhythm of God's creation and going deep into the mystery of the universe.

Ranvir said that it would take some months before he knew where he would be posted. She had admitted to him that she did not really relish the idea of living in the same town as he lived in with his wife. He said he understood her feelings. "How I wish you understood them years ago when I was merely a reflection of you and had not learned to look beyond you," she thought.

But she could not bring any resentment against Ranvir into her heart now. He could still evoke the softest emotions in her and she knew that, to an extent, it was this love in her heart for Ranvir which had prevented her from making place in Prashant's life. But that was not the whole truth, it never could be. Prashant's conduct had been of an extreme nature. Had he been even a little considerate and caring, it would have helped both of them. It was a combination of various factors which had denied them the right kind of rapport.

And with Prashant being so ill-tempered and blunt with her, she had never been able to separate herself from Ranvir, spiritually and emotionally. They had truly been soulmates.

He promised her that he would send her an audio recording of the show. And she was looking forward to that. He was planning to sing a ghazal of Bahadur Shah Zafar, "*Lagta nahin hai jee mera ujade dayaar mein*" and a semi-classical composition from an old Hindi film "*Ajhun na aaye baalma, saawan beeta jaaye.*" When he told her this, she felt a tug at her heart. She remembered singing this song with him several times. Their friends always used to appreciate it greatly. "I would substitute saawan with jeevan … life is really passing us by, Ranvir," she said. "Ranvir, without any reason, I have waited for you for so many years. It's really strange! When I know that we can never be together as we were then."

"I feel so good when I speak to you. Let's not talk about the past now. I know that I will always be in your thoughts as will you be in mine. I am in love with life again," replied Ranvir.

She could not deny the surge of joy in her heart whenever she heard the well-beloved voice of her long lost love. When they spoke to each other, Megha's existence simply did not matter. Theirs was a small, closed world without a place for any presence which was out of tune with it. Sunaina wanted to indulge herself once again in the warmth of sincere love. But she didn't realize that all she was indulging in were memories of that beautiful experience of years ago!

Maaliji had gone to his village after a long time. Now that he knew that Ramesh and Deena would look after everything, he had no worries. His village was beyond Lucknow, near Rae Bareilly where his old brother and his family lived and looked after the small piece of land where they grew paddy and pulses. Earlier, Maaliji used to go home for a month every year but for the past two or three years, he had not been able to manage it. Deena had been in trouble and Maaliji felt he should be somewhere near her if she needed his help. Now that the matter had been set to rest, he could go and visit his relatives in a relaxed frame of mind. "I'll be getting rice and arhar ki daal from home," he told Mrs. Bakshi who enjoyed the pulses from Maaliji's village.

Sunaina gave him an extra sum of money for his travel and other expenses, though he never once asked for anything. In fact, she had never given him the chance even to ask for his salary. She would quietly slip it into his hands at the beginning of the month. That's what Professor Bakshi had always done and taught Sunaina to do as well. She made sure that the traditions set by her dad carried on as far as possible.

In fact, Ishaan and his wife thought that Mrs. Bakshi and Sunaina did too much for those working for them. They could not understand their efforts to make the workers feel part of the family.

"They get swollen heads and start taking you for granted if you do so," Ishaan had told Sunaina several times.

"But have you ever seen any of our people doing that?" she would ask him.

He had not actually. But it was clear that he didn't agree with Sunaina and his mom on this issue and was a staunch believer in keeping servants in their place. Sunaina was surprised because he had also been brought up in the same home, by the same parents and given the same values as she. "The training given to him after he went away from here proved to be more effective in his case," her mother explained to her. That was the only explanation which Sunaina could fit.

But Ishaan or no Ishaan, she would never be able to treat anyone with indignity. People who had served their family for years and had given up their homes to live with them deserved the utmost respect. She never let anyone's advice on this matter affect her way of looking at Maaliji and his family. They would always be a part of this household, a part of this home.

Deena assured her father that she would look after Mrs. Bakshi's family as well as the little ones. Ramesh went to see him off at the railway station and Sunaina marveled at the way this almost illiterate family had sorted out all the imbalances in their relationships. "Perhaps too much learning and education hampers the natural flow of life and relationships," she thought on many occasions. Simplicity in life was a blessing often denied to those who knew too much.

Life was moving further away from simplicity every day and this was the cause of many maladies which had earlier been unknown.

Doon's sleepy quality had ensured idyllic times for her in her schooldays. Away from the national focus, the valley was then in its Golden Era. It was this lazy little foothill town of grey heads and green hedges which had caught Professor Bakshi's fancy when he came here for some work at the university. It captured his heart so he decided to make it his home forever. Sunaina had old black and white and sepia-tinted photographs from the days when Professor Bakshi had come here for the first time. Sunaina had been in Lucknow then, a four year old moppet.

During their early years in Doon, her mother, together with Mrs. Vidya Saluja, their neighbor, used to take Sunaina to Paltan Bazaar where they did their routine shopping once a week, on Saturday mornings. Mrs. Saluja's son, Pravin, went too. He was a year older than Sunaina. All of them would sit in a tonga which they hired for just a rupee! Thinking of it now, she found it like a scene out of some fairy tale. "Once upon a time, there were colorful tongas in this valley," she would tell Roop and Shashank who loved to hear these stories about old Dehra Dun. Stories of huge litchi and mango orchards, gushing and sparkling rivers, gurgling canals, azure blue skies and dark and deep woods.

While Mrs. Bakshi and Mrs. Saluja bought wool, tea, rice or fruit, Sunaina and Pravin would have various Doon specialty goodies. A small bottle of ginger ale or rose sherbet at a quaint old café called "Tip Top" or a scoop of homemade vanilla or chocolate icecream sold in a cosy little shop by an old Parsi lady. Both these shops had long since disappeared and posh restaurants had replaced them. But in her mind's eye, Sunaina still saw them whenever she passed those spots in the bazaar.

Once a week, most families visited the cinema. That was the high point of their week. Few people in Doon owned television sets. Sunaina waited all week to be taken to the movies on Saturday or Sunday. It was a special occasion for which one dressed nicely, bought chips and popcorn and even made paranthas to take along for dinner as they usually went for the late night show.

It was an extremely simple life with few choices. Soap had meant *Lifebuoy* for bathing and *Sunlight* for washing clothes, toothpaste meant *Colgate* or *Binaca*, shampoo meant *Tiara*. Then there was *Brylcream* and *Colgate's Red Oil* for the hair. It was a far cry from today's consumerist society where an over-abundance of choices caused confusion and chaos.

36

Sunaina met Tanu one morning. Tanu was free after a long time today and had come over especially to have a heart to heart chat with Naina. It was Rakshabandhan and a holiday for *Sarang* for the day. It was a holiday in school and Mrs. Bakshi had taken Roop to the market when Tanu arrived. Sunaina was really happy to see her after so many days. Deena made them coffee and they settled down in the verandah for their cosy talk. It was drizzling a bit adding to the fun of having coffee.

Tanu was wearing a yellow kurta and white salwar, with a yellow and white dupatta, and was looking quite pretty and relaxed. She had found the right balance between her responsibilities and relationships and had no confusion left in her life, for the moment at least.

She told Sunaina how her in-laws had changed and had begun valuing her for the person she was. "My sister-in-law from Lucknow visited them last month and gave them a dressing down about their strange behavior. It seems to have had quite an impact!" she said.

Sunaina kept listening, nodding her head or smiling while Tanu, who was always eloquent, narrated stories about Sumeet's relatives. She also talked about her work at the bank which had increased on her promotion.

When she asked Sunaina to tell what had happened with her, Sunaina wondered for a minute what Tanu would have to say about her feelings that had overtaken her well-charted life. Instinctively, she knew that her dear old friend would not approve of her emotional behavior over the last few days.

After Tanu heard about how Sunaina had been talking to Ranvir and how she had even shown Manas her feelings, Tanu was visibly upset. Despite her intentions not to tell all to Tanu, Sunaina could not hold much back. It was just not in her to conceal anything from her childhood friend, her second self.

It was Sunaina's day to get a pep talk from her friend. In her characteristically wise manner, Tanu began telling her to come back to reality and not to daydream or dwell in the past which had rudely divorced itself from her a decade ago.

"Why are you making friends with Ranvir all over again? Wasn't what he did enough to last you a lifetime?" asked Tanu, almost harshly. "Please, Naina, do not fall into any of these traps now. At least now be wise."

Naina listened carefully, sitting with her eyes cast down but looking up and seeing Tanu's expressive face at times.

Tanu had always shown her the mirror. She had strayed away from the straight path often, and was capable of great foolishness, but Tanu was the one who could see the consequences of such actions beforehand and warn her in time to halt her steps. She had known for several days that this was what Tanu would say when she heard of the revival of ties with Ranvir.

"Manas is a true friend and by looking for Ranvir in him, you have lowered the dignity of that friendship!" said her friend. This gave her a jolt though she knew it was true.

"And by telling Manas about Ranvir and even more so sending Manas to meet Ranvir, you have made a blunder," she went on. Sunaina's eyes were moist.

"But Tanu, it was not my intention to put down Manas or his friendship," she said, in a low voice.

"You have done that, whether it was your intention or not. Please clear this with Manas so that he does not feel belittled," replied Tanu. "He has helped you in setting up the school and putting it on its feet and has always come forward to support your endeavors. You have gone and mixed him up with your past," Tanu went on. "I am really annoyed with you."

Sunaina had tears in her eyes now. Tanu saw that but didn't relent. "You'll cry much more if things go out of hand as they did in the past. Stop right now and begin focusing on the life path you had chosen for yourself," she said.

"If at all you want to make up with anyone, you should try it with Prashant. He is alone too and I'm sure that he is ready to start life on a fresh note with you and Roop. But you have just not tried hard enough," she reprimanded Sunaina.

Tanu didn't stop. "I was only joking with you about Manas looking like Ranvir. You took it too seriously, I think."

"But Tanu, please listen to me, Manas said he understood when I told him that I respected him for what he was and not due to his resemblance to Ranvir" Sunaina put in a quick word in her defense.

"Everything doesn't have to be said in words, my friend," Tanu replied, "He will not let you know exactly what he must have felt."

This was getting worse and Sunaina felt terrible now. "I wish I had come and met you some days ago," said Tanu ruefully. "You've made quite a mess, my dear."

"Please Tanu, don't say that. It was just that I was carried away in a flood of emotion after having lived in a vacuum for so long. Don't make me feel like a horror, please," she almost pleaded with her friend, just a couple of months older than her but far more worldly wise than the impulsive Sunaina.

At all crucial moments of Sunaina's life, Tanu had shown her where she was going wrong. Sunaina had great faith in her wisdom and experience and knew that whatever she said was for her own good. And she never minced words at such moments. Tanu was indeed a true friend. She was feeling sorry that she had not told her about all this while she had been talking to Ranvir and getting emotional before Manas. Her tears showed her regret.

"Come on, now don't cry. Let's have another hot coffee now that I know you'll do what is best for you. No more discussions on all this," said Tanu who could comfort her friend in a way no one else could. "It will all be fine. It's good that even now I could tell you that you were losing your way once again in life."

By this time, Roop had returned with Mrs. Bakshi. "Its almost lunch time. Have lunch with us, beta," said Mrs. Bakshi to Tanu.

But Tanu wanted to go back to her dad and after lunch she had to go with Shashank to her in-laws' place for Rakhi. "Shashank and Dad are waiting for me, Aunty. I'll have lunch here another day," she said.

It was another important day in Sunaina's life. A turning point, once again! She felt that she had been transported back to the days when Ranvir had walked out of her life. Would she have to face the same agony once again? Was there no way that she could carry on living in the dream she had created over the last few months? She felt as if life had not much meaning for her any more.

In the afternoon, she was in her study, trying to check some school exercise books but she was very distracted and her mind was still foggy. She rested for a while. But her mind was racing over all the events of the past month. She knew Tanu was right. She could not be so weak again. After all that she had undergone to build up spiritual and emotional strength, this foolishness would just not do.

Almost ashamed of her behavior, Sunaina wept. She wondered what Ranvir and Manas must have thought of her. Oh God! They must have laughed at her inwardly. And what if her mother came to know what had happened? She wouldn't think much of her either! Although Sunaina felt that she had an idea about it, she was not sure how much she knew. She had not said anything to her.

What had happened must not continue. This was what she had decided after her meeting with Tanu. Tonight, she would call up Manas and express her regret at what she had demonstrated in those weaker moments. She was sure he would understand.

She knew that she had managed to delude herself once again by things that had no connection with the present. She could not even say that she didn't want to. If Ranvir was deluding himself, there was no need for her to be carried along. It was his daydream. How could she let herself become a part of it? This was what her mind told her. But her heart hardly agreed. Such confusing thoughts and feelings haunted her and she spent the day in a trance. Tanu's words had shaken her up badly but she was grateful for them.

They had woken her up from a dream which would bring only misery. These were not university days! And the sooner she woke up to this fact, the better it would be. Whether Megha came up to Ranvir's expectations or not, whether Prashant had made her happy or unhappy were questions that were unimportant. What was important now was that she must not share any illusions created for the sake of nostalgia either by her or Ranvir. She had not focused on the wonderful qualities of Manas and had made the great mistake of looking for Ranvir in him.

Sunaina was extremely restless and found it difficult to overcome the acute feeling of regret which had overtaken her since morning. She had already been feeling uncomfortable but when Tanu put it all down in black and white, she felt terrible. At the same time, she also felt a sense of relief that she would now be able to come out of the false existence she had been carrying on for some time now. She felt free. But sad.

37

It was a wet Saturday afternoon when the students of *Sarang* finally put on their small show. Sunaina had managed to hold a final rehearsal with them which made her realize how well Manas had trained her students. When Mrs. Neelima Sinha sang a Sufi kalaam, Sunaina asked her where she had learnt it. "Kaul Sir taught me and it took me several days to pick it up," she said.

Sunaina felt a pang of guilt when she heard this. She had not even bothered to find out what he had been teaching. She had been so taken up with her own feelings and confusion.

She had talked to Manas about her agony. The way he explained everything to her cleared cobwebs from her disturbed mind. He had won her over as his friend all over again. This was not a reflection of Ranvir talking to her but a person who had a clear and wonderful heart and a unique way of looking at relationships. He had spoken to her at length and reassured her that he held her in great regard as a friend and she should just wipe all those thoughts from her mind and rest easy. "You will always be my friend and a co-traveler on the music marga," he told her, trying to make her feel better.

"As far as your past is concerned, even I would tell you not to be wrapped in it. Life moves ahead every minute and no one can go back in time. You know that. There's so much you have taught me about life and here I am, teaching you!" he began laughing.

She thanked him several times over for his assurance and his clarity of thought. "Please convey my best wishes to the *Sarang* team for their first show," he said. "I really wish I could be with them now."

Sunaina felt much easier than before. It had been tough to explain everything to him, to admit her emotional weakness and her mistakes. But he had made her feel so much at ease that she felt proud to have him for a friend. "We are all looking forward to meeting you," she said.

"I might have some very good news for you when I come for Diwali," he said "But please don't ask me to tell you now. It's a surprise!"

"Okay Manas, we'll wait for your surprise," she told him.

Sunaina was now over with the school examinations. She would be taking leave for three or four days in September to see off Prashant. So she was working harder these days to do as much as she could before that. Prashant had called her last night and reminded her of her promise to come and meet him in Delhi before he left. He was more relaxed these days as most of his work in India was now complete. He had to hand over the house to the company. There was an independent project he had taken up and he was also giving it some finishing touches.

The *Sarang* performance drew a sizeable audience consisting of Sunaina's friends and colleagues, Mrs. Bakshi's friends, Tanu and her father and their friends and also Roop's friends. Families of the students also flocked to the show. Deena had helped Sunaina organize tea and snacks to be served after the show.

Raj Singhji, dressed in a brand new, embroidered Kurta Pyjama bought especially for the occasion, compered the show. Sunaina took over from him when it was his turn to perform. As usual, he sang excellently. His family had come for the concert and they applauded the loudest.

Sunaina could not stop herself from marveling at the great enthusiasm which Raj Singhji always exuded. His love for life and for music was so profound that anyone who came in contact with him could not remain untouched by it. He had made *Sarang* come alive so that on any day he was absent from the school, it seemed rather quiet and dull.

He had chosen to sing a Thhumri in Raga Vihag and an old bhajan "*Vrindawan ka Krishna Kanhaiya, sab ki aankhon kaa taara*" which Sunaina remembered her grandfather singing. She had always loved it. Raj Singhji had taught the little ones at *Sarang* to sing this bhajan everyday. And even at the concert, they began singing along with him.

Roop also sang. She was quite confident and as she knew most of the audience very well, she sang without any hesitation.

"This song is for my naanaji who used to love it so much that even if it was playing in a shop in the market, he used to rush quickly to that place and sit and listen," said Roop before starting her song.

Sunaina was surprised as Roop had not told her anything about this. She had chosen Professor Bakshi's great favorite "*Aji Roothh Kar Ab Kahaan Jaayiega*" from *Arzoo*, especially learnt from Mrs. Bakshi for the occasion. Later, Sunaina came to know that this had been done secretly to surprise her.

She was really touched by this gesture of her little daughter. This showed how she loved her mother and her grandfather and how dear she held his memory in her heart.

At the end of the show, Sunaina hugged and kissed Roop and thanked her. She had tears in her eyes after listening to the song in Roop's voice.

Tanu's Dad gave away the prizes. Sunaina and Tanu had bought a small gift for each of the students to appreciate the progress they had made.

Manas had called up his parents and they had also come to the show. They congratulated Mrs. Bakshi and Sunaina for the great show put up by *Sarang*. Mrs. Bakshi said, "Manas has also worked hard with the students and a lot of credit goes to him."

Sunaina kept looking at Tanu who was smiling widely today. She had told her friend about what Manas had said. "He was always clearheaded. It was you who were all mixed up," she said and again laughed, trying to pass it off as a joke, though she knew that it had been very tough for Sunaina to go through all this.

"Well I have spent most of my life mixed up," said Sunaina.

"It's never too late to learn," said the wise Tanu.

38

The monsoon was at its peak and, at times, despite the umbrellas and raincoats, they would get wet going to school. Sunaina never wore saris during monsoons. It was really difficult to manage them. Even otherwise, she was more used to wearing churidar-kurtas or salwar kameez which had been her dress code since the time she had been in college. What had changed now was that she no longer wore glass bangles and ornate bindis with her clothes.

At college, she used to carry bindis of various kinds, stick-ons, powdered as well as liquid ones, in all possible hues in her bag. Before the first lecture, her friends gathered in the Ladies Common Room every morning and she would design special bindis for all her friends to match with their clothes. Ranvir had not liked the bindis at all and wanted her not to wear them. "They do not match your personality," he used to say.

But she had worn them until Roop was around three or four years old. Then she had stopped putting them on. It was something which just happened. One fine day, she did not feel like placing any color on her forehead. Something stopped her, she didn't know what.

In her closet, there were boxes full of glass bangles and all sorts of bindis which were now toys for Roop who often brought out these carved wooden boxes and explored the things that had been so dear to her mother in her student days. Dreaming of how she would wear such kaanch ki choodis and bindis when she grew up and went to college.

Doon was great fun in the rains. Roasted Bhuttas, hot coffee, spicy samosas and sizzling pakoras were all available in the school canteen and students as well as teachers enjoyed these monsoon goodies.

Sunaina always compared this canteen with her own school canteen. It was a small cosy room with no tables or chairs but only a counter which was always crowded with hungry girls clamoring for Bun-Samosas and chutney sweets.

Behind the counter was one fatherly looking man whom they all knew as "Sweetman" and it was with this name that he was fondly addressed by hundreds of girls over the years. Deftly handing over "Bun-Samosas" or the few other items he sold, Sweetman never looked harassed by the crowd of girls screaming "Sweetman! Sweetman!" in a constant chorus. His hands kept working like a machine, taking money and handing over the food to the children. His magnanimous smile made them feel so good. Never had buns with samosas, a popular combination in Doon, tasted so good to Sunaina after she left school.

When she told Roop about the chutney sweets that used to taste something like the imli and gur chutney they made at home, Roop wanted to taste them. But Sunaina had not been able to get them, even in her old school.

The nuns used to bake cakes and make a special "Stick jaw" (which really used to stick one's tongue to the roof of one's mouth) which was sold to the students on special occasions like the annual school fete and sports day.

Once Cathy, who had access to the residential rooms of the Irish nuns, took Sunaina along to this mysterious and fascinating land from where an amazing aroma of baking used to emanate as the sisters baked their own special breads and cookies. Tip-toeing nervously, Sunaina followed Cathy into the high roofed corridors, terrified of being caught trespassing.

Cathy went inside and spoke to Sister Rita. Sunaina was peeping into the room when Sister Rosa came out of the kitchen and spotted her.

"Child! What are you doing here?" she asked in a stern voice.

Cathy came to her rescue. "Sister, this is my friend, Sunaina."

"We all know Sunaina. What she is doing here is what we want to know."

"Sister, she had a bad tummy ache and we came looking for some medicine," said Cathy who always had a rich stock of excuses.

"Well then, please take her to the infirmary!" said Sister Rita, looking suspiciously at them over her spectacles, which were placed precariously low on her beaky nose.

"But Sister, there's no one at the infirmary," said Sunaina, trying to look as if she was in great pain.

Sister Rosa brought out a concoction from the kitchen which looked absolutely fatal to Sunaina. "Drink it up dear and the tummy ache will vanish," she told Sunaina while holding out the small glass to her.

"What's this, Sister?" she asked in a weak, shaky voice.

"It's a mixture of herbs and will do you a world of good."

Sunaina was given no choice but to drink it. It tasted like hell and she was afraid she would vomit then and there.

She didn't remember how they both came out of that forbidden territory to go to their classroom. After this misadventure, she could never associate the Sisters' quarters with the exotic fragrance of baking. She could think of only the weird, dark green, herbal concoction she had to gulp down, thanks to Cathy and her great excuses!

The monsoon days in the valley often looked like late evening in the early morning. The dark clouds would cover the Doon skies and shut out most of the light. This resulted in beautiful grey-green days, full of moisture-laden air when it wasn't raining. Sunaina and her students enjoyed their singing greatly during those days.

"Even the trees and grass of Doon look so happy and bright after the rain," said Roop who also loved the rain.

Sunaina was driving the car, going back home from school, looking forward to the dosas and hot spicy sambhar which Deena had promised to make for lunch.

She had been dreading getting a call from Ranvir ever since she had spoken to Tanu and had her mind cleared of her illusions. Somehow, there was no call from him since then. Perhaps he was busy with his office work and meetings. She felt quite relieved about that as she didn't know how to convey her change of attitude to him without sounding rude. She would cross that bridge when she came to it!

39

Prashant had already sent train tickets to her by courier as she had applied for leave and informed him of the dates when they could go to Delhi. Looking at the tickets, she wondered at how amazingly people could change with time in some ways. She remembered what tantrums he would throw in the past if she ever wanted him to do anything to help her. He had considered it beneath his dignity even to go and buy some groceries for the house.

"Do you think that I will actually go and buy bread and eggs for you?" he would say in the harsh tone which she detested. "In your home, your dad and brother must be doing all these silly jobs but don't expect such things from me!"

Her sensibilities were shocked at such treatment. She felt highly insulted and inadequate. She had been young and extremely sensitive. Prashant's domineering nature shattered her confidence. It had then been beyond her imagination that such people and ideas also existed in the same world where people like her father lived. It had broken her spirit to co-exist with a stubborn and harsh person like Prashant in the same house. She could never call it a home as it was run more like a hostel and she felt an inmate.

She stopped her chain of thought and tried to think that perhaps Prashant had learnt over the years to get his priorities in order. Even if he had, she knew he would not admit this to her because of the king-sized ego he had nurtured ever since she could remember.

After Tanu's talk about her relationships in life, Sunaina had been quite shaken up and had begun thinking more seriously about her daughter's future. She wondered whether she was not depriving Roop of a very important aspect of her life. She tried putting herself in Roop's place and imagining how she would have felt staying away at that age from her own dad. This gave her the jitters. Would she want Roop to have no memories of childhood associated with her dad when she herself had such wonderful ones of her own father?

It became clear to her that she was in the wrong by equating Roop's relationship with her dad with her own relationship with Prashant. She must not look at their relationship through her own eyes but through Roop's eyes.

This opened up a little part of her heart as well as mind and she began thinking in a direction which she had always completely shut out. Perhaps she could relent and, for Roop's sake, go back to the relationship with a clean slate. But her apprehensions regarding Prashant and his behavior at once checked this thought.

She told herself that she would think about it another day. This reminded her of Scarlett O'Hara of *Gone with the Wind*, one of her favorite works of literature. Sunaina had always noticed this trait in herself ... of trying to postpone unpleasant decisions ... trying to pretend that they didn't exist.

When she had read the classic which her mother had recommended, the last page where Scarlett puts off thinking about Rhett until the next day, reminded Sunaina of herself. "I'll think of it all tomorrow. I can stand it then. Tomorrow, I'll think of some way to get him back. After all, tomorrow is another day."

She admired Scarlett's spirit and courage greatly and almost thought of her as a friend whom she had met. This book was a kind of a gospel to her.

There were some others, like *The Thornbirds*, *The Mill on the Floss*, *Song of Sixpence*, *Rebecca*, *Far From The Madding Crowd* and *Doctor Zhivago* which her parents had read numberless times and handed down to Sunaina as family heirlooms. She, too, had read them many times and preserved every word of them in her heart.

Well, she would take inspiration from Scarlett and think of Prashant tomorrow. This was her last thought as she went to sleep. That night she dreamt again of a remorseful Prashant who was shedding tears at the airport and saying that he wanted to go to Hauz Khaas, the colony where Sunaina and Prashant had lived in a small flat in the first year of their marriage. Sunaina woke up. It was only 2:20. She wondered what this dream meant. Was it a result of her thoughts or was it a precursor of things to come? She didn't want to think anymore and tried going back to sleep, hoping for a dreamless slumber.

Ranvir called up the next day and wanted to know what she had been doing all this time. He told her that he missed her a lot. He also told her about his preparation for the concert. Sunaina would now have to make him understand what she had been thinking and about the turmoil she had been undergoing. It was not going to be easy but today she would have to gather the kind of courage which he had shown when he had told her that he would not be able to defy his parents and marry her. This would be his day of shock, though she didn't feel like hurting him at all.

"I've been quite busy," she said and didn't want to say anything more.

"You're sounding a bit strange. Are you tired?' he asked. The trouble was that he could read her moods just listening to her voice.

"Ranvir, I have been thinking about our recent friendship and find it a little awkward," she said, trying to make every word sound clear and loud.

"Don't say that. Where do you find the awkwardness?" he asked, disturbed by her words.

"Ranvir, we must think of others who trust us and for whom this kind of thing would come as a shock. I feel uncomfortable now regarding this friendship about which our families do not know."

"But this is a beautiful world we can both share without anyone knowing," he said, trying to reason with her.

"But Ranvir, I do not want to live in an illusory world at this stage of my life. It's true that I've been an escapist often in life but I've seen the consequences."

When he kept quiet, she knew that he had understood. It was this dreamy quality of hers which had prevented her from understanding the reality of her situation regarding Ranvir's family. While she had remained in her own sweet world of poetry and music, his parents had discovered their closeness and made other plans for Ranvir. She had tried to find another dream by saying "Yes" to Prashant's proposal and had been rudely awakened by his queer and often mean conduct.

No more illusions for her. She was grateful to Tanu for waking her up. She might have created yet another mess and would have hurt not only her mother but also her little, sweet daughter. She shuddered to think of where this revived friendship could have led.

It was difficult to make him see her point of view. "Please Sunaina, it's not that we'll be meeting; just talking to you gives me so much of joy. Don't take it away from me now," he almost pleaded.

"Please Ranvir, I don't want to have this kind of half-friendship with you. I am sorry I realized it late but now that I have the correct perspective, I cannot let you talk me into anything," she said, softly but firmly.

There was almost a minute of silence. "Are you listening to me? Are you on the line?" she asked.

"I am, but it's very tough to let go of your closeness like this," he said, sounding extremely low. Was it tears she felt in his voice? She hoped not.

It was with a heavy heart that she ended that phone call. But she expected him to try again, though she had made it clear to him that she would now prefer to cherish the memories of the years of innocence they had spent together in their youth.

"Let's not let go of those precious memories too," she said. "Remember Ranvir, that a raga sung out of its fixed time always sounds strange and doesn't touch the heart."

She blamed herself no less than she blamed Ranvir for having been rather childish in sharing their lives again with each other. Sandcastles, when rebuilt, often looked ugly. A beautiful dream must end with the night; stretched to the daylight, there were chances of it turning into a nightmare. This was one bitter pill Ranvir would have to swallow. But she felt terrible that she made him do it.

40

She felt sad to be unable to get guidance for her Sufi songs from her guruji who was now lost in the city of dreams where a quirk of fate could turn a beggar into a king and vice versa within moments. What was this magic of Mumbai people often spoke about? she wondered. She had not visited, not surprising, given her tendency to stay put in Doon most of the time.

But whatever she had heard from people she knew made her feel that despite it being overcrowded and living at a pace which was unthinkable for her, there was something in Mumbai which was extremely special. Perhaps she should go and see for herself some day.

Manas had still not told her about the surprise he wanted to give all of them. Perhaps he had made up with his girlfriend and was going to get engaged, thought Sunaina. But she couldn't be sure until he said so.

"Please carry on with your riyaz, Sunaina," he kept telling her whenever they spoke.

"I think I will also have to make *All India Radio* my guru like Raj Singhji," she said, and they both laughed.

And then suddenly one day she received a courier from Mumbai which carried a CD. She was surprised as he had not mentioned anything about sending it. She was sure that this wasn't the surprise he had been talking about.

When she played the CD, she was overjoyed to find he had recorded some lessons for her which she was to practice until he returned. This was so thoughtful of him and the kind of thing she would have expected Tanu to do. All good friends acted alike, she thought.

At this moment, she remembered the books which Ranvir had sent her through Manas. Wasn't that also a wonderful gesture of friendship? But there was no denying that their relationship went beyond friendship and this was what would one day perhaps ruin the friendship between them. Their past and their present could not stand together in this world. She often wondered whether it would have been better if she had not met Ranvir again. It would have saved her from this fresh pain which kept nagging her ... a pain of an old wound reopened. "*Phool khiley shaakhon pe naye aur dard puraane yaad aaye*" was how an Urdu poet had put it beautifully. "*Tum yaad aaye, aur tumhaare saath zamaane yaad aaye*!"

Prashant was waiting to see Sunaina and Roop. He had almost completed his independent assignment and had freedom these days, something he had not enjoyed for years.

Living with his thoughts, he felt a little uncomfortable. He was not used to reflection and usually shunned idleness. He had never had much of an inner life, depending greatly on external factors to keep himself going. Parties, colleagues, tennis, fast driving, soccer matches on TV and conferences at office – all these were part of his life at any given time and he often found people like Sunaina unbelievable.

But he also realized that she was content with herself. That quiet at the centre of her being was what he really envied. He had never been able to attain it. Perhaps, to achieve that, loving solitude was the first condition.

She wanted him to be more settled in his mind. Though she herself was an emotional, impulsive creature, there was something which gave her focus so she had never been restless like Prashant. It was her music, her love for nature and for books which had made her inner being a tranquil lake. Or, perhaps, she had been just born like that. And to think that Prashant's name meant "peaceful!"

Sunaina sometimes saw this restlessness in Roop, too, and prayed that as she grew up, it would go away instead of growing along with her. It was a Singh trait she did not want her daughter to inherit.

Prashant now tried to get his thoughts together. He was leaving the country, leaving Sunaina and Roop behind. For at least six months, he would not be back. There was fear in his heart which had been fuelled by Sunaina's attitude during his last visit to Doon. Somewhere, deep inside, he was insecure. And he also knew that, today, he was far more insecure than Sunaina had ever been in this marriage. There was something in her personality, he could see now, which made him feel that she was prepared for anything which life brought her. Her emotional stature made him feel ill at ease and he wondered how she would take any of his efforts, if he made them, to make things good between them.

He had spoken to Adi about this recently. Adi was his friend and Sunaina's favorite cousin and would be able to tell Prashant how to go about things.

"I sincerely think that both of you, for Roop's sake, should talk at length and sort out everything," said Adi, a simple person who could not understand what went wrong between the two of them. Sunaina had never told him. Nor had his aunt. Ishaan had told him a few things but he still felt that the marriage could be successful. Simple Adi!

"I'll talk to her when she comes here," said Prashant in a manner which showed that he had very little hope, from her as well as from himself.

"Do you want me to speak to her?" asked Adi, looking at his downcast face.

"No Adi, I will talk to her this time. She always shirks listening to what I have to say. But this time, I will request her to hear me out."

Adi wished him luck. They were both having dinner at Prashant's company guest house where he was now, after leaving the house.

"If you were not going abroad, we could have both planned something together in Doon. The business opportunities are increasing there now," said Adi.

"We can always plan later. I'll be coming back in two years," said Prashant.

"Are you serious?" asked his friend looking incredulously at him because he had known him to react negatively to such an idea until now.

"Yes Adi, we'll plan it over the next two years and begin work as soon as I'm back," Prashant said, so confidently that Adi asked no more questions.

41

Tanu met Sunaina in the market one evening. She was shopping and was thrilled to see Sunaina who was buying some music VCDs in the departmental store where they met. Tanu was after readymade clothes.

"Guess what, Sunaina, we're all going to Dubai for a holiday. For once, Sumeet says he will not work while we are there!" Sunaina could see how excited her friend was.

"Who are going and when?" asked Sunaina, surprised at this sudden development.

"The three of us, my Dad, his mother and his sister – all of us. We'll be leaving next week and return two weeks later."

"Wow, Tanu, I'm happy for you but am going to miss you so much," she said.

"But I'll be back soon. Please give me a list of things you need from there. I'll get them all for you, like Santa Claus!" she tried cheering her up.

"Bring me good luck and peace of mind," said Sunaina with a smile.

Tanu smiled and then hugged her.

Suddenly Sunaina's eyes filled with tears. She had been putting herself through so much emotional turmoil lately.

Tanu didn't say anything as there was a crowd around them at the store. "I'll come and see you before I leave. I hope you are not going off to Delhi yet."

"No, later," said Sunaina and went back to choosing her music. There was a new album with a rare selection of Sufiyana Gaeke which she picked up and wondered whether Manas had seen it yet. It featured a Kashmiri singer so she made a mental note of informing him about it.

Tanu was waiting for Sumeet to go over to his mother's home. Sunaina had come alone to the market and drove back after having made her purchases.

It was a dark cloudy evening, the kind which made one gloomy and pensive. She was listening to some instrumental music in the car which was an ideal background for her thoughts that evening. When she had been in school, she had loved to daydream while sitting in class when the clouds gathered and, suddenly, it became dark inside the classroom.

The lights would be put on and it would change the atmosphere radically. On such days, even Sunaina, who had the reputation of being the best behaved and most conscientious student, turned a little mischievous.

On one such day, Mrs. Jasjit Sandhu had been taking their English class. It had been a winter day and Sunaina and Tanuja, in their deep maroon school blazers, sat in class next to each other. They had been in Class Nine then.

On an impulse, Tanuja placed her right hand in Sunaina's right hand coat pocket looking for walnuts and kishmish there. Without giving it a thought, Sunaina put her hand in Tanu's left hand pocket. And at that moment, Mrs. Sandhu asked Sunaina to answer a question. As she tried getting up to answer, it became difficult to disengage her hand quickly.

Finally, they both stood up and started answering the question. It was a funny sight! The class had a hearty laugh on that dark wintry day. Mrs. Sandhu, who knew how good both were at their work, just asked them not to repeat such nonsense and went on with the lesson.

In Sunaina's mind, the incident was still as fresh as if it had happened only yesterday. And when she thought about how their hands were still in each other's pockets, she felt really lucky to have a friend who had stood with her like a rock, though she had not always found kishmish in Naina's pockets. Many a time, she had found the broken pieces of her dreams injuring her hands and heart. But Tanu had not let that stop her from keeping a hand in Naina's pockets. Sunaina knew that she had also done the same. How far had she succeeded, she could not say.

The books Ranvir had sent were now in Sunaina's special cupboard which held all her precious memories. In this cupboard of the past were souvenirs from her childhood, her school, college days and all the loose ends which she could not deal with in this harsh real world. They all sat together, safely, in this blue-green iron almirah which no one except Sunaina had ever opened until today.

A plastic doll called "Hellie" which her eldest mausi had brought from France when Sunaina had been five years old was still sleeping here, her bluegreen eyes still opening and closing as she was made to stand up or lie down. The box in which she came had her name written on it.

In this little treasure house of her life, Sunaina had gathered letters from her father, her mother, Ranvir, Tanu, Adi and Ishaan. Some of the letters were very old and the paper had begun yellowing. Many a time Sunaina wondered about preserving them or not. But she didn't have the heart to destroy any. How aptly the poet had written "*Teri Khusbhoo mein basey khat main jalaata kaise? Pyaar mein doobey hue khat main jalaata kaise?*"

Each letter conveyed how much all these special people in her life cared for her, how much they loved her and missed her. It was impossible for her to part with this treasure chest of emotions! She guarded it like a lioness and nobody even dared to touch it.

Roop had always been after her mom to see what was hidden in the old almirah. Sunaina had shown her old photographs, her university degree, birthday cards, new year greetings, costumes she had worn in school plays and dances, Roop's first school uniform, her maroon and gold wedding salwar kameez and a host of other things hidden from the eyes of the world which could never understand what these meant to her. She could not bear them to be exposed to the harshness of life which she had had to go through.

By placing Ranvir's latest gift among her treasure trove, Sunaina wanted to convince herself that this was now past. She hoped she realized that life could not move backwards. Nor could one sing a raga starting from the bandish and moving towards the alaap. Things turned backwards always became strained and unnatural, she told herself, trying to imagine what words Tanu would have used to explain this to her.

42

Ranvir was now suffering terribly. He could not share this pain with anyone. He felt that this was Nemesis catching up. How many times had he repented his decision to please his parents! Had he asserted himself, they would have come around. But what was done was done.

When he had been living in an emotional vacuum, there was hope in him that one day things would change. God would end his pain and loneliness.

Where this hope came from even he didn't know. But it was there, nestling in some corner of his heart where memories of Sunaina had a quiet home. He had lived by that. It was like a small white bird of hope whose presence he felt in his soul. It was like an exquisite raga which would lose its unique beauty if it was ever sung in this world.

He had been waiting for some kind of a miracle which would wipe away his sorrow and regret. And, for him, his meeting with Sunaina in Mussoorie had been that miracle. It had made him believe that if one really admitted wrongdoing and repented in one's spirit, there was a power which came to the rescue.

Sunaina had now made him realize that there was to be no end to his suffering, at the last. She had shown him joy and then plunged him into misery.

"Why Sunaina, why? Why have you done this? I have suffered enough all these years." These were the words which rang in his heart again and again. He cursed his destiny. He cursed himself. There was nothing in his life to be happy about or nurture hopes of being happy ever again.

He had called up Sunaina again and she had told him the same again. "Please go back to your music," she had advised him, like a grandmother. He didn't know whether to laugh or to cry at this practical stance. Had it been Tanu who had made her see sense? He wondered.

He knew how concerned Tanu always was for the welfare of her childhood friend. He had seen her upset when she saw them together in Mussoorie. But somewhere, deep down, he knew Sunaina was right. Finally, his crazy, impulsive, gypsy-like Sunaina had grown up and become sensible! But this time, he had to bear the brunt of this.

Ranvir was a great fan of Jagjit Singh, the ghazal king, and at that moment, one of the ghazals sung by him was in his mind ... "*Tere baarey mein jab socha nahin thha, main tanha thha magar itna nahin thaa.*" True, he had been lonely before he met her at Mussoorie but not as he was today! He felt trapped in his own existence.

Could one wrong step in life lead to such endless sorrow?

Sunaina took a few extra classes in school as she would soon be going to Delhi to see Prashant.

Smriti, her best student, was now in Class Twelve and always made the school and Sunaina proud by standing first in all inter-school music contests held in the state.

She was a joy to teach and a great pleasure to hear. She always became one with the song she sang and had the rare quality of losing herself completely in the soul of the raga she sang. Sunaina had seen many grown-up artistes who did not have this attribute.

Whenever she taught her something new, Sunaina was amazed at how fast she picked it up and excelled. At such times, Sunaina understood how worthwhile and valuable her music teaching could be.

"Ma'am, how is it that at times when I try to sing a composition with great effort, it just eludes me and when I almost forget about it, it suddenly comes out of me effortlessly and beautifully?" Smriti asked her once.

That was a question whose answer even Sunaina had not completely found. "It has something to do with inspiration and the fact that true art always shirks pressure," she told her bright young student. "It's all up to the Muse," she said with a smile.

"It happens like this in life too, Smriti. If you want something desperately, it never comes to you. But when you finally focus on other things, some day that old wish surprisingly gets fulfilled suddenly," said Sunaina, trying to believe in this philosophy of life herself. Indeed, it had held true for her.

But she wanted Smriti to believe it. There were so many of these beliefs her parents had given her when she had been Smriti's age which had stood by her in later years. She had no other pearls but these.

She realized that such words of wisdom from her dad during her schooldays had been more useful to her in later life. Some of the memorable ones were "Hope for the best but be prepared for the worst," "The value of a wise man's words and the real taste of an amla (gooseberry) are always registered late" and "Why ask about the way to a village one doesn't have to visit?" Sometimes he would quote Urdu couplets to inspire or comfort her. If she ever fell down or had to face some defeat, he would say, "Girte hain shay sawaar hi maidaan-ejang mein; woh tifl kya girenge joh ghutnon ke bal chalein?" Another favorite of his was Mohammad Iqbal's "Khudi ko kar buland itna ki har taqdeer se pehle, khuda bandey se khud poochhe, bata teri razaa kya hai?"

So often in various situations in her life had Sunaina remembered these gems of practical wisdom and drew strength from them. There were some sayings which her dad had passed on from his treasure house of homespun ideas inherited from his own parents.

Each time she fell back on this wisdom, she felt close to her dad. She tried to share this with Roop but knew that her daughter was too young as yet. But she kept trying and knew that, gradually, the sayings would mean something to Roop, too.

Smriti was mature for her years and often talked to Sunaina about her dreams and ambitions. She wanted to be a classical artist and later try playback singing in the films.

"Just be true to your music and the rest will follow," Sunaina often said to her. This was wisdom conveyed to a girl whose eyes were as full of dreams as Sunaina's had once been and whose voice had the beauty of innocence and the light of goodness.

43

Tanu had left and her dad's house was now locked. Hari was in the outhouse and looking after the premises. Tanu asked Sunaina to keep an eye on the house, too. The sprawling house looked sad without its inmates and a haunting silence engulfed it. Whenever Sunaina passed it on her way, she could sense it feeling forlorn.

She was not too keen on leaving her mother and going to Delhi. Deena had assured her that she would look after everything but she would have felt better if Maaliji had been around, too. Ramesh was learning and had become quite an expert at managing work at home and in the gardens. He did a lot of purchasing, both for Sunaina and his own house.

Sunaina thought she would return soon. It was with confused feelings that she prepared herself for this trip to meet Prashant and see him off. She had noticed his recent efforts at changing her views about him, to make her relent. It was not that she had not noticed ... only, she wanted to ignore them.

If she acknowledged his efforts, it would mean making changes in her life and vision once again. She was not really inclined towards doing that.

There was an old Kishore Kumar masterpiece based on Raga Vihaag, from the Mumtaaz-Rajesh Khanna starrer *Aap Ki Kasam* which put this across so well ... "*Zindagi ke safar mein guzar jaatey hain jo mukaam, woh phir nahin aatey, woh phir nahin aatey.*" The poignant rendering of this song expressed the feelings and thoughts of many a person who had been through painful relationships, tossed about on the sea of intense feelings which were shattering and extremely destructive. "*Waqt chalta hi rehta hai, rukta nahin, ek pal mein yeh aagey nikal jaata hai, aadmi thheek se dekh paata nahin aur parde pe manzar badal jaata hai.*"

Alas! Time kept moving steadily onwards while one made mistakes, while others walked all over you, while beautiful winters disappeared giving place to torturous summers, while one wallowed in sorrow and misery, impulsive decisions kept making existence a mess, while one repented yet again. Time never waited.

Prashant had definitely changed considerably. But they were not living under the same roof and she always believed that to know a person's behavior well, you had to live with him or her. There was no other way. The masks people wore when they met each other for a few hours could be highly misleading.

When she used to meet Prashant before and after their engagement, she could not have imagined his terrible temper in her wildest dreams. And perhaps, Ranvir might not have been as charming as she thought had he married her and spent his life with her. She would never know.

This was especially applicable to a man-woman relationship. High expectations, rosy dreams and promises of undying love all crumbled and led to boredom, conflict and a cynical attitude towards love.

Friendship knew nothing of all this sordid stuff. She and Tanu had been together since they were children. But the bond between them had become stronger. They had stayed with each other for years, meeting almost every day. Yet their friendship was as fresh and strong as it had ever been, perhaps stronger now with the passing years.

"Whatever happens to either of us, we will always be there for each other no matter what other people do or say," Tanu stated to her at various stages of their lives and she had echoed this resolve in all sincerity and truth. Sunaina had once read a beautiful piece about the closeness sisters shared. She had no sister and neither had Tanu. But they were closer than sisters to each other; more like twins as far as standing by each other was concerned.

The piece said, "Life happens. Distance separates. Children grow up. Jobs come and go. Love waxes and wanes. Men don't always do what they're supposed to. Hearts break. Parents die. Careers end. BUT ... sisters are always there, no matter how much time and how many miles are between. A sister is never further away than needing her can reach."

Even when she was in the train to Delhi, she remembered how difficult her journey of relationships had been and how far she was from her college time dream of a perfect marriage where everything would be like a picturebook. She had always worn rose-tinted glasses to see the world.

But she had to give that up the day Ranvir went back on his word. And she threw the glasses away the day she discovered the dark and scary side of Prashant. She had tried looking for them after she met Ranvir at Mussoorie but had to stop when Tanu woke her up just in time from her beautifully deceptive dream.

44

The guest house where Prashant was staying was near Connaught Place. It was prominent among the few places Sunaina liked in Delhi. She had a long-standing relationship with C.P. going back to her childhood.

Sunaina remembered visiting Janpath in C.P. as a little girl with her mother, mausis and cousins. They used to call it Queen's Way even years after it had been renamed.

All of them had their favorite little shops here but the shop selling khatta and meethha aam papad was a common favorite. And Sunaina knew that it was still there to visit and take back the amazing black and yellow aam papad for her friends and students in Doon.

Just as she always carried pista and coffee biscuits and chocolate walnut cookies from the well-known bakeries of Doon for Prashant, Mausi and Adi, all of whom loved these mouth-watering delicacies based on exotic European recipes. Several locals had picked these up from the European settlers and handed them down to the next generation. These recipes had led to bakeries coming up in the valley. Crisp brown rusks, macaroons that melted in the mouth, light and tangy lemon and orange tarts, sinfully tempting Chocolate Brownies ... The list was unending.

The streets of the valley, at around eleven every morning, were full of the aroma of baking as there were one or two bakeries on each road. This aroma took Sunaina back to the Doon of her childhood when people used to take flour, sugar and butter from home to leave at their neighborhood baker's. Within a few hours, one could bring home freshly baked Atta Biscuits which tasted like manna from heaven. She remembered going with her dad to the old Sunshine Bakers which was about a kilometer away from their house. The shop was still there but the baking unit had been shifted elsewhere.

At times, she used to sit at the bakery, having deliciously rich creamy Badaam Milk with Dad while the delicious fragrance of baking cookies enveloped her. Atta biscuits were even now available at all bakers and even at grocery shops in Doon today. But the taste of the atta biscuits made from the stuff taken from home could never be matched.

It was all this that endeared Doon to her. Memories in every corner, her childhood peeping at her from every little street and shop. Despite all the changes, these were things which still lived on in her hometown. Hidden from the mainstream, they existed somewhere in the interior of the city, refusing to be moved by the onslaught of the designer culture and the multinational setups.

Prashant had been really happy to meet them at the railway station and as they drove towards the guest house, Roop talked nineteen to the dozen and updated her dad on all the recent happenings in Doon including Tanu Mausi's family holiday in Dubai, the *Sarang* concert and little Manno's progress at school.

"Didn't you sing at the concert?" he asked Sunaina. She shook her head and said that she had wanted it to be, totally and completely, the students' show.

"Have you finished all your work?" she asked him.

"Yes, I have and now I want to spend my time with Roop and you. It's a break which I've wanted for a long time," he replied, looking at her intently and giving her one of his dimpled smiles.

Sunaina was quiet as Roop continued her conversation with him. She was a little tired as she had been taking classes until an hour before she boarded the train. The almost six hour journey made her feel extremely sleepy, but she could not sleep in the train as she had to keep an eye on Roop and the luggage all the time.

At the Guest House they had their dinner in the room. It was almost midnight and Sunaina had some sandwiches and tea while Roop had sambhar vada.

"We must all have been South Indians in our previous birth to be so fond of their cuisine," said Prashant. This made Sunaina smile and feel a little more comfortable in his company. She had been living away from him for so long that he seemed almost a stranger.

Another problem was that both Sunaina as well as Prashant were not great talkers. They were both more given to listening. Perhaps that was why they had never been able to communicate well with each other.

Sunaina was asleep before she could think of anything else that night. Prashant read for a while and then carried Roop from the sofa, where she had fallen asleep, to the bed. He looked at his wife and his daughter and suddenly a strange sinking feeling gripped him. He felt that he was about to enter a huge vacuum where his voice would not be able to be heard by Sunaina and Roop, that he was about to lose something most precious.

He thought it strange that he had never realized until now how much his wife and daughter had meant to him. While he was in Delhi and they in Doon, he had the feeling that they were quite close and he could meet them whenever he wished. It was just a comfortable five hour drive.

But now, when he was moving out of the country, it would not be like that any more. A feeling of dread overtook him. It was almost nightmarish!

"Would he be able to live so far away from them without knowing that there would be a future together for the three of them?"

This question had come to his mind before but now, with Roop and Sunaina so close to him physically, it shook him up badly. He wanted to wake them up and share this fear with them and to hear words which would console him, giving him hope and cheer.

It was quite a long time before he could sleep. He slept with the resolve that tomorrow morning he would talk to Sunaina as a friend and not as the typical husband which she shirked. He had come to know what she avoided and he would make sure he didn't repeat any of that.

Delhi was getting some share of the rains. What seemed like a mere drizzle to Sunaina was taken seriously by the people there who made much ado about nothing. It was raining that morning. It was Friday and Prashant had to visit his clients only on Monday. He would have three clear days to spend with them.

Adi came to see them at breakfast and Sunaina was pleased to meet him after so long. Adi had always been the elder brother she had looked up to. Ishaan was much younger than her and had not joined in the childhood games and fun she had shared with Adi. Even now, they both teased Ishaan and said they had childhood secrets of which he knew nothing.

"You know, Roop, your mom and Adi Mama used to treat me like a slave. I was made to do menial jobs while they had a gala time in every game," Ishaan used to tell his niece. Roop loved to hear about these stories where Ishaan Mama was deliberately given roles in a game which had no meaning.

"In school, I was always the poor student while they were the teachers and principal. Sometimes I was just a peon," Ishaan used to recall and still felt bad about it.

"But Mama, students have an important role in a school," Roop would try to tell him logically. But this never consoled him. He always held it against Sunaina and Adi that they used to make a fool of him when he was an innocent and trusting youngster and made him believe all they said.

This morning, Adi narrated to Roop about the time he and Sunaina made Ishaan sit in a makebelieve doctor's waiting room as a patient and disappeared through the other room (which was supposed to be the doctor's consulting room) to go and play on their own.

Roop went with Adi to her Mausi Naani's house to meet her cousin. Sunaina and Prashant would meet her there in the evening. Somehow, Sunaina got a feeling that this had been subtly done so that she and Prashant could get some time alone to talk over things.

Well, if that was the case, it was fine with her. She would say some things to Prashant which she didn't want Roop to hear and so would Prashant, she thought. Her mother as well as Tanu had told her not to be impatient when Prashant tried talking to her about their relationship and its future. She really hoped that she would be able to keep her promise of being cool.

After Adi left with Roop, Sunaina and Prashant went to the Triveni Kala Sangam near Mandi House where they often went when they both lived in Delhi. Sunaina was a frequent visitor to Triveni when she was at the university and the place had not changed a bit since then. It was one of the few havens of tranquility in busy Delhi where one could get new energy to face the rushed life.

There had been a cute little bookshop by the name of "The Nook" at Triveni where she had browsed for hours. A South Indian lady had been then in charge and she came to know Sunaina quite well. She had most of the books and cassettes with her till now with "Bought at Triveni" written neatly in her hand on them.

Sitting today at those same little tables amid the greenery and sipping nimbu paani with the good old paranthas and zeera aloo served happily by an old waiter whom she remembered from college days, Sunaina had a feeling of déjà vu. It brought tears to her eyes.

It was still raining and this added to the beauty of the cosy place which was the only one of its kind she had ever known.

"Why are you so thoughtful? I thought you'd be happy to be here," Prashant asked as she was looking dreamily at the steps facing the semi-circular stage where she and her friends often used to sit and watch folk dancers practice in the carefree days of their youth. Even Manas had often talked about this place and how he loved its lively ambience.

"I am. Really happy and thankful that we came here of all the places in Delhi," she told him. "I was feeling nostalgic."

"Well, that's your favorite pastime, isn't it?" he asked with a knowing smile. But Sunaina could see that he wasn't being sarcastic this time, as was his wont usually.

She smiled back at him and, after so long, he felt comfortable in her presence. Perhaps it was due to the fact that they were meeting at a place which both of them liked and were away from reminders of ugly past incidents.

Whatever the reason, Prashant was glad to know that there was still a place for both to find a common meeting ground and express their views.

"Did Adi tell you anything about my future plan?" he asked her, hesitatingly.

She looked up at him and shook her head. Adi had no chance to tell her anything. In fact, Prashant himself had told him not to tell her.

"When I return to India in a couple of years, Adi and I will set up our company in Doon," he said.

Sunaina was quite taken aback. He had told her twice earlier about such a plan but had then taken up the job offer from abroad. She looked carefully at his face and then into his eyes. Was this another one of his whims and idiosyncrasies? If so, it was a bad joke he was indulging in, she thought.

But his eyes told her that he was as serious as he had never been about anything until now. It took her a few moments to grasp the meaning of his words and then react to them.

"How have you come to this decision?" she asked, still looking at him a little unbelievingly.

"I've had enough time by myself, Sunaina, to mull over the past and analyze my own behavior and role in making things so bad between us. When I look back on everything, I find that it was immaturity on the part of both of us which prevented our coming to an understanding," he said.

He stopped a moment and went on, "Time has made me realize how senseless some of my actions were. I admit that you only used to react to my actions most of the time, but I want to give another chance to our relationship."

She didn't say anything. "If not for anything else, then for Roop's sake," he continued.

"What do you want me to do?" she asked, still not ready to believe his words.

"Nothing. I do not want you to do anything. I will be in touch with you constantly while I'm abroad and will visit you often. All I ask is that you open your heart to me to give a sincere try to our marriage," he said. "I've seen plenty of the corporate life and after these two years, I'll have enough experience to run my own setup."

This was something Sunaina had not expected. She had believed all this while that it was only her to whom life had taught lessons. She had forgotten that with each passing day, life was also bringing new experiences and thoughts to Prashant. Why had she been so narrow-minded? It was, perhaps, because she had shut him out from her life to an extent where those developments didn't matter to her. He had shattered her self-respect and, for this, she had not forgiven him. She had forgotten but not forgiven, even now.

His views had opened up a totally new avenue of possibilities. She had thought that he would ask her to shift to Muscat or to make a decision once and for all about the marriage. But he had taken her unawares by his plan which sounded quite reasonable, provided he didn't change his mind over the next two years. If they could all live in Doon, she would be able to look after her mom and also carry on with the good work she had started. And in case Prashant chose to be difficult, she always had the option of withdrawing into herself again or walking away from the marriage.

"Think over it and tell me what you feel. I'll wait. For now, let's just enjoy this delicious lunch," said Prashant. All of a sudden, she felt like weeping. Out of relief or out of surprise, she couldn't make out. But she would not give in to this urge she thought. She must not appear weak in front of Prashant.

He had once injured her ego and dignity. Up to now, she could not show him the extent of the hurt and misery he had caused her, her parents and Roop. It would be a long time before she would be able to share her emotions with him! It was mainly due to his behavior that she had cut herself off from her emotions and chosen to live almost in a vacuum, withdraw into a shell.

She told him that she would tell him what she thought before she went back to Doon, the same day he was scheduled to leave for Muscat.

45

Now back in Doon, Sunaina could settle down earnestly to her work and plan her trip to Srinagar to meet Dr. Bajpai regarding her doctorate.

It was past the height of the rains and the weather was mostly clear. She had asked Deena to place all the rugs and cushions of the *Sarang* rooms out in the sunshine today as the sun was out after several days.

September, at one time, had been almost part of the monsoons in Doon but the climatic changes over the last few years had resulted in less rain in September.

"I think this would be a good time to travel up to Srinagar," Mrs. Bakshi told Sunaina. "Will you come with me," she asked her mother. "Tanu hasn't come back or I would have taken her along. She loves to go to the hills."

"All three of us can go this Sunday," said her mom.

"I'll ask Dr. Bajpai whether that would suit him," she answered.

It was a Thursday and she had planned to go over to the bazaar after school and look up some books on music at her favorite bookshop in the heart of the city which she used to visit even as a little girl.

The shop's old proprietor had known her dad since the time he had settled in Doon. He had been Dad's friend and often met him during their morning walk on Rapper Road. Both he and her dad were no more but she was still linked to that family.

The present owner was her dad's friend's son and was well known to her and her mother. In fact, he used to visit them sometimes with his dad when Professor Bakshi was alive. His dad had passed away a few years before Sunaina's father.

On special occasions and festivals, both families tried to visit each other and keep alive the old ties.

When she reached the shop, she spent some time sitting in one of the three cosy chairs for special guests and customers who happened to drop in to buy books or just to "say hello" (in the owner's words). She often felt that this shop, still the same as it had been years ago, was a symbol of the city as it had been in pre-capital days.

Old, carved bookshelves and stools, deliberately and lovingly preserved, a cosy and informal atmosphere which encouraged browsers to stay longer than they intended, extremely polite and helpful staff, and an environment which made one feel that there was nothing better than books in this world.

Surrounded by several highly stylized and modern setups, this bookshop was like a beacon of hope … hope that book lovers would always be around, that hospitality and politeness would remain placed above commerce in this city which had always been known for its warm and caring denizens.

Hope that even when the old order changeth, there was always a place in the new regime for the best of that old order.

"Here are the books you ordered," said a shop-assistant. She spent an enjoyable hour going through the entire stock of music books and selecting the best.

She also gave him a list of books the school's librarian had given her. These were to be sent over to the school by the shop. Soon, the owner, Mr. Nitin Jaiswal, walked in and greeted her warmly, asking after her mother's health.

Discussing music and the school where she taught, they talked for a while over a cup of hot coffee, laced with chocolate powder, which was a specialty of "Buffet" the small coffee shop next door. This little shop had existed for as long as she could remember and had neither changed its look nor the taste of its coffee and popular crisp "vegetable rolls" which were extremely tempting, especially in winters and during the monsoon season.

This unique "coffee and roll" combination had been competing successfully with the best of dishes being offered by the jazzy restaurants that had come up over the years around "Buffet". Sunaina was always happy to see such simple old joints doing well on the basis of quality in the face of stiff competition from the ostentatiously done-up places.

Tanu came back the day before Sunaina was to leave for Srinagar. She was full of excitement and called up Sunaina to exchange news. They met for a while that evening but Tanu said she was too tired to go along with her to Srinagar the next day. Her exploits in Dubai were described in great detail, reminding Sunaina of the old Hindi film stories Tanu had narrated to her in school.

"Have you heard of something called editing," she asked Tanu, with a straight face, after she had listened for about an hour.

Tanu looked at her for a moment, not understanding immediately what she was implying. And then, as her question sank in, she began laughing loudly, just as she had done in school. This made Sunaina laugh too. Tanu's laughter had always been so infectious!

Sunaina talked about what Prashant had said to her before leaving. Tanu was really happy to know that she had heard him out without behaving rashly as she sometimes did. "I think it's a great step forward on his part and you should meet him half way," she said, glad that things would calm down for Sunaina now, with a promise from Prashant that he would settle down in Doon. "It's great news and there should be no hesitation on your part to let bygones be bygones," said Tanu.

"My dear, I've already conveyed to him that I'm ready to close the past and begin anew. On a fresh note," said Sunaina.

"And all this while, you didn't give me this news and kept listening to my Dubai story!" said Tanu, marveling at her friend's patience.

"Did you give me a chance?" she said and they both laughed again. Tanu wanted to know every little detail of her conversation with Prashant. "So, you finally had The Talk?" she asked and smiled.

Hearing what Sunaina had to say, Tanu, too, was quite surprised at Prashant's changed behavior and asked her again whether it was true. When she was finally convinced, she expressed great satisfaction. "Didn't I always tell you that things would be fine ultimately?"

That was true. Tanu had always believed that bad happenings could not be the fate of good people. And in her eyes, there could be nobody who was better than Sunaina. Her selfless love for her friend had always made her see her innate goodness and innocence and ignore the flaws in her personality. "I may be biased but I will always say that you deserve the best," she often said.

Sunaina walked a little with Tanu and bought a few things for the house on her way back at dinner time. She had decided to go alone to Srinagar as her mother was not quite well yet.

Manas spoke to her that night and she told him about her Delhi visit and also about what Prashant had decided. He found it a wonderful idea. When she asked him about his surprise, he again said she would come to know around Diwali time.

"Will you help me sometimes with my thesis?" she asked him. "Once you begin your research, you'll be my guruji," he said, trying to sound serious but making her laugh at the way he said it. He invited her to come to Mumbai for some days but she said she wouldn't be able to get any leave at the moment. "Later, I'll try to make it," she added.

Leaving for Srinagar alone next morning, Sunaina was relaxed, listening to the cassette she had handed over to the taxi driver, enjoying the classical music-based songs from Hindi films. Two of the songs were especially suited for this season ... one was "*Bole Re Papihara, Papihara*" in Vani Jairam's husky voice. It was from the film *Guddi* and was based on Miyan Ki Malhaar, the Malhaar raga created by Miyan Tansen. This was a ritu raga (season-based raga) which sounded good any time during the rainy season. It was similar to Raga Bahaar. Another ritu raga she loved was Raga Basant.

The second song was "*Megha chhaaye aadhi raat*" of Lata Mangeshkar from the film *Sharmilee* based on Raga Patdeep. It was a poignant rendering of the raga and always moved her greatly.

Her meeting with Dr. Bajpai was a valuable experience. A lifetime devoted completely to classical music was evident in his home. Musical instruments, a library of music books from all over the world, cassettes and CDs lying around the room and love for music written all over his impressive personality.

Dr. Bajpai and his wife welcomed her warmly and she felt very much at home. They were simple people. His wife, Sunanda, was also a singer but had not been singing for the past few years as she didn't enjoy good health. She was really happy to meet Sunaina and it showed in her behavior. There was no place for formality or pretence in their simple home.

Most of their conversation revolved around music and musicians. Dr. Bajpai already had the university forms required for her registration with him. She filled them in and promised him that she would send him the synopsis for her research soon from Doon. He found her subject, "Intermingling Classical and Sufi Music" interesting and said he would be glad to guide her. "But you'll have to come up to Srinagar frequently," he said.

"I think I'll be able to manage that," she said, deciding that she would give up devoting much time to *Sarang*. Mom and Ustad Saab would look after it. She could even consider giving up working for a few months. Take a break from teaching and learn more about the depth of the ocean of music that had always fascinated her. She would do so if the need arose, she resolved.

After a great lunch, while they were having tea, Mrs. Bajpai began humming something and when Sunaina requested her to sing, she readily began singing a composition which Dr. Bajpai had set to music some years ago.

It was in Raga Bahaar and the words were "*Bhanwara dolat kunj kunj, aye paat paat pe Bahaar.*" As she listened, Sunaina was astounded. It was a golden voice and she was simply mesmerized. Even when the song ended, she could not speak for a while. The room resounded with the song.

"I have no words to praise your singing," she said, at a loss for words to describe the beautiful voice she had just heard. This was a voice which should have been known all over the world!

"I know what you want to say, Sunainaji. Anyone who hears Sunanda sing always reacts like this. But that's the beauty of her singing. It's only for herself and her near and dear ones," said Dr. Bajpai.

"But how could you not let this voice be heard by all music lovers in the world?" she asked her, still in a trance. She felt that Sunanda's very spirit was composed of pure musical notes.

"Well, I used to sing at university functions and some social gatherings," she said. "But somehow, I was never comfortable performing before crowds."

"She sings best when she's with the family or alone," said her husband, looking really proud of her. "Surprisingly, both our sons are not at all musically inclined," he told Sunaina.

But Sunaina was too absorbed in her thoughts. She had realized that her thirst for making a niche in the world of music was not something which every singer experienced. For people like Sunanda, music was not a means to an end but an end in itself. Sunaina also felt peaceful when she sang for herself and for her special ones. But the need to let others hear her song, appreciate it and enjoy it was quite strong in her and the need to be known as a good singer as well. She wondered if she could ever become like Sunanda, and in fact, would she enjoy becoming like Sunanda?

By the time she reached home, it was quite late. Her mother was the only one still awake, waiting for her. Sunaina was tired but happy that she had taken another step forward on her journey. What had Manas called it? The Sangeet Marga? It was time to become a student again and wade through the sea of knowledge related to sur, taal and raga. There was so much to do. It intrigued her ... the myriad possibilities of growth, of learning, of making a mark. There seemed to be no end to them, and also no end to her dwelling on them! This was an ocean whose depths one could plumb endlessly and surface each time with the choicest of pearls. The more you searched and explored, the more the range and ambit offered expanded to offer you new vistas, new insights, new pleasures, in fact knowledge anew. She could totally lose herself in this maze and yet never feel lost! She was thankful to life for giving her a chance afresh to realize her dreams!

46

While she was in school the next day, there was a call from Ranvir on her cell phone. He was calling after quite a few days. She sent him a message that she was taking a class, although she had been sitting in the music room by herself and could have spoken to him for a few minutes.

She hated to do this. If they could be just good friends as she was with others, things would be fine. But it was not possible. There were too many emotions – of the past and present – involved in the relationship and the only way to avoid problems would be a clean break. Though Ranvir might promise to be only a friend, she knew that for her it was not possible to treat him like that. She was very clear on that point.

She kept wondering how he fared at that concert he was to perform at and about which he had been so excited. She didn't know that he had cancelled his participation in it after she had spoken to him about her second thoughts on the revival of communication between them. Had she known, she would have felt extremely sad. For Sunaina, many times in her life, ignorance had been bliss.

His message to her said, "Do call me once. Really want to speak to you."

Tanu had often told her to delete his messages without reading them. "That's the only way you'll be out of that vicious circle," her friend had told her crisply.

She had tried to follow this advice but curiosity always got the better of her and eventually she would read every single word written by him. She wished that he would forget about her now and let her forget him. She wanted him to be content with the present and to cherish some good memories of their years together, instead of hankering after something which was not feasible.

She realized now that trying to catch up with the past was like trying to live on, after waking up, in a dream which one had while asleep. She had often tried to do that. When she dreamt of her father, which was very usual, she would want to keep reliving the incidents of the dream. But as the events of the day began, the dream faded and reality, with its rough and tough hands, wiped the impressions of the night from her consciousness.

When she reached home that evening, she noticed a lot of activity at *Sarang*, as if there was a celebration underway. She wondered why some students were running here and there and talking in loud, excited voices among themselves. She thought it must be some student's birthday.

She went to the house first and freshened up. While she was having her tulsi tea, she asked Deena where her mother and Roop had gone. "They are in the school, Didi," she replied, trying to hide a smile.

Sunaina found that quite strange. "This is Roop's homework time. What is she doing in the school?" she said to herself as Deena had gone back into the kitchen.

"Didi, why don't you also go there and bring her back?" said Deena, suddenly coming out of the kitchen like a Jack-in-the-Box.

She picked up her music notebook and thought she would take a class this evening. She hadn't taught the little ones for quite a few days.

While she was walking towards the little school, she suddenly noticed that things were quiet. All seemed to have settled down.

As she entered the room, she found not a soul there. This was too much! She called out to Roop several times but there was no response. She then walked into the adjoining smaller room where the instruments were kept. What she saw mystified her completely. Was this a silly dream? The students were in a circle. The moment they saw her they gave a wild shout and broke their circle. And she was face to face with Manas, who was sitting there with Roop in his lap, and Mrs. Bakshi sitting next to him.

She was speechless. Was this the surprise Manas had been talking about? It was indeed a great surprise for her. Diwali was still more than a month away. She was happy to see him. The surprise arrival had added to the happiness. The students were thrilled to see her taken aback and they danced and jumped. She could only laugh at their celebration. It showed how much they had missed Manas. This was their way of showing it.

"It's a holiday for *Sarang* today," declared Manas, getting up from the little stool and coming forward to meet her.

"And please do not think even for a moment that this was my surprise!" he told her as they walked towards the house. She was quiet but all the same, she was looking forward to the next surprise he had planned to give them.

"How did you prepone your program?" she asked him as they sat down for their coffee on the verandah, just like old times.

"Because I could not wait any longer to see your reaction to the actual surprise," he said, looking like the cat who had just licked a pot full of delicious cream. There was not an iota of awkwardness between them and she felt as if she was meeting a childhood friend of hers, with whom she had grown up. The shadow of Ranvir was no longer between them and everything was natural and good. She was thankful that he had not misunderstood her or she would have lost a true and dear friend.

She kept looking at him, waiting for the grand revelation for which he had come all the way from Mumbai, which made it impossible for him to wait for Diwali.

"Auntie, Roop, please come here and sit with us," he called out. They both readily came and joined them on the verandah.

"And now, here is the great news ... the new album which I was planning has a new artist to accompany me in the two duets."

"That's nice," said Sunaina. "But what's so surprising in that, Manas?"

"Hmm ... That artist is you!"

Sunaina thought he was joking. Teasing her. But he looked quite serious.

She got up from her chair and looked completely stunned. "How did that happen? When?"

"As soon as it was finalized, I took the train to Doon," he said, looking really happy.

"The sponsors and the music director heard your concert audio and suggested that you should be part of the album," he said.

"It is totally their idea. I never suggested anything at all," he said, a bit scared that Sunaina might think that he had recommended her name.

As the idea began sinking in, she became excited and nervous all at once and asked him several questions. Her mother and daughter were ecstatic.

"It's the best thing I've heard in years," said Mrs. Bakshi. "It calls for a grand celebration!"

"But how will I do all this? I simply can't think straight. You've put me in shock, Manas," said Sunaina.

"And there's another small surprise," he said.

"NO! Not any more please!" she said, pretending that she would faint if she heard any more.

"Just one little bit more. A film being released in December will introduce a new playback singer named Manas Kaul," he said so softly that she could barely hear him. But she caught what he said and there were no words she could find to congratulate him on this major success in life.

"It's a Sufiyana song which the hero's friend will be seen singing at a dargah," he went on.

Mrs. Bakshi and Roop had not heard what he had said. When they realized what had happened, they were simply thrilled. "Trust them to be so overjoyed. They're really film crazy," said Sunaina, delighted about the wonderful things that she learned this beautiful evening. Finally, her daydreams were getting a shape. Her doctorate would begin soon and so would her recording for the album. *Sarang* was doing well and her students in school were high achievers. She thanked her god for letting her music blossom like this, unlike her love life. There were always compensations in life.

Manas kept talking about the various things in Mumbai which had led to his becoming part of an under production film which was introducing several new artists. "I'll be going back in four or five days but before that, we'll have to work out everything for the album," he told Sunaina.

It was late by now, around 10:00. "I'd better go back home. My parents will be waiting for me at dinner," said Manas, promising to have a meal with them the next day. It had indeed been one of the most eventful evenings in the Bakshi Household in the past few years.

47

Prashant had settled down in his new job and called up several times to talk to Roop and Sunaina. Roop was quite thrilled that her dad was living abroad and was looking forward to visit him there. Her planning had already started, though her mother had not even spoken about it as yet.

Prashant's mother had come to meet him and help him settle in his new home in a new country. She hadn't met him for long and found this a good time to do so. She had also told Sunaina and Roop that their new home was absolutely beautiful and was looking forward to their arrival. Sunaina wondered whether this was a subtle way of telling her that she should now shift to Muscat as soon as she could.

She must not be suspicious and biased about Prashant's mom who had always been very loving towards her and had been extremely pained when she had come to know of the ugly incidents that had occurred between her son and daughter-in-law. She had written a long letter to Sunaina which showed how much she cared for her and how Prashant's behavior had been troubling her. Sunaina still had that letter with her. Though her dad had been a bit cynical about it. "They should have written a letter to him and not to you," he said. He had been very hurt and could not take the letter in the right spirit.

Roop had told her dad and daadi about her mother's latest achievement ... of having received an offer to record songs for an album. They had both congratulated her on this and wished her good luck for the recordings.

Sunaina was glad to know that the recording would be done in Delhi and not in Mumbai. During the Dussehra and Diwali vacation, she could easily spare some days for it. Manas had spoken to the producer and he agreed that they could give them dates in October.

"I'll come down to Delhi from Mumbai. But, in that case, I must leave as soon as I can and complete my other assignments," he said. Sunaina admired the way he was so focused on his music and his assignments. "Give me a little of your commitment and I'll do so much better with my music," she told him.

"You do have your focused phases. They just need to become more frequent," said the young guruji who had ventured again into the world of cinema and begun making a niche for himself there. "You left my Sufi phase incomplete, my friend," she said teasingly.

"I'm sure you can carry on well enough. And there is no question of completion in music. The yearning to make it complete and perfect is what makes it so inspiring and enchanting."

"Words of wisdom, no doubt," she said.

"But few artists know that it is this hankering after perfection which is always needed in an artistic journey. Once you believe that you are perfect, it is all finished," he said.

How correct he was! It was a simple thing that he was saying and yet it had such a deep meaning which could be applied to every aspect of life. Once a person stopped placing targets for himself or herself, once he or she felt that there was nothing more to do, to follow in life, it was indeed a sorry situation. Now she could also understand why Prashant was so focused on his work. His work was as dear to him as music was to her.

"Thanks, Guruji, for reminding me of these gems of truth which I sometimes lose sight of," she told him, seriously.

"I only hope you are not pulling my leg when you talk like this," he said and smiled. They were both sitting on the lawn as Sunaina had just finished checking some unit test papers of Class Eleven students when Manas arrived. He wanted to discuss the album with her. It was a mixed bag of music, with a semi-classical composition, a Sufiyana kalaam, a ghazal, two nazms and a geet thrown in for a rich variety. The ghazal was a duet and had been written by an upcoming poet from Allahabad. Sunaina had loved the lyrics ... "*Itna yaad aaye woh, ham zindagi se door ho gaye, saare jahaan ko bhoolne pe ham majboor ho gaye*". They both went over the duets twice in the evening and practiced until late in the night in the *Sarang* room.

She realized that for a classical singer, it was quite simple to pick up light-classical compositions, ghazals and geets. They seemed like child's play to her. And yet there was so much noise about anyone who cut an album while nobody ever spoke much about someone who devoted his life to classical music. She thought it would be best for her to try and maintain a balance between her classical work and light classical singing. That would be the golden mean, she felt.

She also knew that the opportunity she had thanks to Manas did not come easily to every singer. Some had to struggle for years to come anywhere near it. And though Manas would not hear a word of gratitude, she was very thankful to him. She had noticed that never had she had any kind of negative feeling towards him, not even for a second.

"Sunaina, when Prashantji comes to Doon to settle down, will you keep up your concentration on your music or will it be affected?" Manas asked her while they were having tea.

"How can I say anything? I'll cross that bridge when I come to it. But it will take a lot of effort on anyone's part now to make me neglect my music," she said, wondering how Manas had begun thinking of something which had not even occurred to her yet.

Tanu came and met her yesterday and had greatly appreciated her effort to begin working for her doctorate. And had been equally thrilled to hear about the forthcoming music album of Manas and Sunaina. "So the nightingale of Doon is finally going to reach out to the world!" she teased her friend, but at the same time, Sunaina could see that Tanu's love and good wishes for her were evident even in those playful words. "And you know Manas? This nightingale of ours sings best in the autumn. She is an autumn bird and in this season her soul is at its most sensitive."

"Tanuja, I didn't know that until now. Now that you have told me, I'd like to know more about this," he said, while all of them were sitting in the little instrument room at *Sarang*.

"Autumn is her favorite time of the year and, ever since we were in school, she used to long for September and October to arrive while I was the one always looking forward to Holi," said Tanu.

Sunaina kept smiling while she remembered how she and Tanu used go to their annual school fete in October. The autumn evening in the valley would enchant Sunaina and make her melancholy, too. Even at that age, she could feel the deep sadness inherent in autumn. And yet she was aware of the quiet beauty of this season. At that time, she had neither much knowledge of poetry nor of music.

It was much later when she realized that autumn was a special season for artists. It touched their sensibilities in a way in which no other season could. It had a slow-burning fire within its sad heart and in its tears lay a joy which was far sweeter than the celebration of spring and its glory. Her dad's love for Keats " Ode to Autumn" also sprang from his love of poetry as well as the pensive splendor of the season. And it was one of her favorite poems too. She liked it much better than the "Ode to a Nightingale" which she had studied in school and college. Shelley's line from *To a Skylark*, "Our sweetest songs are those that tell of our saddest thoughts" also fascinated her and brought the sad beauty of autumn to mind. "*Hain sab se madhur woh geet jinhein ham dard ke sur mein gaatey hain*," was the Hindi version of this sung by Talat Mehmood in his soft melodious voice.

"Manas, is there no Raga to celebrate autumn as there is Bahaar and Basant for spring time gaiety?" asked Sunaina, coming out of her reverie. "Even Keats tells autumn, "Thou hast thy music too."

She strongly felt the need for such a ritu raga which would express all the subtle colors, all the delicate emotions and quiet thoughts associated with this season. Keats' ode to the "Season of mists and mellow fruitfulness" had done this in a way which, she felt, could only be matched by the beauty of a raga specially created for autumn or sharad ritu as it was called.

"As far as I can remember, there is no such raga. Some of the *Sarang* ragas do have a melancholy strain which reminds one of autumn afternoons and evenings but nothing specifically for sharad," said Manas.

"Naina will create this raga," said Tanu, who didn't know much about music but knew a lot about Sunaina and her love for autumn and music.

"Sunaina's Autumn Raga! That sounds wonderful!" said Manas. "What do you say, Sunaina?"

She looked at both of them. They had much more confidence in her than she had in herself. They really were her well-wishers and perhaps the soulmates which she used to talk about once without even knowing what the words meant. Their confidence in her ability, their pure and unsullied faith in her talent and depth of knowledge, rubbed off on her and suddenly she felt that she could do it, could compose the raga which nestled in the depths of her soul.

She smiled her warm smile. "Yes, Autumn Raga will be mine. Why must the spring and rains have all the attention? I will create something which will always be associated with Patjhar, the Fall, with the navy blue, orange and pink skies of autumn, with the nip in the evening and morning air and with the hope of a beautiful winter ahead," she said. She knew this raga well, though she had never heard about it. She had sung it within her for years. Her soul had hummed it every autumn.

"Enough about Autumn. Let's discuss the album which will be recorded in autumn, too!" said Manas, sounding a bit like a schoolmaster.

"And her birthday is also in autumn," put in Tanu.

"Yes. But the album will be recorded before her birthday," said Manas.

"Okay masterji," said Tanu and they all laughed, disturbing the students who were practicing in the music room.

Sunaina was happy. Nay, she was on top of the world. Sobering up, bidding Tanu goodbye, she and Manas sat down to serious work. Music was great, it touched the soul, but it also demanded dedication and dedicated hard work from those who chose to tread the path, the music marga.

48

Ranvir had not called her for quite some time. But he had sent her a few messages on the phone including some really mushy verses in Urdu. She felt that, at long last, she had been able to get him out of her system completely. She no longer hankered after the old memories nor did she feel any remorse about having told him not to hope for anything from her now. It was finally all over for her mentally, emotionally and also spiritually. The memories had lingered on too long and kept her away from various experiences of life, binding her closely to the past with a silken thread.

She had not made any effort to come out of that. It had happened on its own which is why it was so final. Anything forced to go away always turns up again in life. But things that went away on their own left one feeling better and easier in the mind.

Gradually, her focus narrowed down. All distracting thoughts were melting away and just the essentials of her existence were now getting her attention. She realized that music was her mission, her reason for living. She must do full justice to this gift from God, leaving the conflicts and constraints of everyday life behind her.

Her papers required for registration at the university were ready and would be dispatched to Srinagar tomorrow. That would be the beginning of another of her journeys in music.

Maaliji was back from the village. He had overstayed his visit and attended the weddings of his grand niece and his friend's grandson. He had informed Mrs. Bakshi from the village that he would be coming by the end of September and had kept his word. Ramesh had worked hard in his absence and Maaliji was delighted to see that all the gardens he worked in had been maintained well by his son-in-law. He had no words to express his feelings but his eyes told everyone how proud he was of Ramesh.

"Sunaina beti, I've got plenty of arhar ki daal this time. You can give it to Tanu and also to some other friends in your school," he told Sunaina the day he arrived.

For Roop, Maalji had brought home beaten wheat with which she loved to make porridge. It was good to have Maaliji back home. His benign presence gave everyone a feeling of comfort and security. Though he was a man of few words, the aura of goodness around him created an atmosphere of cheer and hope.

Manas would go back to Mumbai the following day and meet Sunaina in Delhi in October for the rehearsals and recording. This time, she saw him off happily and wished him great luck for his career in films. He had brought so much good news and moments of joy for all of them. His mother wanted him to stay as she was again unwell these days. He promised that he would be back for Diwali, even if only for a couple of days. Manas had become such an important part of the *Sarang* group that it would always be incomplete without him.

"When we start a big music college, you'll have to leave everything and come and take over as principal," Mrs. Bakshi told him.

"I will definitely do that," he replied. "After I retire from my cinema career."

"There is no retiring from there. The mayanagri and its magic never wears off. I wonder if you'll ever be able to leave Mumbai for long now," said Sunaina.

"There is no magic stronger than the magic of sur and I will go wherever it takes me," he said, looking serious.

"Okay, traveler of the music marga! Let's practice for a couple of hours before you go and get your packing done," she said. Sometimes she felt as if it was Ishaan and not Manas she was talking to and bullying.

Ishaan and Manas were almost the same age and she had always bullied her little brother when they had been in school. Later too, at times.

They had been extremely close to each other during the years when he was in school and she in college. He used to miss her when she was in college at Delhi. He used to wait for her university breaks so that she could come home to Doon with plenty of love and a bagful of gifts for him. He used to write sweet letters to her in which he gave her all the news about his friends, his school, Maaliji and his family and how he was doing at school. She still had those letters in her treasure chest and sometimes when she read them she missed her little brother who had now greatly changed and didn't show much emotion either to her or to their mom.

Perhaps all men were like that, she would sometimes think.

While they were boys, they were demonstrative, warm, spontaneous and sentimental. And later, they took up the image of being strong and silent, bereft of feeling. But she was glad that Ishaan's childhood and early youth were captured in these letters forever. She could read them over again and savor the unpretentious expressions of her little brother. She had tried showing these to him once or twice but he just smiled and changed the topic. Was he now embarrassed by what he used to write? She didn't ask him but changed the topic too.

After Manas left, she called up Dr. Bajpai to ask him whether he had received the papers she had sent. He said he had and was about to call her. She told him about the album. He congratulated her and wished that he would be able to buy it very soon in the market. "For me, you are already a star. For the way you have been carrying on with your music and for your love for the spirit of classical music," he said.

For a moment she thought she would tell Ranvir about the album. But she immediately checked herself. With great effort, she had been able to cut contact. Why put herself in a difficult situation? He would be only too happy to hear about it and would then go on to persuade her that they must be in touch with each other always. No, it was better this way. Why had it come to her mind at all that she must tell him?

There were still about ten days before going to Delhi for the recording. October had arrived, bringing with it a host of good tidings. It was the time of the year she had always loved. For the nostalgic evenings it brought, for being the harbinger of bright winter days, for the sweet, fragrant chill its mornings carried, for the festivals that came with it, for the rust and orange hues it gave to the landscape and for all the things which she could feel strongly but not express in words. It was in her songs that she could express this beauty and enigma of October. It was this rare loveliness which she wanted to capture for the whole world through her Autumn Raga.

SOME AUTUMNS LATER ...

Roop had come home with an Inter-School Music competition trophy. It was a great day for Mrs. Bakshi and Sunaina when the fifteen year old girl had done them proud. Prashant had taken time off from work to attend the competition. It had been four years since he had come and launched his company in Doon. It was difficult for him, returning from Muscat and starting once again, on his own. But he knew that once this was done, things would be smoother and better for him and his family. And he worked hard at it for two years. The last two years had seen them all settling down to a life as close to normal as possible.

Sunaina had completed her doctorate and had been overjoyed at this achievement. Three of her albums, including the first one with Manas, had done well and she had been getting many offers for concerts and for music albums. But, unlike Manas, she had mostly stayed away from the public eye and concentrated on her thesis and on setting up the *Sarang Post Graduate Institute of Classical Music.*

Roop had become very serious about music at the age of ten and besides her studies, had devoted several hours a day to it. With training from her naani, Ustad Saåb and Sunaina, Roop had developed a style which was a rare combination of the richness of experience of her teachers and the freshness of her young voice. She was a serious girl now, with most of her childish chattering gone. In fact, she had turned into a beautiful young lady who sometimes surprised even her mother with her maturity and good sense.

This was not the first time that she had won the trophy in an inter-school concert. She had several prizes lined up neatly in her room and each time Sunaina saw them she could not help feeling thrilled at her daughter's talent and perseverance.

Ever since Prashant came to Doon to stay, things had changed even while they themselves stayed quite the same.

Sunaina had resolved not to let Prashant mete out his dictatorial treatment all over again. And Prashant had also changed. Sunaina didn't give up any of her activities. She made her trips to Srinagar to meet Dr. Bajpai and she also took classes at *Sarang*. She had taken a year's study leave from her school and had now rejoined after achieving her doctorate and a promotion.

For the last six months she had also been working on the institute project. Manas, who had done well for himself in Mumbai, had come to Doon to help her for a month in this. He had done six films and had emerged as one of the new voices of the film industry. His albums had also done well and were a hit with the youngsters. But Sunaina could see that he was restless and lacked the joy which came with success in a chosen field. He hadn't married and, from what Sunaina could make out, he had no plans either. His mother had passed away the year before and his dad had stopped saying anything about marriage to him.

"Whatever one may think, whatever one may plan, joy sometimes eludes you despite getting worldly success," he told her during his recent visit home.

"Manas, if you ever get tired of the big bad city and its problems, you know that you can always come and join the institute. You are such a wonderful teacher," she said to him.

By now, she had also realized that the commercial music world was not her destination and had begun consciously withdrawing from it. She was now able to understand the feelings of Sunanda Bajpai who sang only for herself.

"When one sings for others, it's a song. But when one sings for oneself or for God, it becomes a spiritual experience," Sunanda had told her once.

Living under the same roof and in an atmosphere of music, even Prashant had now come to appreciate this world, which was previously so alien to him. He was amazed at the intricacies and subtleties of this new world revealed before him with each passing day. There was no one more proud of Roop's music than he. Though he didn't have too much understanding of music, he now appreciated what it meant to people for whom it was a way of life.

Whenever he looked at Roop, he felt sad that he had lived for so many years without her, had missed out so much of her childhood.

But he would then tell himself that, even now, it wasn't too late for him to have joined his family. Roop was only fifteen and perhaps needed him more than she had as a little child. He decided that he would be there for her whenever she felt the need to turn to him. Adi had stayed in Doon for a year and a half in the beginning and had then decided that he would work in Delhi as well. He would keep coming to Doon and looked after the company's dealings in Delhi where he had opened an office from home.

In the beginning, Prashant had found it rather difficult to adjust to this city where Sunaina's and Roop's hearts lay. He used to go to Delhi quite often. But by now, the charm of Doon had begun working on him and he had begun to realize what it was about the place which was rather special. The rains, the mountains all around the valley, the beautiful evenings and the interesting people ... it was an amalgam of all these and much more which made up the magic of this town.

It was perhaps for the first time that he had begun identifying himself with the place he was living in and by accepting Doon, removing all kinds of barriers between himself and Sunaina. He found it strange but didn't really mind.

He had suggested that the family move into a bigger house in another part of the town. But Mrs. Bakshi had not been prepared to leave "Anurag". She told Prashant and Sunaina to shift out with Roop. But none of them would hear of this so here they all were, cosy and settled in the old house of Professor Bakshi which he had loved and cherished greatly. The school rooms were now empty as all students had been shifted to the new institute which was still being decorated nicely. They had rented a building in an area which was crowded but so central. "It's going to be the only such institute in the entire state. It must be conspicuous," Mrs. Bakshi had told Sunaina and she agreed.

Sunaina had changed in some ways in the last few years. She was less of a gypsy and was more settled in her mind and spirit. She had come to terms with life. She had now learnt almost all lessons life could teach her, she believed.

Tanu had been in Srinagar, where she had been posted two years ago. Sumeet was in Doon, looking after Tanu's father who was old now and needing attention. Hari was working sincerely and Tanu used to come at the weekends and other bank holidays.

She was staying at the Bank's Guest House which was close to the university campus. Sunaina had been meeting her there every time she visited the university. They had gone to some nearby picnic spots and had a great time, just like schooldays.

"Our kids are now teenagers but I feel like a little girl inside so many times," Tanu would say. Shashank was in Class Twelve now.

"That's true, Tanu – the child hiding away in your heart never quite goes away. And I think it would be terrible if it did," said Sunaina who often felt an overwhelming sense of responsibility towards Roop's life and was scared whether she was capable of fulfilling it.

Her life had suddenly fallen into place and all the chaotic thoughts and experiences had miraculously disappeared. It was almost the autumn of her life. At least, she thought of it like that. Autumn, with its "mellow fruitfulness" and silences, with its sad music and red, brown and rust hues in the hills and vales, with its promise of a rich winter and long restful nights.

She could see the beauty of autumn in her life and felt it in her music. She could see it in her thoughts and way of life. The restlessness and frivolity of spring and the heat and dust of summer had taken leave of her existence and she could now look forward to things in maturity. Every day was like a tranquil river on which she moved her boat smoothly, using the oars slowly and sensibly.

But sometimes, she did miss the stormy phases. The sudden impulses which made life so unpredictable. The rash decisions that rocked the boat on troubled waters. They had taught her so much and left her in the safe seas.

Sometimes, when she looked back, she would suddenly yearn for those days of her early youth when she had taken her beauty and talent for granted, when she had wanted the whole world and had cried when she had ugly experiences. She longed for those days which had actually thrown her into the ocean of life and made her learn to swim. At least those days had not been so somber and even, so much like each other.

But soon she would realize that this was what she had received as a reward from life after all those distracted times she had lived through. Life had come full circle. She was again in Doon and again sheltered from negative influences. After all the strife, Doon had given an even tenor to her life. She knew what she wanted and was working towards it, as she had done when she was a schoolgirl living here with her parents, safe and happy.

Dehra had, no doubt, changed to such an extent that she often wondered whether anyone could remember what an amazingly lovely place it had once been. However, when she went on the terrace in the evenings, she would see the houses and other buildings of Mussoorie light up one by one as darkness fell.

And gradually, the entire hill station would seem like a fairy town with stars of various hues shining brightly all over the place. This was an uplifting sight and took her back to her childhood when her dad used to point out places on the Mall Road to her from the terrace, judging by the lights. They would go up on the terrace every night to see the Mussoorie lights. The lights had multiplied several times over now. But the joy the sight gave her had not changed. It always made her feel like a little girl again.

The view of the valley from Mussoorie at night was even more exhilarating. It was incredibly, breathtakingly beautiful! Like a huge bedspread full of sparkling jewels ... a black bedspread lined with precious colored stones magnified to enchant viewers, to make them catch their breath. Seen from the hills, Dehra was like a bedecked bride on her wedding night. The fact that it was fast turning into a jungle of concrete had not taken away from this breathtaking sight of the valley.

The hills hadn't changed much. They gave her a sense of belonging which her changing city had taken away from her. They stood like custodians of the valley, giving inspiration and strength to all those who looked up at them. The red and pink kaphals were still around whenever one went up to Mussoorie, and the crisp mountain air still enthralled her soul. The pine-scented breeze welcomed anyone who chose to come away from the fret and fever of the busy city. Like the autumn fragrances, these were things that remained just as they had been when the world was a land of magic for Sunaina.

They were more than enough to keep one's faith in beauty alive. Enough to nourish the spirit which thirsted for nature's succor.

Sunaina often thought of all the people who had made her life so rich. Her parents, Tanu, Roop, Ishaan, Manas and her students were at the top of the list. If she thought of Prashant and Ranvir, she could say that they had put her through experiences which had made her wiser. Today, she had come to terms with an existence which, with this richness, had brought her to a quiet shore where the routine movement of day and night was enough contentment. No new ventures or experiments were needed to ignite the soul.

She sometimes thought that had she not stopped herself and Ranvir at that particular point of her life, things might have gone out of hand and life would have taken a drastic turn. She could not have held back her emotions had she given herself an opportunity to get closer to him. But, in a way, it had been better that she had met him again, got a little close to him and then withdrawn. This had helped her in releasing all the pent up feelings from her heart.

That had been the third turning point of her life after the first one, when he had decided not to marry her and the second one, when she had decided to leave Prashant's house. The fourth had come later, when she had settled down to life again with Prashant who had now created a relationship between them which was more of a friendship than a marriage. They had both mellowed and could clearly understand the mistakes they had made in the early years of their marriage. They both wanted to see Roop grow into a good and successful individual. They saw that, in her, they had together created a person who was most precious to them and about whom, they could never have any differences.

She and Manas had tried creating a raga which would sound like autumn. He had given up as he had to go back to Mumbai. But she had managed to create a long composition with a combination of notes which did sound wonderfully autumnal. A sequence of notes that evoked the beauty of the exciting Dussehra and Durga Pooja evenings, the bazaars decorated for the festivals and emotions that relaxed one's mind as did the festive days of September and October. Music which took one to the dusk of autumn with the feeling that days had suddenly become too short and winter was just around the corner.

But it was actually in her soul that she had created the Autumn Raga. Her warm brown eyes sang it, her heart moved to its beat and her mind felt its melody. It echoed in her being.

The ups and downs of her life had been the "aaroha" (ascent) and "avroha" (descent) of this raga. The exuberance of Spring and the celebrations of Basant with its riot of flowers had never been a time she could identify with. Writers, poets, singers and composers had always eulogized Spring with its vibrancy and rejoicing. Why, she always wondered, had the silent beauty of autumn not touched them? As it had moved her ever since she had been a child? Her dad had gone through an exchange program of teachers to Russia and brought back a painting which depicted tall trees alongside a river, with their leaves brown and falling. The painting was called "Autumn in Moscow" and could also be called "Moscow in Autumn", the gallery owner had told her dad. She had been just ten years old then, but still, it was her favorite painting and lovingly preserved by her.

Though Spring has numerous followers and admirers, there are some who are born to sing the praises of Autumn. Sunaina was one of those. She had been born to sing the *Autumn Raga*.